Dating A Metro Man

Book Four of the NEVER TOO LATE Series

By

Donna McDonald

Acknowledgements

I would like to thank my editor, Toby Minton, and my proofreader, Karen Lawson. I know you both are doing your best to help me get out the best books possible. I continue to try to do justice to your hard work.

I would like to thank my fiancée, Bruce McDonald. Your love and support helped me make this dream a reality. You are always the best of every hero to me.

Dedications

This fourth book of the Never Too Late Series is dedicated to my readers.

Many of you contacted me after reading the other three books in the series to ask me about when this one would be done. You emailed, tweeted, and sent me queries and messages on Facebook, Twitter, my Website, and my blog. Every time I saw another query, I was laughing, planning, and plotting how soon I could get back to writing the fourth book in this series.

Thanks to each of you for reading my books. I hope you enjoy this one.

Chapter 1

There was complete silence in the car as they drove away from Alexa and Casey's house. Allen was okay with that because it gave him time to think of what he intended to say to Jenna Ranger when he broke up with her in a few minutes. Lauren's celebration dinner had been a lot of fun right up to the part where Jenna put her hands in Seth Carter's lap to brush food from his crotch.

The shock on Seth's face at Jenna's unexpected action had been comical. Seth had actually grabbed Jenna's hand to stop her from stroking him but it had been too late to stop the inevitable from happening. Allen had wanted to laugh at Seth, who looked torn between embarrassment and open lust.

The blush on Jenna's face when she realized what she was causing to happen to Seth had also been inevitable, as was the stammering apology she gave Seth as she ran away from him to the kitchen.

The idiocy Allen felt for agreeing one more time to being Jenna's token date was immeasurable. He intended to never be such an idiot again. It wasn't helping any of them.

"I'm sorry, Allen. I swear I've not been leading you on or anything like that. I like you, *really* like you, but I'm certifiably insane where Seth Carter is concerned," Jenna said as Allen parked the car in front of her apartment. "I don't want to feel anything for him. I don't even know anymore what I do feel. He's made a second career out of rejecting me, and I still can't seem to stop being stupidly drawn to him."

Allen turned his body in the seat until he was facing Jenna completely. He did his best to draw her gaze to his, but she was looking everywhere she could but at his face.

"Seth wasn't rejecting you at your mother's wedding reception," Allen reminded her. "Any fool could see he wanted to drag you out of there, and that you wanted the same thing. I'm probably the only reason he didn't act on that feeling."

"Not true. Seth didn't act because he never follows through on his feelings. Still, I didn't mean to embarrass you then—or tonight," Jenna said sincerely, her voice tight with unshed tears.

Allen Stedman, the best looking heterosexual man she knew, was sitting across from her and she wanted to cry because she had absolutely no interest in taking him to bed. For the first time in her life, Jenna truly wished she were more like her mother.

"Embarrassment is temporary, but you and I are not going to date anymore. We're moving this relationship into friendship where it belongs, and here's my first friendly piece of advice for you. Give Seth another chance. You need to explore whatever it is that's between you," Allen ordered. "Hell, if I had even a small chance at that much attraction to someone, I'd be all over that person."

Allen saw his emphatic declaration brought Jenna's gaze to his at last. Stubborn resistance wrinkled her forehead and made her frown. Jenna Ranger might often look like her glamorous mother, but she was a lot more emotionally complex and not nearly as nice. While that challenge held allure at first, over time it could wear a patient man out.

"No," Jenna said, shaking her head in denial. "I can't go back to Seth. The other forty or fifty chances were enough humiliation for a lifetime. I wish I could be the woman you're looking for, and I mean that more than I'm going to be able to convince you."

Allen leaned across the seat and put his lips on Jenna's knowing it was probably going to be the last time. He thoroughly explored their taste and texture before pulling away. She was a beautiful, kissable woman, but obviously one more that wasn't for him.

"I'm not stupid and neither are you, Jenna. You didn't get even a little bit turned on by my kiss just now, and Seth Carter is the reason. That's not a truth you can run from for long, no matter how stubborn you want to be," Allen said, resignation heavy in his voice.

"I'm sorry, Allen. I want to want you," Jenna said quietly.

"I know, honey, but that's not how the real thing seems to work," Allen said, smiling broadly in the darkness that had fallen around them now.

It had been months since he'd been with a woman, and Allen had spent two months dating only this one. He figured he deserved a damn medal for not taking advantage of Jenna's vulnerability. Carter owed him forever, and one day he was going to make the man pay.

"If I had tried hard enough to get you into bed, I might have changed your mind for a short period of time. I couldn't let our relationship play out like that because I like your mother, Casey, Seth, and you. Now I'm glad I didn't press you for more because we can be real friends. I'm going to date other people, and you are going to face your destiny," Allen said firmly.

"Seth Carter is *not* my destiny. He's my damn nemesis," Jenna said bitterly.

"Yeah and maybe you're his. I loved reading mythology in college. Nemesis was the Greek goddess of retribution," Allen said, grinning.

He poked her arm with a finger, pushing Jenna toward the door. Normally, it would have made her laugh. The woman was moody as hell and you never knew where you stood with her.

"Go exact your just punishment, Goddess Jenna, and get it out of your system. Then forgive Carter and live happily ever after. I want him back in the gym with me in a few weeks. It's your job to get him there."

"Allen, you're such a romantic. Seth is never going to put business plans on hold long enough to have a normal relationship with me. I've kissed you more times in the month or two we've been dating than I kissed Seth in the four months I dated him," Jenna exclaimed, tears about the truth of that statement blurring the anger and hurt until they were indivisible from the pain in her heart.

She looked out the car window and away from Allen's pitying gaze. "Seth Carter only cares about what he can accomplish in life. Being intimate with me has never been high up on his priority list. Even if I did manage to share his bed for a while, do you think sex is going to magically change his attitude about his work coming first? I don't."

"Jenna, have more faith in yourself and what you two can have together. Give up this negative thinking thing you always do about Seth. You're just feeling sorry for yourself," Allen said softly.

"That's because no one else feels sorry for me at all. When rejection happens to you one day, maybe then you'll believe me about how much it hurts to be dying with desire for someone who sets aside what you're offering and walks away every time," Jenna told him, opening the car door and stepping out.

Tears were going to start flowing rapidly soon, and Jenna wanted to escape before the flood came.

Allen snorted and shook his head about Jenna's rejection comment. She was a good person in most ways, but hadn't matured enough to realize that she had spent two months rejecting everything Allen had done to win her.

Or maybe she was just that wounded from Carter's rejection.

Allen thought it was sad that someone as beautiful as Jenna Ranger was so insecure about herself.

"Look—call me next week and we'll do dinner," Allen said, sighing with frustration even as part of him was still feeling extremely relieved by the break-up. He was tired of being alone and wanted to start looking for someone who might actually want him—just him.

"Sure," Jenna answered, knowing it would be a long time before she could call Allen again.

Maybe she was repeating her mother's mistakes after all, she thought. Maybe she was destined to move restlessly from one man to the next while she longed for the one that didn't really want her.

It was the only explanation for why the most attractive man she'd ever known had become yet another casualty of her toxic dating life.

Chapter 2

Dr. Regina Logan stopped outside her next consultation room and lifted the chart from the door. New one, she thought, noting the green flag placed on the edge of the folder. She flipped open the chart and scanned the information quickly. She always waited until she had finished before she looked at the name of the person.

Her eyes grew wide as she saw Seth Carter's name written at the top.

She swore silently in shock as she scanned the information again quickly, this time with a different eye. Taking a deep breath, she knocked and stepped inside.

Seth stood as she walked into the room.

"Dr. Logan," he acknowledged. He tucked his cell phone into his pants pocket. Regina noted the action and smiled her approval of his politeness.

"Hello, Seth," she said smiling, and then waved a hand at the chair. "Please have a seat. You can call me Regina here if you like. I want you to be comfortable with me."

"I guess you're probably surprised to see me." Seth sat again in the chair and studied her face, looking for shock, disapproval, surprise, or any other emotion. All he could see in her gaze was kindness and patience.

Regina shrugged to indicate her neutrality on the matter. "If I am surprised, it's pleasantly. I hope that I can help you with whatever brought you here today."

Seth looked at her a long time before he spoke. "I don't know where to start." His gaze dropped from hers to study his hands.

Regina was used to the initial discomfort that most of her patients felt. She was working to shut out the knowledge that this was Casey's cousin and Jenna's great love. She focused instead on Seth's bowed head and the nervousness in his hands.

"How about I ask you some simple questions and you answer them?" Regina suggested.

Seth nodded. "Sure," he said.

"In your client profile, you mentioned that you were experiencing some problems. Do you know if you have a physical problem? Have you seen your regular physician?"

Seth shook his head. "It's not physical. I don't have any problems with getting—well," he paused to look for the right words.

"—getting or maintaining an erection?" Regina supplied, helping Seth get past the verbiage.

"Right," Seth said, glad he hadn't had to explain it himself. "The problem isn't physical. It's something else, but I don't know exactly what it is."

"Can you describe the problem to me?" Regina closed his file. She linked her fingers together and rested her hands on top of the folder to show her willingness to wait while Seth searched for words.

"Can I use her name?" Seth asked, not sure if it was some sort of violation or not since Regina knew Jenna.

"You need to say things in any manner that works for you. You can say absolutely anything in this room and it will go no further. I don't even put the details in your file. I use codes in my notes that are known only to me and one other deeply trusted member of my staff. I take many precautions in protecting a client's privacy." Regina stopped and waited to see what he would say next.

Seth nodded his head in acknowledgement, letting Regina know that he understood and believed her.

"My problem is with Jenna." Seth looked away from Regina to a window that looked over the street in front of her building.

Regina could see Seth's mind had gone somewhere far away as he was looking for a way to explain. She well knew how difficult it was to ask for help.

"Jenna thinks I don't want her, and I can't ever seem to change her mind. The night of Casey and Alexa's engagement party I was alone with Jenna in her room. We started kissing. Things got heated between us very quickly, but I stopped because I hadn't brought any protection with me. I would have helped—shit," Seth blushed and swallowed, "I would have been happy to help her—this is incredibly hard to talk about with someone other than her."

He leaned forward in the chair and rubbed his face.

Regina made a considering hum in her throat. "Let me see if I can fill in the blanks and help you a bit. You and Jenna were making out, but you stopped because you didn't want to have unprotected intercourse with her. You were willing to do other things, but I take it Jenna had a bad reaction to that."

"I didn't even get to suggest it. She wouldn't even hear me out about why I'd stopped. She was already mad when I showed up, but after that she was angry and cold. I could tell that she completely shut out the possibility of being with me in any manner. I don't get what I did wrong. I thought stopping was the right thing to do; the thing a nice guy would do. I tried to ask what was wrong, but all I got was more anger. Seems like anger is the strongest feeling she has toward me," Seth finished.

"Have there been other exchanges since then?" Regina asked.

"Nothing worth mentioning," Seth said sadly. "I embarrassed her at Casey and Alexa's wedding reception. Fortunately, I walked away before anything really bad happened."

"Okay. This is the part where I have to ask some really personal questions. You dated Jenna for quite some time. Did you ever have intercourse with Jenna?" Regina looked at the grim set of his jaw and knew the answer before he replied.

"No."

"Did you express your sexuality with her other ways, such as heavy petting or oral gratification?" Regina took out a pen and pretended to make a note on her chart while Seth struggled with the pained expression on his face.

"No."

"So it sounds like you were abstaining. Was abstinence from sex a mutual decision, or did one of you have a moral or religious prohibition?" Regina looked up when Seth laughed.

"No," Seth shook his head, "neither of us had any moral or religious prohibitions. Or at least not that I knew."

"So abstaining was a mutual decision then?" Regina asked, pen poised above the file.

Seth studied his hands again. "I guess it was my call more than Jenna's. At least, that's what she says about it."

"Okay. Jenna didn't want to abstain. Why did you want to? You were together for several months in what appeared to be a serious dating relationship," Regina recounted.

"When I met Jenna, I thought she was the most incredibly hot woman I had ever met in my life, but I also thought it was terrible timing for me for that kind of relationship. I know how intense that first rush of passion is and how all consuming it can be. I was busy all the time with my business. I got phone calls from several different time zones at all hours of the day and night."

Seth looked toward the window again as he tried to find a way to describe the situation that was fair to both him and Jenna.

"Jenna would get really upset when I wasn't paying a hundred percent attention to her. I guess while we were dating I was trying to have just a friendly relationship with Jenna until I had the time to give myself freely to a more passionate one. I have always wanted to marry her. I've known that since the moment we met." Seth leaned back in the chair and sighed at finally getting to say it out loud, even if it was just to a doctor.

"Did Jenna return your passionate interest?" Regina asked, knowing this answer already, but wondering if Seth did.

"Yes." Seth didn't hesitate. "She still wants me, but she doesn't want to want me. I finally believe her. She's seeing other men and trying to get over me, but I don't think she's slept with any of them yet. At least, she hadn't up to the night of Lauren's product party. She accidentally told me."

Regina looked thoughtful as she tapped the end of the pen on her chin. "Okay. Here's my next question. While you were still actively dating Jenna, what did you do with the passion you felt, but that neither of you were exercising within your relationship? Even priests have a lot of trouble turning off sexual arousal, and they have elaborate ways to handle it. Most normal people merely subjugate the sexual urge by channeling it to another less risky person, to self-gratification, or to substitute activities such as overeating. You look healthy and fit, so I'm going to guess that you don't overeat."

Seth flushed to the roots of his hair, closed his eyes, and groaned in embarrassment. "Do you have to know the specific information?"

When he opened his eyes again, Regina nodded in sympathy but was firm in her reply. "Yes. I do. I think it's important to this discussion."

"Self-gratification," Seth said, mortified.

"How frequently?" Regina returned her attention to the file, wrote a couple of codes, and saw Seth moving restlessly in the chair. She looked up to see his flaming red face.

"Seth, there's nothing wrong with self-gratification. I'd be a remarkably rich woman if I had a nickel for each time I've had to explain this. The alternative to sex that you chose was a testament to your feelings for Jenna. You could have taken that passion to another person. Many, many people do that. Some of us would think that self-gratification was a more honorable choice. It is the one I recommend to people most frequently in situations where one or the other partner cannot be sexual for some extended period of time. So tell me how often and how consistently. I wouldn't ask if I didn't think I truly needed to know."

Regina watched his high color fade a bit as he looked toward the window and sighed. Facing truths about sexual feelings was hard for everyone.

"Four or five times a week, sometimes more. I guess it's been every week since I met her." Seth leaned his head back in the chair and closed his eyes.

"Perfectly reasonable," Regina said, smiling a little at her folder. "Do you know what Jenna did to handle it?"

Seth's head came up and his eyes locked on Regina's. "What do you mean?"

"Well, if Jenna returned your passionate interest, then it's reasonable to assume she would need to find an outlet as well if neither of you were helping the other achieve sexual release," Regina said, trying to make her voice a balance of logic and kindness.

Seth frowned, remembering the power of Jenna's desperate kiss in the bedroom the day of the party and recalling how she had turned off her response as soon as he put on the brakes. What did that mean?

"I guess I never thought about it. I don't know what Jenna did. I guess I thought she did nothing. Women seem to handle sexual frustration better than men, don't they?" Seth asked.

Regina shook her head from side to side and sighed at the lack of true understanding in his response. She saw this all the time.

"Well, let me set you straight and tell you that your thinking is completely wrong. First, single women without regular sexual partners self-gratify as much as men. If you don't think I'm right, check out the sales of vibrators. That's not even counting the women who don't use them. Secondly, let's talk about sexual arousal for a woman Jenna's age. Her sexual arousal when she is turned on is probably five times stronger than your arousal at your age. If she's not doing anything to seek relief from the sexual tension she has around you, then she's probably been in the world's worst mood for a very, very long time." Regina laughed as Seth processed the information.

"Shit," Seth said, as the errors in his thinking were becoming clear. "You're saying Jenna's perpetually mad at me because I get her wound up and never follow through?"

"Mad is probably the mildest word you could use to describe her frustration level. If I were you, I would avoid being alone with Jenna in rooms with large throwable objects, sharp knives, or ball bats." Regina smiled as understanding finally dawned in Seth's eyes.

"When I followed her to the bedroom, she was throwing her shoes against the wall. I thought she was just having a temper tantrum. You're telling me it could have been more than that?" Seth asked, still trying to take it all in.

Regina shrugged, "Possibly. Since I don't have Jenna's side of the story, I can't confirm."

"She said she was done with me. My God, she's dating other guys. She's trying to take her passion to another person because I—oh shit, Regina. What the hell am I going to do? How am I going to fix this?" Seth looked at her desperately.

Regina got up and walked to a shelf with a fish bowl full of small colorful foil packets. She scooped a handful out, walked to Seth, and dropped them into his hands.

"Here. Never be without at least one of these in your pocket. If you're not willing to take any risks, then at least be prepared at all times to follow through." Regina laughed as Seth looked surprised at the various colors and textures.

Seth closed his hands around the packets of condoms and nodded. "I feel like I'm in a high school sex education course. I can't believe I have to be told something so simple at age thirty."

Regina laughed. "That's because you currently have little or no sympathy for what Jenna is suffering. We need to change that, make you not just sympathetic but empathetic. As often as you've been achieving sexual release on your own, you've literally forgotten how bad it can be to be churned up and not have an outlet. So I want you to completely stop self-gratification for the next week, and then come back and see me. And I want you to not approach Jenna again until you see me."

"You're kidding, right?" Seth couldn't believe what he was hearing, couldn't believe what she was asking of him.

"Do you want to fix this or not?" Regina asked quietly, smiling at his shock.

"Well yes. I'm willing to do as you ask, but I don't see how that's going to make a difference," Seth said.

Regina laughed and wondered just how bad off Seth would be in a week and how soon it would take him to figure it out. She'd almost said two weeks, but experience and instinct told her Seth Carter would never make it two weeks.

"Seth, you're going to want to put away anything around your house that is valuable and that you don't want broken. Getting back in touch with your sexual tension will be a bit like going through the worst parts of puberty again. When you start getting frustrated in a few days, your mood is going to shift dramatically. You may have trouble sleeping. You may be irritable with people around you. Some men have told me that they destroyed things."

Seth snorted. "I don't think it's going to get that bad in a week."

"Think of it this way," Regina said, eyes twinkling, "an average single man self-gratifies once or twice a week. You're above the average. This means your sexual frustration will be proportional and likely start the first day you abstain. I could be wrong, but I'm rarely wrong. I've asked lots of men to do this. It is torturous, but effective one hundred percent of the time."

She wrote something on a form and handed it to Seth. "Tell the front office I said to schedule you in the morning exactly a week from today. If you have any questions before then, call me."

Seth nodded. "What if Jenna sleeps with someone before the week is up? She's still dating Stedman."

"I don't know. Only you can answer that question, Seth."
Regina said softly.

Seth nodded and walked out the door. Regina sighed and
laid her head back in her chair.

Lord, what people did to each other, she thought.

The simplicity of her relationship with Ben never failed
to bring a rush of gratitude to her. All the years she had spent
looking had been validated the day Ben Kaiser walked into
her life. The right person simply made all the difference. She
found herself wondering if Seth was going to prove to be the
right person for Jenna and vice versa.

Even with her skills, Regina knew all she could do was
tell the truth and hope her clients were smart enough to
figure it out. She sighed again and rose to go see the next one.

Chapter 3

"Are you okay?" Casey asked, searching Seth's face for signs of illness. He was standing in the kitchen of Seth's condo, setting out the Chinese food he'd brought for their dinner.

"Of course. Why?" Seth asked, frowning. He stuck his hands in his pockets only to remove them quickly.

"Well, you've walked to the patio door and back about fifty times in the last ten minutes. It's not like you to pace. You keep putting your hands in your pockets and pulling them out. You seem nervous or something. Talk to me. I've been helping you solve problems for a long time now, remember?" Casey watched Seth stop walking and run a hand over his face. Seth looked like he wanted to say something, but didn't.

"I need a beer. Want one?" Seth asked, walking to the refrigerator. He didn't know how to answer Casey's question or even if he wanted to confide what was going on.

"I'll take a small glass of red wine if you have it. I'm still doing the physical therapy and have to limit my alcohol intake," Casey said.

Seth nodded and pulled a bottle of wine out.

Casey watched him pour the wine and saw Seth's hands tremble holding the bottle.

"Seth, why the hell are your hands shaking? What's wrong?"

Seth set down the wine bottle with more force than he intended and liquid sloshed inside.

"It's only been two days and I'm a wreck, that's why. I can't function like this." Seth ran a hand through his hair, turned toward the patio door, and drank the beer straight down without stopping.

Casey grinned and laughed softly.

"What?" Seth asked. "What's funny?"

"Just an old memory. For a moment, something about you reminded me of when you were seventeen. You had this major thing for a girl you'd been dating, who wouldn't let you get past second base. I used to wonder if you were going to explode before you got to have sex with her. You tended to wear your sexual frustration on your sleeve. It was hard to watch, even though it was entertaining at times," Casey said, laughing and spooning food into plates. When he looked up from the food, it was to see that Seth had gone pale.

"Are you saying you can tell that I'm—oh shit," Seth searched for the right words, shocked that Casey so easily saw the problem. If he could, could everyone? "You can tell that I'm sexually frustrated?"

"No. If I didn't know you as well as I do, I'd probably just think you were upset or mad as hell about something." Casey shrugged.

"*Upset?*" Seth repeated, cringing as he remembered saying something to that effect to Jenna. "I am such a damn idiot."

Two days of suffering and he already learned the lesson Regina had wanted him to learn.

He couldn't stand the thought that Jenna had ever felt like he felt right now. What had he been thinking to hold back from her as if they had been nothing more to each other than just good friends? They were a hell of a lot more than friends.

To keep from loathing himself, he needed to maintain the illusion that she hadn't been this miserable. But every time he thought about how unrestrained and desperate

Jenna had been every time she kissed him, Seth knew it was a lie. The thing about her he loved most was the very proof he had ignored because it hadn't fit his freaking plan.

Casey smiled easily. "Since I do know you, and I also care about you, I'm going to just say that I think you need to get laid as soon as possible. Seriously. It can change your entire outlook on life. It could definitely relieve the tension that has you pacing and shaking. Normally, I'm not a fan of casual sex, but you obviously need the relief."

"Trust me—sex with a random woman will not fix this, Casey. I miss Jenna. I only want her." Seth knew he sounded like a child demanding a toy back that had been taken away.

Casey shrugged. "Better look for someone else, Seth. I believe that ship has sailed already. She's seeing some guy Allen set her up with last week."

"*What guy?* I thought she was dating Stedman," Seth said, remembering the man's tanned, muscled perfection with a scowl.

"She and Allen broke up I guess. They seem to be just friends now. Been like that since Lauren's party," Casey finished serving the food and carried the plates to the table. "I know the new guy Jenna's seeing is straight because I saw her kissing him in the garden. It wasn't just a friendly kiss either, if you know what I mean."

Casey thought it best to just put the truth blatantly out there. Seth was going to have to start accepting that his chance with Jenna was long gone. The girl had definitely moved on even if things hadn't worked out with Stedman.

"I can't believe she barely broke up with Stedman and is already kissing another guy," Seth said angrily, hands fisting in his pockets. Neither Jenna nor Allen had bothered to tell Seth they had stopped dating. Stedman hadn't worked out because Seth had been between them—even when he'd tried damn hard not to be. Now Jenna was looking for yet another alternate person.

"How long ago was she kissing the guy?"

"Last weekend," Casey said, looking perplexed at Seth's outrage because he'd never shown it before over her. "Jenna brought him by to meet us. You can't understand much of what he says with his limited English, but he seems okay."

"Oh, fucking great. She's kissing a guy that she already brought home to meet her mother." Seth felt his heartbeat thunder in his chest as the heat rose in his face. He swallowed hard trying to calm himself. "Sorry. I'm just—I wish I'd known she and Allen had broken up, that's all."

Seth wanted to go back to that day in Jenna's bedroom, to have the chance again to sink inside her as he had wanted, as she had so obviously wanted. If Jenna had gotten pregnant with his child then, she for sure wouldn't be kissing someone else now. The thought of Jenna pregnant and being completely his sent a surge of possessiveness through him.

His response answered the question he'd asked Regina about Jenna sleeping with someone else. He didn't care about Allen or the other guy. Jenna was his, simply his. He was going to find a way to make her want to be.

Casey saw the anger in Seth's face and the rigid stance of his body. Normally, Seth was the calmest man he knew. He'd never really seen the adult Seth so agitated or angry over anything. It worried him what he might do in such an agitated frame of mind.

"Seth. Snap out of it. You were never this concerned about what Jenna was doing when you two were dating. There are a lot of women in world. You're a good-looking guy. I'm sure you'll find one soon. Come eat before the food gets cold." Casey picked up his wine and moved to sit at the table.

Seth turned to Casey. "Damn, Casey, you know how it is. There are no other women for me. There's just been Jenna from the first moment I met her. I kissed her the way I wanted to the night of your engagement party. I could have done more, but I stopped. I won't make that mistake again. She still wants me and she's mine. I don't care how many guys she kisses in her mother's garden. Hell, I don't even care how many men she takes to her bed. I'm going to be the last one."

Casey looked at Seth's face and saw that he meant every word. This wasn't a seventeen-year-old boy with a crush. This was man in love.

"What the hell happened to you this week?" Casey asked, his voice quiet and serious.

"I finally figured out what Jenna has been trying to tell me practically since the day we met. I finally understand. I'm just not allowed to do anything about it for a damn week." Seth picked up his fork and took a bite of food. "Thanks for bringing dinner. I've eaten everything in the house and haven't taken the time to go shopping."

"It's not like you to overeat, which just proves my point," Casey said, digging into his food. "You know they say that overeating is just a substitute for other things."

Seth glared at him so hard Casey stopped talking. He looked at Seth as if he was seeing him for the first time. Maybe he was—Seth certainly wasn't acting like his normal self.

Seth dug into his food with restrained anger. "Don't worry. My eating binge will not last longer than a week. I'm going to make sure to put my energies in the right places after next Tuesday. Now shut up and let me enjoy this. Food is the only thing I have left to enjoy right now."

Casey laughed, not quite sure why that remark was so funny. He didn't even know what Seth was talking about, so it must have just been the frustrated look on his face.

"How's the security business?" Seth asked, desperate to change the subject.

Casey started talking about the work that Jim had brought to Ben and him. Seth relaxed enough to polish off his plate and head back for round two.

Chapter 4

Jenna sat with her mother at Eddy's having a drink and a sandwich while they waited on Regina and Lauren to show up. Despite her borderline depression over her lackluster romantic life, she was managing to eat with gusto instead of just picking at her food.

Her attitude had improved some over the last couple of weeks. Breaking up with Allen had been the right thing even though her ego had stung at the time. Letting him fix her up with a gym buddy had been good also, even though she was stalling about another date with the sweet, hunky guy. Cristo was a great kisser and wonderfully attentive. Hopefully in time she would come to appreciate it more.

"Eddy still makes the best turkey club in town," Jenna said, taking another bite from her sandwich. She picked up a pickle and crunched.

"So how are you and Cristo doing?" Alexa asked, noting that Jenna stopped chewing and swallowed hard.

Jenna shrugged. "He's fun. We've gone out a couple more times," she said easily.

"He's very sweet. I like him," Alexa said. "But why did you and Allen break up? You never really said."

"Allen and I weren't going anywhere in our relationship. You know how that is, Mama," Jenna said flatly, not really wanting to get into it or admit the breakup had been Allen's idea.

Alexa nodded, not put off by Jenna's stall tactics. That and she had grilled Allen until he'd finally confessed that he had broken things off with Jenna when he realized she still had a major attraction to Seth.

"Certainly," Alexa said. "I guess I'm just a bit surprised you didn't go back to dating Seth."

Jenna choked on a swallow of beer and glared at her mother when she recovered. "Why would you think I'd go back to Seth? You know how I feel about him."

Alexa shrugged. "No, I don't know. You were smiling at him at Lauren's product launch party and co-conspiring with him about her pregnancy test. The two of you were looking really friendly there for a while."

Alexa smiled and wanted to laugh as her stubborn daughter shook her head furiously in denial. She was as stubborn as Paul and could hold a grudge longer than most people remembered the thing that had made them mad.

"Not going to happen," Jenna said. "I am trying to be friends with him, but that's just for the sake of the family connection. There's no need for the two of us to be fighting at every wedding, funeral, or family dinner for the rest of our lives. We're practically related now that you and Casey are married."

"*Related?* Hardly," Alexa said dryly, truly laughing now. "Anyone with eyes can see that you two are still interested in each other in a major way. The chemistry is obvious, honey."

"*Hardly*," Jenna said, mocking her mother, who only smiled more widely at her sarcasm. "I'm careful to keep my interactions with him strictly PG, or PG-13 if you count the swearing."

Alexa raised one eyebrow. "Really? That crotch grab at the house a couple weeks ago seemed more deserving of an R rating at least," she said, wanting to laugh at the blush creeping up Jenna's face.

"I did not grab. I was brushing food from his lap," Jenna told her sharply.

"I suppose the prominent erection Seth got that we all politely ignored afterward wasn't your fault," Alexa suggested.

"Can't you be like a normal mother and just let me be mad at the man who hurt me?" Jenna demanded.

Alexa laughed and put a hand over Jenna's. "No. I can't. You didn't sleep with Allen, the hottest guy on the planet, when you had over two months' worth of chances. Jenna, we both know why. I don't know what kind of magic spell Seth Carter casts over you, but you are not going to break it by pretending you're not sexually interested in him."

Jenna shook her head. "I don't *want* to be interested in him—sexually or any other way," she said, sounding like a petulant child even to her own ears.

Alexa laughed. "Well, you are. Now go seduce the man so you can make a real decision about your feelings. For all you know, Seth Carter might be terrible in bed. Maybe he can't pay attention long enough to get the job done. Maybe he'll stop to take a phone call in the middle of things. You might find you hate him for making to do lists for work while he's doing you. Who knows?"

Jenna finished the beer and laughed despite her irritation. Her mother was outrageous and awful, rarely like a normal mother at all. But she was also wonderful and caring, even though her comments were totally off about Seth. He was bad—but not that bad. The man kissed with precision, and the slightest erotic touch sent her trembling in his arms. She had no doubt that Seth could more than get her there if he could ever make it a priority.

"Seth would not be terrible in bed," Jenna said firmly, laughing and smiling. There was no reason to be upset with her mother for telling her version of things. It would be easier to get over Seth Carter if she could believe for even a moment one of those awful things would be true.

"Oh, how do you know?" Alexa challenged, lifting her chin and narrowing her eyes. "You told me you never got that far with Seth. I'll bet you that blue dress Sydney specially made for me that the man starts and stops so often during the act that you never get a Seth-Carter-induced orgasm out of him."

"I'm not sleeping with Seth just to win a stupid bet with you," Jenna told her mother, laughing at how unbelievable the conversation was. "Daring me to have sex with men is just wrong. You're a horrible, horrible mother for suggesting such a thing."

"Fine, I'm a horrible mother who cares about her daughter being happy," Alexa said, resigned. "Since you're not interested in Seth *that way*, I guess I won't tell you what Casey said about Seth's new agitated state after they had dinner last week. He told me Seth was acting like a frustrated teenager."

"I'm so definitely not interested in Seth Carter's frustration," Jenna said snidely, lifting her empty bottle to Eddy at the bar and holding up a finger for another one. She was annoyed to notice her hands were shaking. She refused to acknowledge the flicker of hope that jumped in her gut.

Alexa shrugged and sipped her red wine as she waited. Jenna could fool a lot of people, but not her. The girl was dying for the man and wasn't doing a damn thing about it, which was both unhealthy and unwise. While she waited for her daughter to come to her senses, Alexa passed the time counting to see how far she got before Jenna caved and asked more questions.

Jenna squirmed in her seat and wrestled with herself. Her mother was baiting her. That was obvious. The question was why. Her mother had never been a fan of her and Seth's relationship. But now Jenna didn't buy her innocent it-doesn't-matter-to-me look either.

"Do you want me to date Seth? Do you honestly think he deserves another chance to break my heart?" Jenna demanded.

"No. If he breaks your heart again, I'll probably kill him. I liked Allen and was happy you were dating him. He'd have been good for you, and to you. I like Cristo, but I don't think the handsome Spanish weightlifter is going to score either. He's not even half as charming as Allen," Alexa said pointedly.

27

"I want you happy in all aspects of your life, Jenna. Seth is either the answer or he's in the way of it happening. Your obsession with him is making another man an impossibility."

"If I dated Seth it would just be to scratch a long-time sexual itch," Jenna said harshly. "I seriously don't like him. The more I date other men, the more I realize Seth was incredibly rude to me while we were together. He was constantly working and rarely finished more than five minutes of conversation with me before I had to share his attention with a text, an email, or a call. I am not going back to that."

"Good," Alexa said. "You don't deserve to be ignored. No one does. But if you can't keep your hands off the man when he's around, something has to give, honey. Trust me. Denial is not healthy or fun."

"What if I can't move on afterward?" Jenna asked, realizing as she asked that it was her true fear. "What if I like being with Seth so much that I end up being ignored in every other way for the rest of my life? I do not want to be a human slave to a freaking technosexual."

"Never going to happen, baby. That's just you not trusting yourself," Alexa said, reaching out and linking her fingers with her daughter's. "Just because you watched me unsuccessfully pine for a man doesn't mean you can't do better with the one you so obviously want. Maybe you'll end up being the only thing that draws Seth out of business mode to have a real life. My blood flows in your veins. Holding a man's interest will not be a problem for you once you invest yourself in the relationship."

"You have to say that," Jenna said pathetically, so wishing it could be true. "You're my mother."

"No, I have to say that you need to face your emotional fears and move through this challenge one way or another. Some relationships are just meant to be, sweetheart. You've been separated from Seth more months now than you dated him, and he's still the only man you want. That's some pretty strong destiny," Alexa said quietly. "I'd be telling you this even if I hated Seth. You don't want to be stuck dating hot guys that do nothing for you for the rest of your life. They don't make men any hotter than Allen Stedman."

"Okay, as uncomfortable as it makes me to talk about Allen that way with you, I admit you have a point," Jenna admitted. "Maybe I'll think about dating Seth again just so I can get him out of my system."

"Maybe you can start back up by emailing and texting first. After some suitable time, then you can meet for dinner to see if you're still hot to sleep with him," Alexa said, joking. "That process seems to work well for those online dating sites. It should appeal to Seth and his obsession with technology."

Jenna laughed. "I'm never going to get what I want from a technological relationship with the man. I want my hands on more than just his damn data."

"*Data?* Is that what they're calling a man's package these days? Wow, I am really getting old. I'm glad Casey still uses terms I can understand," Alexa said, snorting and laughing as Jenna grinned and drank her beer.

The mother in her was glad that her daughter was at least not being stubborn anymore.

And the friend in her was happy because it looked like Seth Carter was going to get another chance with her daughter after all.

Chapter 5

His week of waiting was up and now Seth stood outside Jenna's apartment contemplating what he would say to her. Regina had declared him sufficiently aware this morning and told him to do what he had to do to fix the rest of his life.

So here he was with his frustrated libido straining at the end of a very short leash, hoping the woman he wanted still wanted him back.

As he raised his hand to knock, Jenna opened the door. It was a toss up which one of them was more surprised.

"Seth? What are you doing here?" Jenna frowned. She so did not need to see him seconds after she had turned down yet another date with Cristo. Her plans for the evening had been to swing by a job site and then head to the mall for some therapeutic shopping.

"Sorry. Looks like you were headed out," Seth said quietly, putting his hands in his pockets. "Can I have just a few minutes?"

He had to work hard to keep his gaze on her face and away from the short khaki skirt that fit every one of Jenna's curves and showed off her legs. She wore a white shirt and short sweater over it that emphasized her breasts. Seth sighed and tried to clear his head of lust so he wouldn't babble like an idiot.

Jenna wanted to refuse to talk to Seth but she was too curious. He was nervous, edgy, and uncomfortable. It was such a contrast to his normal calm that she found herself motioning him inside.

Seth stepped into Jenna's small living room. He didn't sit, but rather stood at the end of her couch.

"You seem upset, Seth. Are you all right?" Jenna asked.

"I'm not upset," Seth denied automatically.

Then realizing what he'd done, Seth laughed without much humor, remembering when he had said the same to her.

"Sorry. Yes, I'm suffering a little, but people don't actually die from my problem. Though I have wished myself dead a few times in the last week," he told her, smiling at the irony.

Instead of laughing, Jenna just looked confused. "But you're not ill?"

"No, I just need to tell you something. I'm trying to figure out how to do it without sounding like a crazy person," Seth told her, running a nervous hand through his hair and sighing.

He watched Jenna walk to a chair and sit while she waited. The skirt slid up her thighs several inches. He closed his eyes and prayed for self-control while he got out the words.

"When we met, you scared the hell out of me. No, that's not right. What I felt for you scared the hell out of me. I was just getting my life together. Casey was coming to live with me. I was in my second year of building a business. It was a crazy time. I—I found a way to handle what I felt for you, but in the process I didn't allow myself to acknowledge your side of things." Seth stopped, searching Jenna's face for some glimmer of comprehension, but didn't find any.

"Look—when you said that I never understood you, I didn't want to believe the problem was me because I was trying so hard to be a nice guy. So I went to therapy to find out what was wrong with us," Seth said, pacing in front of her.

31

Jenna struggled to talk around the lump in her throat. "You—you went into therapy—to talk about—*us*?"

Jenna looked at him as he nodded. Seth looked as gorgeous to her as ever, as calm and controlled as ever, with the exception of his eyes which looked—Jenna couldn't think of a good description. Words like scary, dangerous, and overwrought came to mind.

"Since there is no us anymore, I'm not sure I want to know what you concluded, Seth. I think if you left right now, I'd be okay with you not ever telling me what happened in your therapy," Jenna said honestly, standing again and hooking her purse over her shoulder.

"The problem was mine, Jenna." Seth walked to her and stood just inches away. He could tell she was ready to bolt. He put his hands in his pockets to keep from reaching for her.

Seth watched as Jenna looked at him with a mixture of panic and longing. His body hardened, and he felt exactly like he did the first time he ever laid eyes on her. He belonged to her—with her. And she belonged with him.

It hadn't taken Seth long to discover that Jenna Ranger was smart, hard-working, and incredibly beautiful, even if she didn't seem care about how she looked most of the time. She loved her family, defended her mother even though Alexa drove her crazy, and was a loyal friend when she gave someone a place in her heart.

When she kissed him the first time, Seth had seen his first glimpse of heaven on earth. It had been the same with every kiss since. His world wasn't ever going to be complete until this woman was a part of his life. There were no substitutes for her.

"I worked hard to restrain the desire I felt for you because I thought I didn't have time for it in my life. I got completely back in touch with all that passion this week, and I'm bringing it to you now. Even if you still don't want to date me, I for damn sure don't want you walking around not knowing how much I want you and have always wanted you."

With the panic setting in at his words, pride was the only reason Jenna wasn't running for the door. This was her house. She wasn't going to run away in a panic. She would simply leave with dignity, Jenna decided.

"Seth, I'm leaving now, and you need to also. Maybe we can talk about this later," Jenna said, her voice breaking with nerves.

When she started to step away, Seth's hands shot out of his pockets to catch her arms. His grip was tighter and more desperate than he intended, but now that he was actually touching her, Seth couldn't rein in his need enough to be gentle.

"You can slug me after this if you have to, but I've got to kiss you one time while I feel this way. You've got to know how it really is, how it's been all along. I don't want to scare you, but I have to kiss you," he insisted. "In fact, I think I will die if I don't."

"Seth, I seriously don't think this is a good idea. Not now—not like this," Jenna was panicked at the firm grip he had on her. He was bigger and stronger. She'd have to really hurt him to break away.

"Kiss me back," Seth commanded. "Get it over with and go on if you have to, but kiss me back, Jenna."

"I'm having déjà vu. We did this already. It didn't make a difference," Jenna said, her voice flat and cold.

"I promise you that was a very different version of me," Seth said, absolute sureness ringing clear in his statement. "You will never be kissing that passionless man again."

Jenna's panic climbed another couple of notches.

Seth gripped one of her arms tightly in one of his hands while he pulled off her purse and tossed it in the chair with the other hand. Stepping a fraction closer, Seth cupped Jenna's beautiful face with a hand that trembled in anticipation.

Idiot, he thought. *You could have had this all along.*

Jenna saw Seth's eyes change colors and opened her mouth to say something to make him stop, but his lips were on hers before she could get any words out. There was heat.

God, there was heat coming out of Seth and into her. His lips practically sizzled moving across hers and the sound of satisfaction he made in his throat and chest had excitement dancing along Jenna's nerve endings.

Arousal, always instantaneous when Seth touched her, raced through her blood like lightning.

Too late Jenna realized Seth had not been calm at all since he walked through her door. He had come to seduce her. Panic surged again, followed by the resistance Jenna had spent months building against her own feeling of desire for this man. Both warred with the arousal swiftly building inside her until Jenna thought she would lose her mind fighting him and herself.

Seth's kiss was demanding and proof of his intention was hard and insistent against her belly. Jenna trembled all over, some real fear mixed with a level of excitement she'd never felt before with him. Her mind rebelled at Seth's unrestrained passion, but her body was screaming yes. As Seth's grip tightened and his body grew harder and more insistent against hers, it was obvious that his body had heard.

Seth devoured Jenna's mouth, his lips sliding across hers and his tongue dipping inside to explore. Jenna's mouth was water to him after a long walk across the desert his life had become without her. He put his hand on the back of her head and tangled his fingers in her hair. Tugging up her chin, he left her mouth and kissed her neck across her madly beating pulse. Then he came back to her mouth and felt her tremble in his arms.

Finally, Seth pulled away to look at her. Her skin was flushed, her eyes heavy with desire, and her mouth wet and swollen because of him. Need pulsed between them as he held her in his arms pressed tightly against the truth of how much he wanted her.

"I'm so sorry for making you want me and never—damn, I'm so ashamed of myself I can't even talk about it. You're everything I want and have been since I met you. You have to believe me. You just have to."

Seth kissed her furiously then as if his regret was somehow her fault, and he knew it wasn't right to take his anger at himself out on her mouth. Just like dragging her to floor and pushing her skirt to her waist wasn't right either, but he did that, too. He needed to get to her, needed to make her his before someone else could take his place.

Seth heard Jenna call out to him, but he was beyond the point where he could tame the need he had to make things up to her. But he tried, really tried to stop for moment, to tell Jenna everything he had been thinking and feeling. The words were stuck inside him, blocked by his remorse and an overwhelming fear that Jenna might have truly gotten over him.

Instead of telling her what he was feeling, Seth put his face between her thighs, kissing her legs.

He called her name harshly, part demand and part plea. "Jenna. Let me love you. Let me have you. I need you so badly. *Please*," he begged.

When her legs trembled against his mouth, Seth didn't wait for a better yes. He just ripped her underwear down her legs until he could spread her thighs enough to put his mouth truly on her. Licking inside her was a pleasure so powerful it shocked him. When her body lifted from the floor, he moved firmly over her legs to hold her in place while he did as he pleased.

This is insane, Jenna thought, as she felt Seth dragging her clothes from her. Her mind couldn't even take in that they were finally having sex after all this time.

Then she gasped at the first touch of Seth's mouth on the raw ache that had gone so long without being met. She'd been with men who hurried before. She'd been with men who were proficient lovers. It was just that no man had ever put his mouth on her with such blatant intention of taking what he so obviously wanted and giving her what he seemed to know she needed.

Without warning, her release came so hard and strong that Jenna held her breath in shock until the world starting to turn black. She heard Seth moaning in appreciation against her. Jenna bit her lip until it bled to keep from sobbing his name.

Seth went quietly mad at the taste of Jenna's bliss. When he finally lifted his head from her lap, he had already shed his pants and was sheathing himself in one of the many condoms he'd stashed in his pockets.

Instead of looking sated and relieved, Jenna lay panting, palms flat on the floor, eyes closed tightly.

Seth had a single moment of panic that he pushed away ruthlessly.

"Jenna. Open your eyes. Look at me," he demanded.

Seth heard himself insisting, all but yelling at her, but he desperately wanted her to see him. When she finally did open her eyes, the confusion was still there. She didn't understand, Seth thought sadly, but there was no turning back for him now that he'd gotten this far. She was his and he had to have her, had to show her how much she meant to him.

"Jenna, this is how much I want you," Seth said huskily, sliding inside her as slowly as he could manage with the need to take her swiftly driving him crazy.

Seth heard her moan and felt Jenna kicking her underwear completely off to free herself. Seconds later, she wrapped her legs around his and arched into his strokes. His need was so great and his erection so hard and hurting that Seth could barely feel Jenna pulsing around him. The urge for release was maddening, but at the same time elusive in his overexcited state. It had been so long. He really had been waiting for her, and he wished like hell he could make her believe it.

Seth shook her shoulders to make her open her eyes again when she closed them.

"No. Don't close your eyes. Look at me," Seth demanded. "After watching you date all those others guys, I need to see that you know it's me inside you."

When Jenna opened her eyes this time, Seth saw himself reflected in them. Then he let his passion loose at last, moving in and out of her, trying to make up for all the lonely months, all the times he had sent her away.

He was going to make a baby with her, he promised himself. He was going to make more than one. Seth hoped she saw that intent in his gaze as he kept it focused on hers.

Jenna blanked her mind about what they were doing, even as her traitorous body rose and fell in rhythm with Seth's.

She had no choice but to watch Seth's face. If she closed her eyes, he shook her until she opened them again. He was so hard inside her that it hurt, but if he'd pulled out she would have killed him with her bare hands. The earth could have dissolved around their straining bodies and Jenna wouldn't have cared. Her relief to be with him at last was as profound as it was unwanted.

If only she could have felt emotionally good about being with him. If only this had happened when she had desired him initially, when the promise of happily ever after had been singing through her after they had first met.

But it wasn't like that now, and her heart was still hurting for all the months she had tried to have this with him and never did. Now—now it was just sex.

However relieving this was physically, nothing had really been resolved. If anything, Jenna thought, she detested Seth even more now for holding this amazing connection back from both of them. She was angry with him for finally giving her what she wanted, but even so she still didn't want him to stop.

Her unfightable desire for him shamed her, but she held tightly to him all the same.

Shocked when the first giant tremor hit, Jenna suddenly tightened beneath Seth's plunging body, thrashing and arching as the rest of an incredibly violent climax ripped through her. She even tried to fight it off because unlike the pleasure that raced through her before, this time Seth was branding her with every stroke. She felt him everywhere as he continued to move hard inside her without stopping, even as the pleasure he gave her went on and on. Then as it ebbed away, all that was left was a need to be the one he found release with and she wanted him to so desperately that her heart threatened to explode in her chest.

"Seth, please," she called in a panic that she wouldn't be able to please him, fear of it making her want to weep. She wanted to curl into a ball and cry like a baby until she could come to terms with how overwhelmed and out of control she felt.

"I love you, Jenna. I swear I love you," Seth promised fiercely.

Then he kissed her, pushing his tongue into Jenna's mouth to mate with her as fully as possible as his body finally found sanctuary inside the comfort of hers. This was the only woman, Seth thought, as he gathered her up in his arms and gave in at last to his need for her.

Struggling against his weight and the pressure inside her, Jenna hauled in a needed breath just before Seth collapsed on top of her.

Thank God it's finally over, Jenna thought at last, vastly relieved as she had felt Seth tense and climax.

After what they had just done and what she had felt about it, Jenna felt committed to the man inside her. She didn't want that connection, didn't want to feel the way she did. Her heart was breaking again, and she needed to be alone.

She needed another kind of release now and needed it quickly.

Tears hovered, waiting to fall, but Jenna battled them away. All she had done during the months she hadn't been able to touch Seth like this was cry while she wanted to and he didn't. She had no intention of stripping herself emotionally bare and bawling her eyes out in front of Seth over finally getting what she wanted from him.

After a few long minutes of resting deeply inside her, Seth rolled them to their sides to relieve Jenna of his weight. He was disappointed when she pulled away and disconnected their bodies the first chance she got.

Jenna rolled back to her back again and closed her eyes at last. Unfortunately, it didn't block out the memories she was reliving. She took several deep breaths until she could trust herself to speak without dissolving. "Seth, I want you to leave. When I open my eyes again, I don't want to see you beside me or above me. I'm just going to lie here while you gather your things and go," she said firmly.

"Jenna," Seth began, feeling the hurt and anger rolling off her in waves. It was just like that day he kissed her in her bedroom. He stopped trying to talk when she held up a hand. A single tear rolled out of one eye and down her face to the carpet, making him want to die.

"I'm sorry if I hurt you. I didn't mean to," he said, wretchedly close to tears himself.

"You didn't hurt me, Seth, at least not physically. This— this madness was probably inevitable, but I just wasn't in the same mental place you were about having sex today. I'm— embarrassed about being with you, and maybe a little in shock that it actually happened after all this time. Just go, okay? I need to be alone right now. I'll be fine. Just stay away from me for a while until I come to terms with this."

Seth stood and pulled his clothes back on, thinking how much he really didn't want to leave Jenna this way. But what choice did he have? Jenna lay on the floor with her eyes squeezed tightly shut and wouldn't even look at him.

Somehow he made his feet take him across the room away from her.

After Seth closed her front door softly behind him, he stood in the hallway wondering if he could wait her out and if she would let him back in to talk.

Then he heard Jenna crying, the sound of her loud, tortured sobbing tearing him apart inside.

Shame engulfed him. Had he forced her, he now wondered? Hadn't Jenna wanted him as much he wanted her? Could he have been so wrong about what was between them?

He remembered her two climaxes and knew that she had desired him. Still she had told him more than once that she didn't want to want him anymore.

The emotional pain of listening to her cry and not being able to do anything about it did not help the stress and tension he already felt. Knowing he was going to be physically sick if he stayed to listen much longer, Seth rushed out of her building to avoid leaving a final humiliation in front of her door.

The crowd at Eddy's was thick, and Casey was glad that he'd gotten there early enough to get a quiet booth away from the rest. He saw Seth come through the door and look around for him, so Casey waved a hand until Seth saw him. Seth had a two-day growth of beard and a deep frown that would scare anyone that looked at him.

For the first time, Casey genuinely saw himself in the younger man he had raised. How well he knew that look was not good news for Seth's emotional state. He'd seen that look in the mirror for months after Susan had died.

"Hey," Casey said, as Seth dropped his body into the seat across from him.

"Hey," Seth said back.

"What's up?" Casey said lightly, not wanting to seem too anxious to extract information, even though he was.

"I need you to do something for me," Seth said quietly.

Casey shrugged. "Sure. As long as it's not illegal—well unless it's going to be a lot of fun, and then we can talk," he joked.

Alarm bells went off when Seth didn't even try to fake a laugh. He had parented the boy enough to know that Seth had done something wrong or at least something he perceived as very bad.

"Jenna and I—we had a really serious fight a couple days ago. I hurt her, and worse than when we were dating. When I left, I heard her crying from the hallway outside. I need you to check on her or get someone to check on her. I—I can't tell you what happened between us, but I finally burned every bridge I ever built with her. But I can't stand wondering if she's—hell," Seth said, clenching his jaw. "Will you check on her for me?"

"Sure," Casey said. "You want me to give her a message from you."

Seth shook his head.

"It wouldn't do any good. Jenna is never going to believe anything you tell her about me ever again. It's too late to take back what happened between us. All I can do now is keep my distance like she asked me to, and that's what I'm going to do. I just need to know she's okay so I don't lose what's left of my mind."

"You got it," Casey said, leaning forward and pushing his beer to Seth. "Drink this. It won't solve anything, but it might make you feel less like a bastard for a tiny bit of time. Then cut yourself a break so I don't have to slap you around."

Seth snorted. "I wish you would slap me around right now."

"Too bad," Casey said, focusing a smirk. "You're old enough to face your own consequences. I do have your back though. That's never going to change."

"If I tell you I love you, will you kick my ass then?" Seth said, almost smiling.

"Nah—Alexa has made me all mushy. I'm practically a metro man myself," Casey said, signaling for two more beers. "Scares the hell out of me sometimes. Kaiser in SydneyB clothes can walk that edge. I'm not made that way. I only know one type of manhood. It doesn't include much sensitivity outside of the bedroom."

"*Did you just call me a metro man?* Damn, Casey, is that what you think of me?" Seth said, laughing despite his self-loathing. He rubbed a hand over his bristly chin. "Well, I guess I can see where you get that impression, and maybe it's mostly true. Though I have to say I've recently been in touch with my inner Neanderthal. It ultimately cost me my last chance with Jenna."

"Maybe not," Casey said, grinning. "Alexa said she'd talked Jenna into dating you again, but she wasn't sure how long it was going to take Jenna to come around to the idea."

Seth closed his eyes in mental anguish. Once again his timing with Jenna sucked more than he could handle knowing. "Well, I ruined that, but tell Alexa I said thanks for trying."

The beers landed on the table and they each picked up a cold one.

"Here's to you staying in touch with your inner Neanderthal. It makes me feel like you're actually related to me," Casey said, laughing and clinking his glass on Seth's.

"Here's to you figuring out clean fingernails and nice clothes don't make a damn difference to how good you are in bed," Seth said, grinning for the first time in several days.

"You sound like Kaiser," Casey said dryly, "but then come to think of it, he ended up being the only man good enough in bed for the sex therapist."

"Yeah, Regina is amazing. I'm guessing her standards are pretty high," Seth said, looking at the ceiling as he contemplated the extent of what Dr. Regina Logan knew and what kind of man could possibly keep up with her.

Both Casey's eyebrows shot up. "Something else you want to tell me about, Seth?"

"I'm just saying—oh hell, forget it. I'm in a weird damn mood," Seth said morosely, sipping his beer and heaving out a breath.

If he kept on talking, he was going to end up telling Casey everything. He wasn't ready to confess to anyone, not even Regina, who deserved to know how right she had been about everything.

Chapter 6

Plagued with occasional insomnia when she was stressed whether for good or bad reasons, sleep had always been a challenge for Jenna and her restless nature. Lately, sleep was impossible because she couldn't stop dreaming about Seth. She had vivid sex dreams that woke her and reduced her to a quivering mass of female angst.

When the last of the orgasm had faded from the current one, Jenna pulled herself upright in the bed. She looked at the clock, groaning when she saw it was only four-thirty.

Wrapping her arms around her knees, she squeezed her eyes tight to keep from crying. She had dreamed of him again, dreamed of him moving so hard inside her that it hurt, dreamed of his desperation as he took her on her own living room floor. Yet the climax she'd had in her sleep hadn't taken the edge off of her real longing.

Despite all the lectures she'd given herself about how wrong it was on so many, many levels, Jenna longed to be with Seth again.

He challenged her at every turn, irritated her with his unshakable self-confidence, but still she longed for him. She wanted to feel that deep unrestrained connection, even though she had sorely resented it when it happened the first time.

Seth's physical rejections when they dated had wounded the woman in her and made her feel unwanted. His reluctance had made her insecure and distrustful of her ability to hold the interest of the men she had dated while attempting to replace him.

But the problem now was simply pride.

Only a few minutes of Seth's lovemaking had proven irrevocably that all those endless months and days of working to get over him had meant nothing. She especially hated that she'd had a total orgasmic meltdown from just his mouth on her, and hated that Seth had gloried in it though the end result had been to her benefit.

And her heart still hurt from having sex without the emotional closeness she dreamed would accompany the act with a man she wanted that much. Though Jenna had to admit that an absence of love on her part certainly wasn't stopping her from wanting everything else.

No. What they had wasn't love, Jenna thought. She didn't know what it was, but it wasn't love—or least it wasn't what Jenna thought of as love. There was no genuine concern for each other's lives, no mutual plans, or shared goals as a couple. What they had was nothing like the relationship she had imagined with him when they had met, but there was only one bottom line that needed to be addressed now. She had been intimate with Seth Carter once, and she wanted him again. The decision now was about whether or not it was worth trying to have him again.

Jenna swung shaking legs out of bed and trudged to the bathroom, turning on the hot water in the shower before pausing to glare at her own reflection over the sink.

This was the third time this week she'd awakened before five in the middle of a climax, feeling an invisible and extremely aroused Seth moving in and out of her like—well, she didn't know what it was like. It had never been like that for her before. But he'd been determined. Relentless. Harder and more precise inside her than any man she'd ever known.

Stop it, Jenna scolded herself, feeling herself quiver in anticipation just thinking about it.

Sex with Seth was a like a drug she'd accidentally ingested, and now she was in desperate need of another fix.

At seven that evening, Jenna stood resolutely outside Seth's apartment looking for the courage to ring the doorbell. Her hesitation reminded her too much of the last time she'd stood out here worrying in that stupid tight blue dress and torturous heels hoping to seduce him. Evidently he'd been in a different mental place about them then because she had failed, and failed miserably.

It had been a month after that failure before she had been able to bring herself to wear any kind of damn dress again. And when she did manage it finally, all she'd thought about was him.

Lifting her chin, Jenna firmly chastised herself for going there. That was water under the bridge, she told herself. A different time. Certainly a different story and outcome.

She'd come to talk with Seth and figure out where they stood now that they knew what was between them and what could be again. Whatever came of the conversation Jenna fully intended to have with him this evening, she hoped that it at least would dispel the dreams that were costing her sleep.

You are not an emotional coward, Jenna Ranger, she reminded herself.

To prove it, she pushed the doorbell several times to make sure Seth heard it no matter where he was in the house.

The doorbell woke Seth from his second or third depressed nap on the couch that day. He wasn't expecting anyone, and random sales people were banned from his housing complex.

Thinking Casey must have left his key at home, he got up and stumbled to the door, bleary-eyed and resigned to talking to his worried cousin. Lack of sleep was starting to take its toll, but he knew Casey would never leave him alone if he didn't convince him he was at least marginally surviving.

"What the hell, Casey? Did you forget your key again?" Seth demanded, yanking open the door.

The last person he expected to see was standing in front in him.

"Can I come in?" Jenna asked quietly. She tore her gaze away from his to look over his shoulder, which wasn't easy to do with the differences in their heights.

"I thought you were Casey," Seth said, fading off. He couldn't stop staring at Jenna.

Blood was pumping hard to get his brain to register her presence even though he remained frozen and unable to move. In the last week, Seth had concluded that Jenna was never going to speak to him again in this life. Not after what he had done to her. She hadn't even been able to look at him when he slunk away that day.

"Sorry," Seth said, shaking his head and reining in his emotions so he could act mostly civilized with her. "Sure. Come on in. Excuse the house, I've—my housekeeper left me to run off and marry your mother. I have to find a new one."

His attempt at humor had Jenna smiling slightly, but it didn't diffuse the tension between them. It also didn't stop his heart from trying to beat its way out of his chest.

Jenna walked by Seth, careful not to touch him, but hyper aware anyway. She noticed Seth was unshaven and dressed in ratty clothes that looked two sizes too big on his lean frame. Something soft for him nudged her to care, but she pushed away the concern.

Her reaction was probably because she'd never seen Seth this unkempt in the whole time they'd dated. Seth had been all manicured, business perfection each time they'd been together. Most of the time the man had looked better maintained than she in his dress clothes and business suits. Jenna had felt obligated to get her mother's help to improve her own appearance when she was with him.

"I think we need to talk," Jenna began.

Then Jenna looked hard at him before stopping to sigh as she closed her eyes in self-defense. It was really hard to look at Seth without wanting to climb him like a tree and demand that he have sex with her again, even in his present condition. She was completely ashamed of the urge, but truth was, Jenna would tolerate just about anything to have the man for real one more time.

She looked at the floor instead of him, and thought of her own floor. Jenna closed her eyes once more, this time cursing her imagination. This was so not going the way she wanted.

"Okay—here's the thing, Seth. I can't stop thinking about the day we were together. I even dream about it," Jenna said baldly.

Seth walked away from Jenna to the patio door, crossing his arms and looking out. *She has a right to be upset about it,* he reminded himself. *Take it like a man and let her have her say.*

Seth nodded, keeping his back to Jenna. "I can't tell you how sorry I am that I didn't control myself that day. What I did was completely selfish, and if I could take back that day I would."

He turned to face her when he could bring himself to look in her face without flinching. "There are a lot of things I would take back if I could just rewind the clock with you. I can only ask you to believe that I never meant to hurt you by anything I did. Maybe one day you'll be able to believe it."

Jenna wiped a hand over her face. She should be enjoying the fact that Seth was tortured and feeling guilty about what had happened. Instead, all she wanted was to soothe him. Damn the man. It was like there was a soft spot in her where concern for him bloomed like a flower in a field of rampant, invasive weeds.

Lots of half-answers and evasions warred inside her before Jenna found the courage to be true to herself, and truthful with him. She was tired of not telling Seth Carter how she really felt—not that she expected it to change anything.

Jenna put her hands on her hips and looked at the tortured man she still longed for.

"Yeah. You were harder inside me than any man I've ever known. It hurt quite a bit that first time, but I still want you again anyway," she said, frowning and sighing. "I guess some women are just stupid about stuff like that. Or at least I seem to be where you're concerned."

Seth couldn't have looked more stunned if Jenna had slapped him. He wasn't even sure he heard her right. Maybe he was just hearing what he wanted to hear.

Jenna would have laughed if the urge to scream hadn't been so pressing. The feeling of shame about how they had come together grew stronger. It only made her more determined to do whatever it took to rid herself of at least that one negative emotion about this man.

"But I heard—" Seth began, swallowing hard against the lump in his throat, "I heard you crying when I left, while I was standing in the hall."

"I was angry and resentful of what happened and—and of how it happened without me being mentally prepared to deal with it," Jenna told him fiercely. "It took me months to get over you, Seth. I was finally starting to get my old life back. You messed that up by forcibly reminding me of the chemistry between us. I'm still angry about the way you seduced me, and I haven't forgiven you yet."

Seth met her gaze, trying to understand, but her logic eluded him. "If you're still that mad about us having sex, then why are you here?"

"Because—damn it, Seth—I still want you," Jenna said sadly, but proudly. "I don't like you. I certainly don't trust you. I don't want to stay all night or date you or anything normal that's supposed to be between two people. This sexual attraction I feel for you pisses me off in ways I can't begin to explain, but heaven help me, I want you inside me again despite all that. I want you so badly I can barely function for thinking about it all the time."

Seth ran a hand over his face. It was his worst nightmare come true. Jenna didn't want to be in his life. But it was also his perfect fantasy that Jenna was aching to be with him.

What did it say about his own self-respect, he wondered, that he was actually thinking that sleeping with her might be enough for him as well? It was barely half of what he truly wanted, but hell—maybe he could at least sleep again.

"So it looks like you and I have the same problem. Are you suggesting we do something to fix it? What exactly do you want from me?" Seth asked carefully. He had to work hard to keep his relief and his rapidly returning excitement from being too obvious.

Jenna kicked a piece of carpet lint with the toe of her leather shoe. She hadn't thought about what would happen if Seth didn't throw a fit or throw her out. His quiet question about what she wanted was a surprise to her. Beyond being sexual with him again, she didn't want anything. How could she ever tell him that without sounding like a heartless bitch?

She looked resentfully at his calm, relaxed stance. Always the businessman, Jenna thought resentfully, watching Seth stand by patiently while she made up her mind. He seemed to be simply waiting to see what kind of deal she wanted to make. Well he was in for a shock.

"I guess I want you to be my damn booty call," Jenna answered at last. "But that's all I want from you."

Jenna thought Seth once again looked like she'd slapped him.

"Your booty call? You mean you want to be involved with me for just sex? Even though you're still mad at me?" Seth watched as Jenna nodded yes. "I have to admit I never saw that offer coming. People don't usually want sex with partners they hate. So how do you see it working? Did you want me to sign a contract?" Seth finally asked, sarcastic and only half joking.

After Casey practically calling him effeminate, Jenna's idea about him being only good for sex was at least a small step up for his ego. The biggest trouble Seth was having with the deal was that Jenna had concluded he was good in bed, but not good enough to spend time with out of it. There had to be more to her feelings for him than just sex, Seth thought. He just couldn't imagine Jenna was that calculating a person or that she had so little faith in love.

"Are you still getting those daily feeds from that dictionary site?" Jenna asked with a hesitant smile, trying to give both of them a little time to think about her suggestion. He'd sent her the link to the booty call contract one day and she'd laughed about it. Now it wasn't so funny.

"Yes," Seth said simply. "Some of the new terms that get submitted still make me laugh."

Jenna smiled for real at that. Seth used to text her the latest new terms and what they meant. It often put a smile on her face as well, but being that kind of friendly would just lead to trouble—and more heartache.

"I wouldn't make you sign a booty call contract if you promise to abide by the spirit of it," Jenna said easily, getting into the idea now, which more and more seemed like a good solution to her. She could get all she wanted of him and finally get Seth out of her system. "Look at my offer as a business arrangement, Seth. I know how serious you are about your business deals. I want to have sex with you, but nothing else. Could you live with that?"

"Give me a minute," Seth said, turning back to look out the patio door. Instead of seeing his courtyard, he ended up watching Jenna bite her lip in the reflection. It was a dead giveaway that Jenna was not at all sure she wanted what she was asking for, which was reason enough to consider it.

Seth figured it'd be a toss up between them as to who got tired of the deal first.

The thing making him hesitate was the thought that maybe he should say no on principle. After all, he was in love with Jenna. He wanted to marry her and make babies with her. He'd told her that. A sex-only relationship was not even in the same ballpark as his other long-term goals for them.

Still—it seemed like it might be a way, especially since it was Jenna's idea and not his, to finish his remaining time-consuming business without offending Jenna with how much time it consumed. Jenna wouldn't be involved enough in his life to be offended by his need to take a phone call at odd times now and again. But maybe he could use their strictly sexual relationship to keep Jenna bound to him in a much stronger way than merely dating as friends ever would have anyway. This might keep her with him until he was completely free to romance her and convince her to marry him.

And while she was in his bed or he in hers, Seth decided, he would make double-damn-sure Jenna never felt the urge to shop around for better. The thought of not having to compete with any more Allen Stedman types was another damn good reason to do this.

But they needed some ground rules so he knew for sure there was only him.

"I won't share you intimately," Seth said firmly, working to keep the venom out of his voice. "Casual dating is okay I guess, but if you want to sleep with another man—just call me and say goodbye."

"Not a problem," Jenna said. "I don't do casual sex. You're the first sex-only relationship that I've ever considered. Let's call our agreement casual, but monogamous."

Seth nodded, fighting to keep from grinning, and fighting hard not to dash across the room and throw the damn stubborn woman to the floor again. Jenna had just confessed to wanting only him, but he sure as hell wasn't going to point that out to her at the moment.

"If either one of us wants out of the deal, what then?" Seth asked, when he could trust himself not to smile like an idiot.

"No harm. No foul." Jenna crossed her chest as she spoke. "I think that's only fair."

"Fine. Since I still want you too—and badly, I can't see not accepting this deal," Seth said, walking across the floor to her, stopping only when they were toe to toe.

"Should I expect a call for sex soon?" Seth asked, hoping the elation wasn't showing so much that he'd scare her away. If Jenna thought he was hard for her last time, the woman was in for an even bigger shock next time around. He'd have to be careful since she had confessed to it hurting before.

Jenna bit her lip, wondering if she dare tell him what she wanted. Again, Seth just seemed to be waiting on her. It was just sex, Jenna reminded herself, and the nature of this type relationship was to just ask—anytime.

"How about now?" The question barely made it out of her mouth, before Seth had his lips searing hers again with the heat she'd been dreaming about for days. Her arms came up to help her wrap herself around him. He felt so damn good. The tension inside her unwound as she groaned his name.

"Take a shower with me," Seth demanded against her mouth as he broke for air. "I need one, and then I need you."

Seth pulled the purse off her shoulder with one hand and pulled off the jacket she was wearing with the other. He tossed both on a nearby chair.

When his cell phone rang, they both froze, staring at each other.

"Take it," Jenna said, lifting her chin. "It doesn't matter. I'm staying. I need this."

Seth clamped a hand around her wrist to be sure she couldn't leave and dragged her with him to the phone on the end table.

Japan, he saw, looking at phone, and then at the clock. Damn it. He had to take the call. He had specifically asked them to call at this time.

"Take it," Jenna said again, not believing the words coming out of her mouth. She was determined never to get upset over a simple phone call again. That was over. No more hurt feelings. "Take the damn call, and then I want you to—"

Seth closed his mouth hard over Jenna's, his tongue dancing against hers before she could say words that would make him forget the call entirely. He wanted to be with her now. It was almost as bad as the first time. The last thing in the world he wanted to do was deal with a business call.

He was going to fix that next.

When Seth broke the kiss, he stared hard at Jenna, contemplating his options. She nodded hard to reassure him she meant what she said. Finally, Seth answered the call, speaking Japanese to the person on the line.

Jenna put her hand on Seth's chest, felt his heart pounding beneath it. The harsh sounding language rolled through him as he spoke, vibrating powerfully through his chest muscles, which were tightening and bunching under her hands. Jenna's thoughts floated in a lust-filled dreamlike state. At least she had something interesting to do this time while Seth took a business call, she thought wildly, letting her free hand roam. Seth still had a death-grip on the other wrist and showed no signs of being willing to release his hold.

Jenna let her roaming hand find its way down and across a flat stomach, and then even farther, exploring new territory. She was barely able to refrain from touching what she wanted to explore, but knew it would destroy his ability to talk on the phone. Seth was already breathing hard. It made her giggle. She wanted to tease him and ask him if he always became short of breath when he spoke Japanese. But that was too friendly a comment to make, and she wouldn't want him to think she was jealous or cared about his business.

Seth watched Jenna exploring his body, and then heard her wicked giggle. He would definitely never take a phone call on the way to bed with her again. There was no cutting short the cultural courtesies that were expected in the call. But damn it, Seth thought, sighing at the heaven her hands were on his body. He wanted her. A ragged sigh spoke volumes about the twisted emotional state Seth was in.

Jenna understood. With her hands on him, she was so tuned to Seth, that she knew instantly when she had pushed him to the edge of their teasing. Tugging Seth by the wrist he still held of hers, Jenna pulled him down to the couch, and did what she hoped would ease the situation slightly for both of them. She crawled into his lap and put her face against his throat while he talked. Seth let go of her wrist to put his arm around her and hold her close.

Stupid, Seth thought. So stupid that he had not been intimate with this woman before.

He had been so very, very stupid to not celebrate all the passion between them.

Some twenty minutes later Seth hung up the phone only to find that Jenna was fast asleep in his arms. Evidently, he hadn't been the only one not sleeping. He wrapped his other arm around her and turned them both until they were lying together on his thankfully large couch.

Jenna wouldn't like this, Seth thought, enjoying the sensation of holding her sleeping body. She also wouldn't like knowing that Seth wanted this intimacy as much as he wanted to be inside her. Lust still was on him, but love for her had him cradling Jenna in his arms and sighing in contentment.

Seth couldn't believe that a mere hour ago he thought he'd never speak to her again, and now he held her. He loved Jenna Ranger, would probably always love her.

It was the last conscious thought Seth had before he fell peacefully asleep as well, relieved to have Jenna in his arms at last.

When Seth woke at ten that evening, it was to find he was alone on the couch. The loneliness without her returned in a rush. Then he saw the note under the phone.

Glad we worked out a deal. See you tomorrow night at nine. J.

Not great, Seth thought, wishing Jenna was still sleeping beside him, or better yet waking up to find him inside her as he would have been if she had stayed. But he'd let tomorrow at nine be good enough. At least Jenna was in his life again.

When it came to something this important, Seth would find a way to be a very a patient man.

Chapter 7

At eight forty-five the next night, shaved and completely ready for the woman coming through the door in fifteen minutes, Seth paced his living room watching the clock. At eight forty-seven the doorbell rang and he all but ripped the knob off opening it.

Jenna stood there smiling and nervous with an apologetic look on her face.

"I'm a little early," she said, clearing her throat and fighting not to blush.

"Early is good," Seth replied hoarsely. Then he grabbed Jenna's wrist, dragged her across the threshold, and slammed the door behind her before crushing her against it. The purse and sweater she carried fell to the floor unheeded. Seth didn't let their bodies follow even though he badly wanted to do so.

"Put your arms around my neck," Seth ordered, lifting her by the hips when she did as he asked. He groaned at the pleasure of having her in his arms for real and lifted her legs to wrap them around his waist. When he pushed Jenna against the door again, Seth pushed himself hard between her legs as well. He could feel the heat of her even through the denim that separated them. The sounds of pleasure Jenna made in her throat had Seth shaking in anticipation.

Mine, he thought. *Thank God. Mine.*

The desperation he suddenly felt to make sure Jenna was completely his was almost as strong as it had been the first time.

"Bed now," Seth said firmly, walking with her still wrapped around him. When they got to his room, he carried her to his king-size bed and followed her down, pressing against her with their clothes still on. He kept her legs around him as his hips moved against hers, using his hands to encourage her to stay wrapped around him.

His whispered demands spoke the truth of how he was feeling about her being willingly with him at last. "Hold on to me. Stay with me. Don't let me go."

"Okay, but this would be so much better naked," Jenna stated logically, her voice breaking with every movement of Seth's body against hers.

"Yes it would," Seth agreed, pushing against the heat between her legs until he was dizzy with the promise of getting inside her.

Then, never ceasing his rhythmic movements, Seth worked the buttons of her shirt until they were all free. When he found a front clasp bra, he unsnapped it as well, pushing all the clothing off her breasts until they were bared to him. Jenna's breasts were small, taut, and perfect.

And all mine, Seth thought again.

He was finally becoming accustomed to how that feeling turned itself into thoughts he never thought to have about any woman. It was all Seth could do not to say the words out loud.

Taking one peaked, excited nipple into his mouth, Seth sucked fiercely as he pressed Jenna harder into his bed with each slide of his body against hers. When the climax hit her, Seth felt her clamoring beneath him to get closer, to wrap herself tighter around him. It was all he could do to keep from yelling out his success. Seth switched his mouth to her other breast and moved his hands to her hips as he carefully rocked the rest of the orgasm away.

That's one, Seth thought. Then he pleased his inner Neanderthal by resting his still aching erection on her now quiet body beneath his. The pride he felt at having satisfied her was second only to the anticipation of making Jenna have another orgasm when he was inside her.

While Seth let her senses settle and her body recover, he lay on Jenna thinking *"mine"* over and over until he suddenly remembered laughing at Casey for saying and thinking the same damn thing about Alexa. Seth ended up laughing at himself even as he pressed harder on Jenna to stake an ownership he finally appreciated and understood.

"Your turn," Jenna said dryly. "But I want more clothes off first. That didn't quite do it for me."

Seth moved hands to her jeans, popping the snap on them and pulling the rest of her shirt free. "That's enough until I can trust myself not to dive right into you."

Jenna said nothing for a moment. She could see from Seth's face he wasn't teasing.

"Maybe I want you to dive right in," Jenna said at last, realizing in that moment she meant every word.

"Maybe you do," Seth said, grinning at the sincerity in her gaze. "That's not necessarily what I want. It's just what would happen if you were completely naked right now."

"Next time I come here I'm going to have on less clothes," Jenna promised, her words more threat than anything else. She was tracing his wide shoulders with her hands as his laughter rumbled through both of their bodies.

"We'll never make it to the bed if you do," he warned, insanely pleased that Jenna had mentioned a next time already. "If you had shown up here in any way naked at all, I would have nailed you against the damn door the moment you stepped through it."

"Good," Jenna said quietly. "I'm empty and I want you to fill me up. I'm tired of feeling this way."

The idea of filling her up had him trembling on top of her. Seth buried his face in her neck, inhaling the scent there. He never wanted Jenna to feel unsatisfied again.

"I'm a starving man, Jenna Ranger. It's not safe to push me past caring about being nice. I might honestly hurt you being too rough," he told her.

Jenna reached down and pulled the very nice and expensive polo Seth wore up and over his head. Then she reached between them and unsnapped his snug-fitting jeans. Reaching inside when she could, Jenna wrapped her hand around the hard evidence of just how much Seth wanted her.

He was absolutely harder than any man she had ever known, and probably could hurt her. Jenna tightened her hand around him, wanting him unrestrained despite the risk. He would hurt her a little and then the discomfort would turn into her finally feeling like everything was right in the world.

As she stroked him inside his clothes, Seth moaned. The sound of his obvious desire for her drove Jenna mad wanting to sate it for him. It made her want to do crazy things like rip his clothes off and beg him to come inside her again. Jenna decided her desire for Seth had to be abnormal, but self-awareness didn't change the reality of what she had to have or die trying to get.

"Seth, I want you inside me. *Now*," Jenna whispered fiercely, "stop making me wait."

Seth rolled off her and away, shucking his jeans and underwear in single motion. He reached out a hand to the bedside table where a handful of condoms were waiting. He opened one, put it on, and then turned back to see Jenna had removed her jeans and underwear, too.

He crawled between her legs and nudged the entrance to where he badly wanted to go again.

"Are you sure about this?" he asked. "If you cry this time, I'm never touching you physically again. I can't bear the thought of really hurting you."

Snorting, Jenna pushed Seth to his side, and then to his back so she could crawl on top on him. "Haven't you ever heard of playing through the pain? It doesn't last long."

She positioned herself over him and slid down, embedding him inside her before Seth could say much about it. When she had taken him in as far as she could, Jenna was breathing hard and fast losing control of herself. She was so in awe of the connection she couldn't bring herself to move on him for a minute.

Even this much was damn satisfying, Jenna concluded, starting at last to move slowly. She didn't want things ending too soon for either of them. Instead, she wanted to keep him inside her, just where he was now. Everything else was a bonus as far as she was concerned.

Her attention was drawn from her thoughts when Seth called her name and clutched her hips tightly. When she repeated the action of rising and falling on him again, Seth held her hips for a couple of heartbeats before letting her repeat it. Finally, she grabbed both his hands and pushed them to the side of his head. Her unbuttoned shirt flapped around her and her bra dangled inside it.

Seth looked at her with raw desire but wasn't acting on what she saw in his gaze.

"Stop being so nice," Jenna said fiercely. "This is not the time. *I need you, Seth.*"

Seth met her furious stare without remorse for his actions, his eyes glazed from the pleasure of being inside her while she rode him.

But not wanting to deny Jenna anything this time—their first mutual time, Seth finally let his body actively seek release. In doing so, he used his greater strength and rolled them over until he could surge in and out of her at will. Reversing their previous situation, Seth now held Jenna's wrists at her sides as his gaze locked itself to hers.

"Jenna," Seth whispered, her name a reverent prayer for what they doing. Words of love were on the tip of his tongue, but Seth held those back, knowing for sure now Jenna didn't want to hear them. He couldn't risk making her upset again. Not now. Not this time. Instead he told her another kind of truth.

"It's never been like this with anyone else," Seth said, sinking completely into her and pushing deep to emphasize the point. "I've never been this hard and aching with a woman before you."

"Good," she keened, lifting her hips and closing her eyes. "Seth—please. Don't hold back."

Seth groaned and gave in to her demands for release, the ones she made out loud and the silent ones her body was making for her. His hands slid from her wrists to link his fingers with hers. He rocked them both over and over until Jenna screamed his name and he groaned in satisfaction at the same time. When he stopped rocking, she was still straining and vibrating around him.

That's two, Seth told himself. Then he let his weight carefully come to rest on her intimately and felt her heart beating madly against his. He wondered how many more times he could push Jenna over the edge tonight.

"Don't move and don't make me let you go yet," Seth ordered softly, needing to absorb the reality of Jenna's body compliant and resting beneath his at last. He wanted time to memorize their first real moment of connection and wanted her to want the same. Their breathing was the only noise in the room for several long minutes.

Eventually, Seth turned loose of her hands and rolled them to their sides. This time Jenna didn't disconnect their bodies or pull away. He wondered what she would think if she knew how much he wanted her still, because it was a shock even to him.

"When do you need to leave," Seth asked, lifting strands of her hair away from her face and tucking them behind her ear. He kept his voice neutral, but was humbled by how difficult it was not to demand she stay. He was never going to be able to make fun of Casey again, and he owed the man who raised him a huge apology for being disrespectful about his feelings.

"Soon," Jenna said firmly. "Why?"

"I'm not done with you yet tonight, but I understand if you need to go—or want to go," Seth told her, watching color bloom in her cheeks. He'd just now noticed the lamp he had left burning was still on.

There hadn't been a lot of men in Jenna's sexual experience that ever went a second round, much less a man like Seth who seemed not to have a limit—or at least not one she could find so far. Embarrassment colored her face, but she well knew you couldn't fix a problem until you knew what kind you had.

"Am I not satisfying you?" Jenna asked, making herself say the words, though they humiliated her. Men had told her she was beautiful, but of the few she had slept with, none had ever praised her skill in bed. It was simply a matter of not knowing, Jenna told herself. She lifted her chin to wait for Seth's answer, regardless of how humbling it was to think she might be less than proficient from his point of view.

Seth considered the earnestness in Jenna's expression when he answered with the simple truth he had no wish to hide from her anyway. His ego didn't need stroking. Other things about him did. He wanted her to want to be the woman who did it, more than he wanted anything else.

"Oh, you satisfy me plenty, baby—I'm just backed up with not having sex for a long time. There hadn't been anyone before you for months, and then—well, there hasn't been anyone since I met you," Seth said, smiling at her.

"Seth, it's been at least eight months since you met me," Jenna said quietly.

"Yes. Probably about a year and half since I had sex with a woman," Seth told her, unashamed. "Casey was here long before I met you, and I spent more time with him than I did dating. He missed Susan terribly during those first few months he was here. I didn't want him to feel more alone by seeing me bring a woman home."

Jenna reached out a finger and put it on the pulse at the base of his throat. It was calmer now than it had been earlier. Calm was a word she always used condescendingly with Seth. She now knew better. He was patient. He was willing to wait and work for what he wanted. That didn't seem as bad to her now that she knew he used that approach to everything—including her.

"How long do you think it will take you to catch up?" Jena asked, her throat tight as she choked out the words. She didn't really want to think of Seth waiting or why he had done so. She wasn't ready to like him again for being there for Casey and suffering with his cousin through his loss.

"I have no idea, but I'm not an animal. I can wait for next time," Seth said, laughing and holding her serious gaze. "I just wanted to explain why I don't seem to be able to get enough of you."

Jenna separated their bodies then, but she did so nicely. "Is your shower big enough for two people?"

Seth rolled out of bed, removed the condom, and held out a hand to her. "Absolutely."

They washed themselves and each other, not lingering too long. The shower felt more intimate than everything else they had done so far. They talked little and Seth handed her a large bath sheet afterward that almost touched her ankles.

The woman was at least five foot seven, he thought, but Jenna seemed really petite to him tonight.

When they finally made it back to the bed, Jenna pushed him back on it with one hand. "I know one thing guaranteed to knock you out and make you sleep," she told him, bending to kiss his knee and up the inside of his thigh.

"Jenna, you don't have to seduce me. I'm already seduced. You certainly don't have to—you know what I mean," Seth said roughly, mind reeling as she continued to explore him with her mouth. "Look—I'm not going to be able to stop you if you keep that up."

"Good," Jenna said, "no condom either. I want this without it. After what you told me, I trust you with this. Let me do what I want."

Seth laughed as she ran her tongue along the other thigh and back up to run it along his hard, aching erection. "You can always do whatever you want with me. I just didn't want you to think—*Jenna.*" With her mouth moving over him and her hair spilling between his legs, all Seth could say was her name.

When her hands got involved, he grabbed the bed sheets trying to maintain some decorum with her. Not long after, he heard someone calling out in a tortured voice and realized with shock it was him. Still her mouth kept moving even after that until he forgot everything but the woman he was happy to let control him.

When Jenna finally let go and kissed her way up Seth's body to his mouth, she devilishly plunged her tongue in deep. It pleased her to hear him whimper into her mouth. His compliance was the headiest pleasure she'd had tonight. If there was pride at his slack jaw and blurred gaze, so what? She'd been motivated, and Seth had been fairly easy to please.

Payback, Jenna decided, just payback for the first orgasm Seth had given her. She refused to give any other definition to what she had just done to and for him. She certainly wasn't going to confess that it had been the first time she'd completed that act with any man, or that she wanted to repeat it with him again.

Drunk on feeling like she was finally in control of at least one thing that happened between them, Jenna quietly acknowledged it was not a sterling character moment for her. But it was a true one for her nature. She was very pleased with herself—and Seth.

"I need to go now," Jenna whispered against his lips. "Can I come back in a few days?"

"Come any time," Seth said, lifting his hand to her hair again, wishing he could ask her stay so he could hold her. "I'm going to think of a hundred ways to please you between now and then. You're obviously better in bed than I am, and I'm very competitive."

Jenna put her face against his shoulder to stifle her laughter and her pink face. Maybe she had been better than she knew, but it hadn't mattered until the man beneath her had confirmed it. Her pleasure at that knowledge was going to her head fast and pushing her into wanting to do rash things—like curl up beside him and stay within reach.

"Sex is not a competition," she told him, still unwilling for him to know that it was just him who inspired her.

"No. I guess sex isn't a competition, but I had plans to give you more orgasms than you gave me. Now we're even," Seth said seriously. "I owe you."

"No, you don't. We don't owe each other anything," Jenna said, pulling away and rolling out of bed to her feet before she could change her mind. "That's one of the best things about our agreement."

Jenna dressed in record time, relenting to come back to bed to kiss Seth once more while he looked at her with heavy lidded eyes still full of appreciation. She appreciated him, too.

"Come back anytime," Seth said, his mouth warm on hers.

"In a few days," Jenna said, straightening, fighting the inclination she had to climb in beside him. Cuddling was not part of their agreement, and she liked what they had. It suited her. "Sleep."

"Text me when you get home. I can't help wanting to know you're safe. Blame Casey—he made me that way," Seth told her, using his cousin as an excuse.

"Okay," Jenna said, sighing. "I'm not going to argue over a simple text. Good night, Seth."

"Good night," he said, stroking her cheek before dropping his hand.

Minutes later, he heard the distinct click of the front door latch locking into place and knew Jenna had truly gone. He stared wide-eyed and silent at the ceiling until he heard the phone vibrate on the nightstand some twenty minutes later. Seth looked at the message and sighed.

Home safe. Sleep now.

He typed back quickly to make sure she would get his text.

Thanks for texting. Good night.

"I love you," Seth said to the phone, tossing it back on the nightstand in frustration.

Then he closed his eyes and let the first relaxed sleep he'd had in a couple of years take him under.

Chapter 8

Jenna was standing at her office window contemplating why in the last two weeks she hadn't been able to wait more than two days to see Seth, when her boss knocked and came into her office.

"Glad you're in," Todd Warren said, smiling smugly at his favorite architect. "It's not every day I get to make someone's dreams come true. Today is your lucky day."

Jenna laughed and walked back to her desk. "Why Todd, you sound almost giddy."

"Giddy—*giddy*? Yeah, I guess that's about right. We just got a new fat contract and you were the reason," Todd said. "Client wants a six-hundred-thousand-dollar house and has allocated one hundred thousand dollars for the lot, which has to be substantial, have some ground around it. Beyond that his list of stipulations is fairly minor. He said to tell you to design the house you wanted to live in yourself and don't be stingy with your dreams. Apparently, he's checked out several things you have done and loves your style."

"His name isn't Kaiser or Gallagher or—what's Jim's other name now? Simpson! It wasn't Simpson, was it?" Jenna demanded, unable to believe a client had randomly selected her from the limited amount of other residential designing she had done.

Her work for Todd was primarily commercial. She certainly wasn't famous, but Jenna thought she did have a unique style that she'd been hoping would catch on in time.

When she pulled herself out of her thoughts, Todd was shaking his head. "There is no name. Client wouldn't identify himself. Deposit was sent electronically from a local bank, but through escrow. His attorney authorized it and will be authorizing all future draws against the work being done. Strange, sure, but the first check still cashed."

"So a mystery man or woman—" Jenna began.

"Man," Todd said confidently. "I talked to the attorney, who wouldn't give the client's name, but did refer to the client as *he*."

"Okay, so the mystery man wants me to design *him* the house of *my* dreams?" Jenna said. "Why?"

"Wrong question. Totally wrong question. This is your chance to do what every architect dreams of doing. Bring your dream house to life and make a design portfolio that will sell your work from here on out," Todd insisted.

"Don't you get an odd feeling about this?" Jenna insisted back.

"You did the Nolan house during your internship at Jagardi and made the cover of *Architect Digest*," Todd reminded her. "That's why I hired you. How is this different? This is another break. Some eccentric dude plucked you out of the architecting ether and wants to let you play with his money. You're going to give him a showpiece afterward and a story to tell people he invites to dinner. That's what people with his kind of money to burn want."

Jenna sighed. "I guess you're right. I'm obviously not going to turn the chance down, Todd. I just got a weird feeling when you told me, that's all. It's the whole mystery-man thing. I'm not opposed to surprises, but I'm not big on secrets."

Todd smiled at her and laughed.

"What?" she asked, wondering what was up with her boss's strange gaze on her face.

"That's the calmest reaction I've ever seen you have. Who's the guy?" Todd asked, narrowing his eyes and studying Jenna's serene face. For a couple of weeks now, Jenna had come to work looking more peaceful and happy than he'd ever seen her. Restless and irritable were Jenna Ranger's usual moods. Some guy was putting that smile on her face. Todd would bet money on it.

"What guy?" Jenna asked back, turning her gaze to some papers on her desk, which she shuffled.

"*The guy* who's got you so mellow you're not pacing and yelling at me," Todd told her. "There has to be a guy."

"That's a very personal comment, Todd," Jenna challenged, glaring at him to discourage his poking into her private life. "And a question I don't have to answer."

"Says the woman who refused to date me and hooked me up with my wife instead," Todd said, smiling. "And for which I remain exceedingly grateful. My wife is both hot and the love of my life."

Charming bastard, Jenna thought, laughing until she snorted at the lovesick look Todd always got talking about his wife Linda. "The guy in my life is no one important. Get off my case, Todd. I'm allowed to have a life outside your company."

"Well, I had high hopes that my hot-headed, stubborn, artistic-minded architect finally had a healthier way to use that restless energy of hers, but hey—at least clients think she's talented," Todd said, frowning and rolling his eyes.

"That's sexual harassment, Mr. Warren," Jenna told him, laughing and arching her eyebrow at him.

"Not when I'm hoping you marry the guy and keep that mellow outlook forever. That's just healthy self-preservation from a boss who values you and the kind of money you're evidently going to bring to my company." Todd jumped up and walked to the door. "Hey—bring that smile on your face and the sexy guy to the Vanguard Ball we're helping sponsor next weekend."

"Can't do it," Jenna said easily, "we're not dating. I don't really like the man. We just have a mutual agreement to let nature take its course for a while. I can still get a date though. Don't worry about me showing up forlorn."

"I don't. I'm worried about the sexy guy," Todd said, grinning. "Even if you didn't look as stunning as your mother, it's sad to think you'll be breaking some poor sap's heart eventually. That soft smile you have now is going to improve your dating life a thousand fold from here on out. Be grateful to the man, Jenna. Let him down easily when the time comes, and then find another just like him. He's good for you."

"Stop worrying about my love life," Jenna said, frowning. "I'll build your damn house and spend every dime efficiently. You need to think about giving me a decent bonus if I make the press for your company."

"Done," Todd said quickly. "You can have the bonus to spend during the two weeks you take off for your honeymoon. Keep that guy, Jenna. He's obviously good in bed. You haven't yelled once since I came in here—no matter what I've said."

"It's called maturity. Besides, I'm getting too old to yell. From now on, I'm just going to throw things," Jenna picked up a pencil and threw it at the door that closed too quickly behind the laughing man she had enjoyed working for until today.

She didn't need anyone pointing out how much Seth had improved her outlook on life. At an average of being with him three to four times a week, it was hard enough just dealing with how much she was becoming used to him.

"I'm sorry to be asking you so late. I just forgot about not having a maid of honor until Sydney asked me about the dress. It was crazy to think I could get the whole wedding planned in two weeks," Lauren said, sighing with every delicious bite of ice cream she put into her mouth.

"Are you sure you don't want Mama or Regina for your maid of honor?" Jenna asked, digging into her ice cream with almost as much gusto as Lauren, who was pregnant.

"No. I want a single woman. You're the only single friend I have left," Lauren told her. "I know you're a lot younger than I am and might not want to do this for an old lady."

"Okay—stop," Jenna said, holding up a hand. "I am nothing but flattered that you asked. I've only ever been a bridesmaid up to now. I just wanted to know you'd made the choice. Regina didn't stand with Mama. I figured you would ask her."

Lauren giggled. "No way. Regina bawls at weddings. Her mascara runs, her makeup melts, and the woman couldn't care less. Can you imagine the wedding photos? When you even bring up the subject of a wedding, Regina's all *count-me-out* before you can ask her anything anyway."

Jenna giggled and polished off the rest of her ice cream in one giant spoonful. Her appetite had greatly improved over the last couple of weeks. She'd always heard great sex could do a lot for a person. She was learning it was true. Her moods had never been better.

"Well, I'm your woman then. I'm single and never cry at weddings. So what's my primary duty for the next few days?" Jenna asked.

"Keep me from having an emotional breakdown, and make sure I don't eat so much that I can't fit my pregnant body into that amazing dress Sydney made for me," Lauren said, her gaze both serious and laughing.

"It's only four more days. I think we can handle it even if you eat round the clock," Jenna said, laughing.

"You've obviously not seen me eat lately," Lauren said, leaning back in her chair and wondering what the harm of seconds on ice cream would be for her.

"No," Jenna said firmly, laughing openly at the look on Lauren's face. "You do not need seconds. I saw that look of longing in your eyes. There—how did I do?"

Lauren laughed. "Great—too great in fact. It's bad enough I have two mind-reading friends. Now you're doing it too. I'm a weak woman and have no willpower. That's what got me into this condition."

"I beg to differ," Jim said, walking into the kitchen and smiling at the two women perched at his granite-topped island. His house was a home now that Lauren was in it every day. "I happen to know for a fact that I'm the cause of your current condition and I'm very proud of it. Just don't tell Regina how proud I am. She still hasn't forgiven me."

Jenna watched Lauren giggle and Jim dip his head to kiss her, laughing against her lips as he did so. She couldn't help sighing in envy at their loving relationship. *One day*, she promised herself. One day she would find that same kind of love.

"Well, I'm at least happy my first go at being an MOH is for a woman who is for sure going to be happily married. I watched friends do this for each other and it was horrendous every time. You're both so sweet. This is going to be a pleasure. So are we doing a bachelorette party and getting a stripper?" Jenna teased the question out, making sure her eyes were enthusiastic as she watched for Jim's reaction. It had been a long time since she'd felt light-hearted enough to tease anyone.

Jim's head jerked up from Lauren's, and he bellowed out, "No. Absolutely no strippers."

Jenna laughed so hard at Jim's declaration, she almost fell off the bar stool. "Why, Jim? Don't you trust the woman you're going to marry?" Her eyes darted to Lauren, who was laughing behind her hand.

"It's not about trust. Lauren just doesn't need the extra—stimulation," Jim said finally, tugging on his laughing bride-to-be's hair before stalking out of the room.

"What's his deal with the stripper?" Jenna asked softly after Jim had exited, whispering the question in case he was still within hearing distance. "Is that about the man Mama kept you from picking up?"

"God no, we got past that long ago," Lauren said, holding her belly while she laughed. "Let's just say it doesn't take much to get me in the mood these days. Jim doesn't even undress in front me anymore. I hear my libido is revving on baby hormones."

"Really?" Jenna asked, shocked. Then she laughed again. "Wow. That's—that's almost too much information." Saying this caused her to laugh again.

Lauren shrugged and leaned closer. "When you're not constantly worried about getting pregnant, the sex is absolutely amazing. Seriously. I can't believe it myself. I could do it two or three times a day lately. I'm figuring it will slow down when I start to show more."

Jenna closed her eyes and sighed. "Something to look forward to when my time comes, I suppose. Thanks for telling me. I didn't mean it when I said it was too much information. I'm just envious."

Lauren reached out and took one of Jenna's hands in hers. "Love will find you, honey. When it does, grab it with both hands. And it's okay to let desire be your guide if that comes first. I think it just works like that for some of us."

Jenna looked away and swallowed hard. "If I ever find myself in that kind of situation, I'll keep it in mind."

Lauren studied Jenna's face, saw the flicker of something like guilt in her gaze, but she said nothing more even though she badly wanted to pry.

"So I told Sydney about asking you, and he said to send you by for a fitting when you said yes," Lauren told her, changing the subject and seeing instant relief in Jenna's eyes. "You can wear any color as long as it's blue."

Jenna laughed again. "My favorite color," she said, leaning over to give Lauren a hug.

Seth ran a fingertip down Jenna's belly, stopping to explore her navel. There wasn't an inch of her he hadn't explored already. Or an inch he wasn't wanting to explore again. Each journey over her was a discovery of something new.

"Are you going to Lauren and Jim's wedding this weekend?" Seth asked.

"Yes, I have to. I'm Lauren's maid of honor," Jenna said. "I've decided not to take a date. I wouldn't have time to spend with anyone anyway."

71

"I wasn't planning to take a date either," Seth said casually, running strands of her hair through his fingers. "I may end up working security with Casey again. Save a dance for me if you can. I promise to behave this time."

Jenna laughed. "I like not fighting with you Seth."

"I like not fighting with you too," Seth said in return, grinning. "Is that a euphemism for sex?"

Jenna snorted at his question.

"Have you told anyone about—us?" she asked. "I never thought to ask, but I'd rather keep this just private—not that I would ask you to lie. If you need to tell Casey I understand, but I'd have to tell my mother, and I would need to do it before Casey did. I don't want Mama mad at me or hurt."

"I'm not telling anyone," Seth said. "As far as I'm concerned, no one needs to know but us. If you decide to tell your mother, let me know. Casey is the only person I care about, and he'd never butt in anyway."

Jenna studied her hands. "I'm not—I'm not ashamed of what we're doing. I don't regret a moment. It's just I don't want the pressure that people would put on us to—date—or whatever."

If her mother, Regina, or Lauren knew, she'd hear endlessly about a potential happily-ever-after. She didn't want happily-ever-after. She wanted this—just Seth and her—happy in bed together.

Seth rolled over on her and kissed the tops of her breasts. "I feel the same the way. I don't want any pressure. I just want this." He kissed his way down between her breasts and across her soft belly. "You are the most beautiful woman I've ever known, and I don't think I've told you that before now. Still it's true. You have your mother's genetics and your father's nature. It's an intimidating combination that endlessly turns me on. I bet you get your way in almost everything you set your mind to in the world."

"Not everything," Jenna sighed, enjoying his lips travelling over her, "but I guess I get most things I go after."

"Let me see you go after something. What do you want from me right now?" Seth asked, his tongue licking down her belly, licking a trail from her navel down and then back up to a breast peaked and waiting for him.

"I seem to want whatever it is you do to me next," she told him honestly. "Use your imagination. Surprise me."

"Fine. Spread your legs," Seth ordered, almost mindless with lust when she did what he asked with no hesitation. The woman gave all every time. He eased inside her, lifting her legs around him as he did.

"Now hold on," Seth said, his voice taut and sharp with the need to move hard in her clawing at the edges of his sanity.

He rolled them until he had Jenna on top, and then he sat up with her in his arms. He owed Allen Stedman for his new muscles—and more for not taking advantage of Jenna when he had the chance. He would just have to settle that debt some other time.

For now, Seth rocked himself up into Jenna, finding a rhythm that was like making music. Jenna's legs unwound until her heels hit the bed. She pulled her legs back until her knees rested beside his hips. She rocked down on him returning the favor as he rocked up into her.

"I like this a lot," Jenna said, rocking down hard on him and watching Seth's eyes narrow to slits.

"So do I," Seth said, pushing upward and lifting himself against the front of her as he did. He felt her breasts pushing against him with every stroke.

"Is this your idea of competition?" Jenna asked breathlessly, on the verge of shattering.

"No," Seth said quietly. "You could stop moving right now and nothing more would happen. This is synchronous. Like dancing—only in bed. It takes two people to get something like this right."

"Is this right?" Jenna said, bearing down on him and rocking forward and back, forward and back, causing Seth to grit his teeth.

"Damn it—yes," he swore, hearing her laughter at his loss of control, which sent him straight over the edge. On Jenna's next slide down on him, Seth held her hips and ground himself up into her and against her until she came unglued, and still he pushed more.

"Enough!" Jenna called, but Seth only laughed. He pulled her down hard, keeping her impaled, and used his hands to rock her hips until he called out and fell backward with Jenna in a heap on top of him.

His heart was hammering. There was even a ringing in his ears.

"Answer that. I have to get going anyway," Jenna said.

"What?" Seth asked, his hands slipping away without his permission as Jenna moved off him. Then he heard the phone. He looked at the clock and closed his eyes briefly. New Zealand. Shit. He'd forgotten.

Seth reached for the phone. His chest was heaving from exertion still, but he answered as calmly as he could. While he conducted the conversation about a product he'd been seeking, Seth watched sadly as Jenna put on her clothes. She tiptoed quietly into his bathroom and closed the door. His attention no longer divided, Seth mostly tuned into the conversation and managed to hang up before Jenna came out.

"Stay," he said. "There should be no more interruptions."

Jenna shook her head. "I need to go. I have the dress fitting tomorrow and a new client at work. I'm getting to design my dream house."

"Wow. That's great." Seth blinked, surprised that Jenna had so easily shared her work with him. "I mean it is great, isn't it?"

Jenna didn't seem very pleased at the prospect, Seth thought. This was her chance to make her dream come true. She'd told him about wanting this kind of opportunity long ago.

Jenna shrugged. "Some mystery man has ordered a custom designed house. I'm going to do my best of course, but it seems very strange to not be able to interact with the client who'll be living in the house eventually."

"You're going do a great job," Seth told her, confidently knowing it was true. "Ever since I met you, I've dreamed of making enough money and letting you build a house for me. I bet you'd know exactly what I would like."

Jenna walked over and perched on the side of the bed. "Probably, but I'd still want to ask you to help me make design choices."

"Well, if your mystery man doesn't step forward, count me in as an alternative opinion," Seth said on a laugh. "I'd love to see the process of building a house and learn what to do when my time comes."

Jenna laughed at his earnestness. "You would do fine," she told him, "but I may take you up on your second opinion offer."

"Call me anytime," Seth offered. "Are you sure you can't stay—for one more time?"

Jenna sighed and leaned in to kiss his mouth. "Not tonight. Maybe after the wedding."

Seth kissed her back, sweeping the hair from her face so he could see her clearly. "I've never had after-the-wedding sex before. Is it good?"

"I don't know," Jenna said, laughing. "I've never had after-the-wedding sex either."

"I'll look it up on the Internet and let you know what we need to do," Seth said, liking her answering giggle.

"I can only imagine what kind of hits will come back on that search. Be careful there. I can't see you again until after Lauren's wedding no matter how churned up you get," Jenna told him.

Seth smiled as she headed to the bedroom door. At least some part of Jenna seemed to recognize that if he was churned up, he'd look to her to take care of it—and him.

"Text me when you get home," Seth ordered. He watched her nod as she left. He listened for the click, and then slid down on the pillow to rest and wait.

A half hour later the phone vibrated.

Home safe. Thinking of wedding sex now and wish I had stayed. Going to be a long 3 days.

Seth's laugh rang out in the empty bedroom as an idea occurred to him.

Wish you had stayed too. Going to be a HARD three days.

He hit send and waited. When the phone buzzed again almost immediately, he laughed harder.

No sexting! I hate walking around in wet underwear. Go to sleep Seth.

Seth chuckled at being admonished, but was happy as hell about making Jenna wet.

It's HARD to sleep when I want you this much, but I'll try. Goodnight, Jenna.

"Damn, lady—I love you so much," he said to the phone and hit send again.

When it buzzed a few moments later, he picked it up reluctantly. He knew their fun moment of texting had ended. For a little bit there, it had almost seemed like she liked him.

Goodnight Seth. See you in 3 days.

"Absolutely," Seth said to the phone. Then he closed his eyes and willed himself to sleep without her.

Chapter 9

Saturday was a great day for the wedding. The country club had donated their facilities in appreciation for all the work that Lauren had done over the years. Though it was interesting to Jenna that the strange change of heart from their board of directors had come suspiciously close on the heels of her mother making a personal visit and buying a lifetime membership for her, her family, and friends. The clear implication being that they could either accept Alex Ranger's family and friends as upstanding members of Falls Church society, or they could end up working for her after she bought the place.

Jenna knew from a distance people would think her mother had used her money to buy loyalty for Lauren's sake. Jenna well knew her mother used her wealth and everything else at her disposal to help her friends and people she loved. It was one trait Jenna admired greatly in her mother. Money was a power tool to Alexa Ranger and she knew how to use it well and to the best advantage.

However clever her mother had been in securing the country club for the wedding, Jenna had quickly learned that opting to have the whole small ceremony under one roof meant both wedding party and guests were never out of each other's sight.

As Jenna smiled for the flashing camera, her thoughts and gaze were with the man across the room talking animatedly on his phone. She couldn't remember ever seeing Seth so excited over a phone call, and heaven only knew, she'd seen him take a lot of damn calls.

"Smile, Jenna," the photographer ordered, pulling her attention back to the wedding party.

When the final photo was snapped, Jenna reached out and took the bouquet of flowers from Lauren's hand. She waved the flowers in the air to a man in a large white hat across the room and received a nod in return.

"Okay, so now this is the part where the bride gets to go stuff her face as much she wants before she has to deal with talking to all her guests," Jenna said easily. "The chef is plating up food for you and Jim right now."

Lauren closed her eyes in bliss. "You are the best MOH ever. I feel like I'll pass out if I don't get food shortly."

Jenna put both bouquets in one of her hands, and then laughed and took Lauren's free hand in hers. It was a two-for-one deal as she tugged Lauren across the room because Jim seemed permanently attached to his bride today. The man wouldn't leave her side. Jenna had to fight sighing in envy every two seconds.

Jenna's smile of pleasure was making her face hurt by the time she finally got the bride and groom over to the food. Her mother and Regina were already nibbling, and they looked up as most of the wedding party approached.

"Sydney outdid himself again. I can't believe he missed another wedding where his clothes were being shown to perfection," Alexa exclaimed, shaking her head. "Lauren, you and Jenna both look so beautiful."

Alexa then turned to Jim with a dazzling smile. "You look good too, handsome."

"I have to say that I do like my suit," Jim agreed. "Sydney Banes is an extortionist, but the fit of this jacket is amazing. I guess I'm going to have to buy more. Damn Kaiser anyway. It's his fault I'm developing a clothes fetish."

Ben walked up laughing. "One great suit does not make a fetish, Gallagher. Trust me—I know these things now. I'm sleeping with a sex therapist."

"Well, we didn't sleep much last night," Regina corrected, laughing softly at the glare her husband gave her.

"Maybe you won't have to worry about that for a week or two," Ben said sagely, his focus only on Regina and her laughing mouth as he spoke.

"Forgive me, Benjamin. I'll behave in public," Regina said, hooking her arm through his.

"And that will cost you a damn month," Ben declared softly, grinning at her outright belly laugh. He was still so much in love, he was stupid with it, Ben thought.

"Sorry," Regina said, finally noticing the whole group was watching and listening to Ben and her. "It's the whole wedding sex thing. It's easy to get caught up in the vibes coming off the bride and groom, especially these two."

The sigh Jenna released was so loud, it had everyone looking at her. Her face flushed at the same time as her breasts buzzed.

Lauren looked down from her six-foot height in heels at the cleavage of her much shorter maid of honor with fascination. "Jenna, honey, that's not where a portable vibrator goes. There are much better places."

"*Lauren!*" Jim protested in a pained voice, even as he had to laugh. Not that he missed the overly polite woman Lauren once was, but Jim still hadn't gotten used to hearing her true thoughts every time she opened her mouth.

Alexa, Regina, and Ben laughed too.

Jenna snorted and then laughed, a mannerism so like her mother's that even she couldn't deny it. "Sorry to disappoint, but it's just my cell phone, Lauren. I have a new client who's going to make me rich and famous. I didn't want to miss any calls from work. Sorry. I thought I was being discreet hiding it in my dress."

Turning her back to the group, Jenna fished the phone out of her bust and hit the button to unlock the screen.

She had to read the message twice to figure it out, and then again to believe what he'd sent.

Wedding sex: a condition where a man wants to F the MOH really HARD until she screams with pleasure. Sound about right?

Jenna made a sound of alarm, and her breathing became erratic as her mind conjured up images of other times she and Seth had—oh God, she thought. This is insane. How did he do this to her?

Her gaze raked the room, but she couldn't find him in the crowd. If she were as tall as her mother, she could have seen over all the people mulling around.

"Jenna? Everything all right?" Alexa asked, concerned at the strangled sound her daughter had made over the message she'd received, and the way Jenna's body was now tensing up.

Jenna turned back to the group and held the phone against her chest, keeping the message private. "It's fine, Mama. Everything's fine. Just—just something I wasn't expecting has come up."

Shit. Now I'm lying to people who know me too well, Jenna thought, feeling the blush creeping higher. Besides—she knew exactly what had come up. It was just that she didn't know the exact location of the man who owned it.

The phone buzzed against her chest again. They all just looked at her when she didn't immediately acknowledge it and check the message. Jenna realized if she didn't do it, they would all start to suspect something other than a business call was going on.

Then the grilling would begin.

"Honey, your MOH duties to me are over. You can take all the calls and messages you need to now. Go ahead," Lauren encouraged, waving her hand that now had a half-eaten roll in it. "You provided food. I'm going to be occupied with this and talking to guests for quite a while."

Jenna pulled the phone away and hit the button to read the message.

Too HARD to wait. Need you NOW!

She groaned and hit reply before anyone could sneak a look at the screen.

Not now. LATER!

Almost a full minute passed before the phone buzzed again. This time Seth told her exactly what he needed to do and how he planned to do it when he got his hands on her. Jenna started to sweat thinking about how it would be, and didn't even want to think about all the things happening under her dress. Walking was now going to be a challenge in her highly aroused state.

She typed furiously and hit send.

Fine. WHERE?

The phone buzzed back and she had to read the message twice to take it in. All she could think about was getting to him.

Meet me in the hall. I know someplace private.

Jenna sighed and looked at Lauren in apology. "I need to go take care of something. It shouldn't take long. Give me twenty minutes. I'll be back for the cake cutting and the dancing."

Lauren patted Jenna's shoulder in understanding before she dashed off.

"Sorry, Lauren. Jenna's been as bad as Seth today about her electronics," Alexa said sharply, rolling her eyes. "Seth has been on the phone since the wedding ended. He's supposed to be helping Casey provide security."

And Alexa had been hoping he'd be paying more attention to her daughter, who didn't bring a damn date for once.

Lauren shrugged. "Jenna's been great. I couldn't ask for a better MOH. She's done a lot and deserves a few minutes of relief," she said, smiling at Alexa.

And if Lauren had read the text message correctly, Jenna was about to get some major relief. Lauren would bet her trust fund and Jim's money that the sender of the sexy message she'd seen on Jenna's phone was Seth.

"So what's with the MOH stuff?" Alexa said laughing. "We have to talk in acronyms now?"

"It's efficient and effective—like sexting—I mean text messaging," Lauren said, looking at her husband and giggling at his blush. "It was a Freudian slip. I swear. I am seriously trying to behave."

"What's wrong with sexting?" Ben asked, looking at Jim's flushed face. "I like it."

"Why is everyone looking at me? I didn't say there was anything wrong with sexting," Jim said, defending himself, and giving his bride a don't-you-say-anything-more look.

Lauren giggled again. She sent sexy messages to Jim all the time. Sometimes he sent her one back, but he'd be embarrassed for anyone to know it.

"Well, I don't know what the big deal is," Alexa said, shrugging her elegant shoulders. "If I want to tell Casey something sexy, I call him up and tell him. I don't know what's so great about seeing it in black and white."

Regina patted her arm. "Some of us like the titillation of reading the words over and over throughout the day. Plus it's fun to play word games," Regina explained. "We're not all as brave as you are about telling men what we want or need. Sometimes it's easier to do when you can't see his face, and it gives him time to think about it."

Alexa snorted. "I guess I like a more direct approach and face-to-face communication."

Ben linked his fingers with Regina's and leaned in to kiss her cheek. "I want to sext you for the rest of my life."

"Kaiser, you're so pathetic," Jim said, smirking at the man he now considered one of his truest friends.

"Gallagher, don't be so insecure on your wedding day. I've spent months giving you my best tips. Now it's time go practice them on your wife," Ben told him with a laugh, loving the way Regina snickered at his side. Her support of him was unconditional, and he was already getting to that point where all he could think about was getting her home and alone with him.

"Don't worry, Ben. Jim will not let your training go to waste. I intend to see to it that he gets to practice every day," Lauren teased, laughing at her husband choking on his drink.

"Am I ever going to get used to that mouth of yours?" Jim exclaimed.

"Maybe—but we'll be so old by then you'll have lost your hearing anyway." Lauren smiled and held her husband's gaze as she happily finished the rest of her food. She sincerely hoped Jenna was having as much fun at her wedding as she was.

"Don't push them down. They snap open on the sides," Jenna whispered, exploring Seth's neck with her hungry mouth. Her breasts were straining inside the complicated bodice of her dress, but there would be no relief for them. She'd have to settle for relief elsewhere.

Seth had both hands under the multiple layers of her formal dress and made a strangled sound of pleasure when the tiny piece of cloth finally fell away from her into his hands. He was sitting in a chair in a storage room with his pants around his ankles and couldn't care less. Pulling Jenna unceremoniously down and onto him, he used her hips to guide her until he had encased the full hard length of his erection completely inside her again. His relief to have her was as profound as his urge to make her scream.

"Finding you under all those layers was like uncovering a treasure," Seth said once he was buried inside her.

Jenna giggled. "You can liberate me from my underwear anytime, but those text messages already have me hovering on the edge. Move it, Carter. You made me want you, now deliver the goods."

"I'm damn glad we practiced this position already," he whispered against her mouth, "I don't want to keep you from your duties. I swear I'll be fast. I just had to do this now. Three days is a long time to wait, but you sure as hell are always worth it—every time."

Jenna rocked back and forth. "I'm not going to last long. I figured out what worked best last time. This time I—Seth. Seth!"

Seth fastened his mouth to Jenna's and rocked up into her, swallowing her sounds of climax with his mouth. Another five seconds of her rocking on him and calling his name, and Seth felt himself falling over the edge into bliss with her. This was a hell of a position for them. Three days of wanting, ten minutes of texting, and then they lasted less than five minutes together. Problem was now that the first wave had crashed on the shore for both of them, Seth didn't want to let go of the ocean. He scooped Jenna's hips into his hands and held her on him to keep the connection.

"Once is never enough with you," Seth told her sincerely, leaning his forehead against hers. "I'm sorry. It just isn't. I hope you don't think I'm just an awful guy who's never satisfied."

Jenna sat astride Seth and laughed at the serious concern in his face. "Do you think I'm dumb enough to think badly of a man who likes sex as much as I do? Your sex drive is not a problem for me—or at least it's not a problem yet. It thrills me every time I climax to have you practically begging for a chance to give me another one. I'd stay now, but if I don't go back to Lauren soon, everyone I know will think something is wrong and come looking for me."

Seth let her hips go and helped her slide off him, having to catch Jenna when she wobbled as she stood. Knowing being with him had made her legs weak brought him a dark, dark pleasure. And Seth wanted nothing more than to make it worse for her. If he thought about it too long, he'd be hard and aching again.

"This was not just wedding sex in a closet for me, Jenna. You have no idea how badly I want to throw you over my shoulder and just leave with you. I want to go someplace I can do what I want to you as often as I want until neither of us can even walk. I want to exhaust you, feed you, sleep with you, and then wake up and do it all over again. I've never felt like this with anyone else. I mean it when I say that I need you. I'd do a lot to keep you in my bed," Seth told her.

"Fortunately for me, and my duties to Lauren, you are not a caveman," Jenna teased, smoothing her dress back into place.

"Caveman. Metro man. Hell—I don't know what kind of man I am anymore," Seth said honestly, making her laugh.

"Caveman about sex. Metro man about everything else. Not a bad combination," Jenna said sincerely, tugging on her dress until it felt almost normal again.

"The only thing I'm sure about is that this longing is about you," Seth told her, but inside he was thinking he knew it exactly what it was. He was finally getting to express some of his love for Jenna, even if it was just the physical part. Problem was—he wanted a hell of a lot more.

Jenna closed her eyes. "Can I come by your house later tonight?"

"Yes. I'll be in to the reception hall in a few minutes to dance with you," Seth told her. "That should keep everyone from asking too many questions."

Jenna nodded and slipped quietly out the door.

Seth finished his own clothing adjustments and slipped out close behind Jenna, closing the door to the storage room with a soft click behind him. He looked around and sighed in relief when he didn't see anyone. But hearing swearing from a few doors down the hall, Seth followed the sound until he walked into a room and found Stedman with his head in his hand.

"Damn it, Carter—a fucking storage room? I ought to beat the crap out of you," Allen said.

Seth hung his head and put his hands in his pockets. "Let me guess. Casey's testing a new camera system."

At Allen's abrupt nod, Seth took out one hand out and ran it through his hair.

"It wasn't—it wasn't our first time. I would never treat Jenna that way. What happened just now was mutual and consensual—and damn necessary for both of us. You're just going to have to take my word on it," Seth explained, feeling a need to defend himself and Jenna.

"Glad to hear that at least. I didn't see either of you go in there, but I saw Jenna come out. At first I didn't think anything about it, even when she adjusted her breasts inside her dress as she walked away. Then you come out less than two minutes later, and what you two did is all over your damn face," Allen said, glaring at Seth.

"So are you pissed or—what?" Seth asked, wishing Allen could have found out in a less sleazy manner, but it was too late for wishful thinking.

"Pissed—yes, but I guess I'll live. I'm still trying to decide if *you* get to or not," Allen told him.

"If you kill me, Jenna's going to be disappointed tonight when I'm not at home waiting on her to show up for round two," Seth told him.

"Stop your damn bragging before I decide to kill you after all. So what's the deal?" Allen demanded. "Are you two dating again?"

Seth pulled out the chair next to Allen and sat. "No. She says she doesn't want to date me. Jenna is just using me for sex and I'm letting her."

"Hell, Jenna could have used me for that," Allen said, bragging himself this time, irritated and not sparing Seth the truth of it. He finally calmed and ended up wanting to laugh when he saw the stark disappointment on Seth's face that the woman he wanted had potentially wanted someone else.

"Yes, I know she could have used you. Thanks for not— you know I'm in love with Jenna, right?" Seth asked, watching Allen's laughing mouth settle into a smirk.

"Yes. Everyone knows—even Jenna, who may never admit it. Is she still mad at you over your work?" Allen asked back.

Seth nodded. "And afraid of what we can be to each other. I don't blame her for that. I'm afraid myself, but I want her more than I'm afraid. It was bad before. Now being without her would be fucking impossible—and that's not a joke."

"Being in love with her, you know that sex-only shit is going to get old soon. You're going to have to have it out with the woman," Allen informed him. "I don't envy you that fight. Even her mother isn't as stubborn as Jenna. Alexa likes you, in case you didn't know. She's been rooting for you over me."

Seth shrugged. "Yeah, I know. I probably don't deserve Alexa's affection, but it's good to know she's going to be okay with me when I marry her daughter."

"Marry Jenna Ranger—the woman who doesn't want to date you? And how are you going to manage that miracle?" Allen asked. "Jenna's already getting what she wants from you for free. She's not going to necessarily want to buy the cow—well, bull in this case."

"I don't know yet," Seth said easily, laughing. "Every idea I come up with makes me sound more and more like Casey. He actually said he considers me a metro male. I'd hate to shoot his male-female paradigm in the ass. Casey might not recover if he finds out I'm like some yuppie version of him."

Allen laughed and nodded. "I wouldn't be too offended by Casey's opinion. He probably thinks the same about me. I'm still designing clothes and working for Alexa. When I mention the designing, Casey cringes. I haven't even told him Sydney is thinking about adding my designs to his line of clothes. Gunny's not going to like it, but hey—it's what I trained for as much as this."

Seth snorted. "I used to blame the military for Casey's thinking. Truthfully, the older I get the more I see that his ideas of what's manly probably came from our parents. Our fathers were brothers. Both were beat-your-chest and scratch-your-balls men. I never thought of myself as much like them, but I've recently discovered one area where I'm just as macho as Casey."

Allen cocked his head and smirked. "I'm intrigued as hell, but I still don't want to watch you scratch your balls."

"I've staked my claim to a woman, and Jenna Ranger is mine," Seth said, not laughing at Allen's comment even though it was damn funny. Instead Seth held Allen's gaze until the man looked away.

"You know I could snap your skinny ass like a damn toothpick," Allen threatened.

"Yeah, you could. Wouldn't change a thing, dude," Seth told him, never blinking.

Allen laughed and shook his head. He could see Gunny's influence in Seth's stance. Not that Jenna felt any differently about him, she was just too stubborn to admit it yet.

"Hell, I knew you loved her from the beginning. That's why all I did was kiss her. You've got nothing to worry about from me," Allen told him, finally able to both say it and mean it. "But if you're going to take the most beautiful woman I've dated so far and keep her for yourself, then you owe me one in return—*dude.*"

Seth laughed. He wished he could get off so easy. "Sure. You know I make a living at finding the impossible, don't you? I'm good at my job. I'll let you know when I find one that's suitable. Any special requests?"

"I have a completely open mind about looks and body types, so long as she's romantic. Not long dresses and brooches, but candles and bubble baths—I like that kind of thing. I guess I like a lot of feminine in my females," Allen said.

Seth snickered. "Finding the feminine in Jenna is like mining for gold. It's rewarding at the end, but you've got to dig like hell, walk through sawdust, and wear a hardhat to find it. Then when you do, you have to be half caveman to get your way.

"Stop your damn bragging. I don't want to know how you got a woman who held me off for two months," Allen said, laughing himself. "You owe me more than you'll ever realize for not pressing her."

"Oh, I realize what I owe you. You can trust me Stedman. I'll find you a woman, but you're on your own after that. It will not be my fault if you strike out again. I'll keep you posted on my search," Seth said jokingly as he stood. "I have to go dance with Jenna now and pretend we're just friends. Do you have to tell Casey you caught us on camera?"

"Oh, hell no. This camera tape is going to be wiped and restarted due to an unfortunate malfunction. You're telling

Gunny about this, not me," Allen said laughing. "I get enough drama working for Alexa and Sydney."

"Thanks, man. See you in the gym this week," Seth said, walking out the door.

"Yeah, okay. Invite me to the wedding," Allen called after him.

"You can be my best man if I get that far. Thanks for the vote of confidence." Seth laughed and headed back to the reception hall for a dance.

"Carter, I am always going to be the best man," Allen called, laughing as Seth walked down the hall.

"Okay Dr. Body-Language-Tells-The-Truth, what's going on? Jenna and Seth are not fighting for once. They're also smiling, but being very careful not to touch each other while they dance. Damn it, are they really becoming friends?" Alexa demanded.

Regina laughed. "Probably. This would disappoint you, Alexa?"

"Yes," Alexa said stiffly. "Don't ask me to explain myself. I can't help rooting for Seth to get her into bed."

"Well, I can't tell you for sure one way or the other what's happening," Regina said regretfully. "You're definitely going to have to wait for the movie to come out now."

"Why?" Alexa asked, surprised Regina wasn't willing to guess, and then it hit her. "Oh, damn it, Regina. Don't even tell me which one of them is your client. I'm just going to take my worrying-mother ass elsewhere and throw a quiet fit of frustration."

Regina laughed and hugged Alexa as hard as she could. "Let go of the outcome, Mama. Enjoy the show."

Alexa said something in Regina's ear that only she could hear and stomped off to the echo of Regina's laughter.

"What was Alexa so mad about?" Lauren asked, coming up to stand next to Regina.

"She's worried about her baby getting hurt," Regina said, snickering still.

"I'm a legally married woman now. She can relax," Lauren said easily.

"Her other baby, honey—Jenna," Regina said, thinking how nice it was that Lauren was so totally focused on herself today.

"Why is she worried about Jenna? I thought she'd be happy that Jenna and Seth were finally sleeping together," Lauren said, shrugging.

Regina looked at Lauren with new eyes. "Well, aren't you the oracle. What makes you so sure of that? Did Jenna say something?"

"No—of course not. They don't want anyone to know. I sneaked a peek at the X-rated text message Seth sent her earlier, or at least my money is on it being him. I just wonder where they snuck off to do it. I'd like to use that hide-away myself and consummate my marriage here. It seems like just the thing a notorious woman like me would do after the board accused me of it and kicked me out of my job here," Lauren said boldly, grinning at Regina's laughter.

"Oh my God, I can't believe you said that out loud in this place," Regina told her, hugging Lauren. "I swear I like you so much better now. I never know what you're going to say next."

"Me neither. Don't tell my husband, okay? If I embarrass him too badly, I'll have to apologize. I'm not in the mood for that today. I want other things," Lauren said, eyes glazing over with her carnal thoughts.

"I have no idea what you're talking about, but you know, I'm actually okay with that for once," Regina said, laughing.

Regina watched Jenna and Seth glide around the floor and saw Seth whisper something in her ear. Jenna blushed, pulled away and looked up at the man with so much longing Regina wanted to cry. It was even worse when Seth looked back like he wanted to drag her off somewhere.

Damn, I'm good, Regina thought.

Not that it meant what they felt would last, but at least they weren't taking their passion for each other to other people. That kind of betrayal was damn hard to fix, as Regina well knew.

But just like Alexa, all Regina could do now was sigh and hope they continued to work things out. Happy endings required a lot of work from both people involved.

Chapter 10

The contract builder her firm worked with freed up unexpectedly. The next thing Jenna knew the foundation was poured and the forty-eight-hundred-square-foot mostly ranch home she planned was being framed.

She had to be on site a good deal during the week it was being done, as there were a few unusual aspects to contend with, such as allowances for skylights in all the bedrooms and baths. There was also a loft area above the great room that would eventually be outfitted for office and library space.

Each day Jenna was on site from 6 a.m. until dark, creeping home in the wee hours to sleep so she could do it all over again the next day. She'd been too tired to even think about calling Seth, but was perturbed that he hadn't called her either. It made her wonder if the longing she felt was just on her end. Didn't he need her? He said he did, but it had been almost six days now.

As if her thoughts had weaved their way to him, the phone buzzed with a message from him.

If you're playing hard to get to make it HARDER, it's working.

Jenna laughed, feeling relieved and several other emotions she wasn't ready to deal with as she answered him.

Working 16 h days this week. No end in sight. Sorry.

She pressed send, and then immediately regretted not responding in kind to his sexy message. Jenna thought for a moment and then typed again.

So how HARD is it?

Jenna pressed send and waited.

And waited.

And waited.

When the phone finally buzzed, she almost dropped it trying to unlock the screen and see the message.

Against the door. On the floor. 3 more times in the bed HARD.

Jenna sighed, held the phone against her belly as she looked around to see if any of the construction workers were watching her face flush.

How about once late tonight? 11 or after. Best I can do.

Jenna closed her eyes. She would probably be too tired to participate, but what the hell. Let Seth do all the work if he was in such bad shape.

When his reply came, Jenna looked at it and laughed. The man was very honest—at least about sex.

Better than taking matters into my own hands. I need you.

Her question completely answered at last, Jenna returned to work hoping she could get away shortly after dark.

At ten that night, Jenna got out of the shower and dressed in as few clothes as possible. She pulled on the khaki shirt she'd worn the first time they'd been together and a blue camisole with no bra, not that she ever needed much of one anyway. Over the camisole that matched the color of her eyes, she pulled a lightweight sweater of the same color and headed out to Seth's.

He was leaning in the doorway of his condo still dressed in formal work clothes when she walked up the sidewalk to his building. Seth motioned with a hand for her to go inside.

She got a whiff of expensive cologne and hot aroused male as she walked by him. It was a mouthwatering combination.

Jenna heard the door close with a decisive click behind her, and then Seth tugged her into his arms. Seconds later she was plastered hard against the door just like he'd threatened. She shook in his arms as she laughed at his enthusiastic greeting.

"I'm not wearing any underwear this time," Jenna whispered boldly against Seth's exploring mouth, which moved from her lips to along her neck and got even more insistent at her words.

"Great. Me neither," Seth whispered back, holding on to his self-control as fiercely as he held on to her. "Don't say I didn't warn you. I'm not letting go of you, so unfasten my pants."

"What if I don't want to yet?" Jenna teased.

Seth's hands slid the skirt up to her waist, and then he used them to lift her legs firmly behind her thighs to spread her open for him without any choice in the matter.

"I let you fall and you take the consequences when I finally do get my pants off," Seth finally answered.

Giggling, Jenna's hands moved hastily to his pants, quickly freeing him from them. Pushing the very nice material off his hips, she let what she knew were the most expensive pants Seth owned fall to the floor in wrinkled heap.

Seth lifted her even higher, bent his knees, and impaled her with a single steely thrust.

"I warned you," he said roughly, letting his inner Neanderthal speak for him as Jenna groaned and wiggled on him to take him in more comfortably. "I can't help how hard I am. Wrap your legs around me."

By that point, Jenna didn't have the willpower to refuse him much of anything, so she simply did as he asked.

"Seth," Jenna called, feeling him move inside her as hard as he had been the very first time they had been together. Weeks later now, she craved his fierce possession, craved it so badly that having him again made her want to weep with relief.

How had she stayed away from him so long this week? How had she come to need him so much?

"Baby, I can't even feel myself inside you. I'm too damn excited," Seth complained. "That's enough of this. I'm sorry, but I need more control."

Seth took them to the floor then, not even making it to the living room carpet. He just fell to his knees with her wrapped around him and laid Jenna down on the wood floor in his foyer before sliding as far into her as far he could.

"Better—much better," he said, moving in slow, but deep strokes.

"Faster—harder," Jenna ordered, squirming under him and arching with each one.

"If anything gets any harder, it won't do either of us any good," Seth said, laughing now at Jenna's wild eyed-expression. "And I don't want to hurt you on this wood floor."

"Seth," Jenna said, "I'm a woman on the edge here. Stop making me wait."

"We're on a damn wood floor. If I lose control, I will hurt you," Seth said firmly, stopping completely. "I am not willing to do that."

"But I don't care," Jenna argued fiercely. "Can't you just do this once without worrying about the circumstances?"

"Never," Seth said firmly. "But I promise to always give you what you want one way or the other." He pushed deep and gently rocked up, repeating the action until Jenna thrashed beneath him.

"Not this way. No. You, too. You, too," she insisted, trying to move away from what he was doing so successfully, but to no avail. Seth already knew her body too well. It was humbling to realize that she couldn't stop him from giving her an orgasm. When had she given him that level of control?

Seth bent and kissed her, and then held completely still when he felt her quivering with release under him. "I will always do what I can to meet your needs," he vowed, as he felt her climax overtake her.

When she quieted, Seth was still inside her as hard as ever. Even in the aftermath of her pleasure, Jenna was mad as hell at Seth for exercising so much control over her response. The situation made her want to scream. The panic inside her was threatening to spew her emotions all over him. Emotional tirades were for a dating couple, not for them. They had a more simple relationship.

"Feeling better now?" Seth asked softly, smiling unconcerned into her face even as she glared furiously at him.

"Damn you," Jenna hissed, her tone harsh and intentionally hurtful. "You had no right to take over like that. It was supposed to be both of us."

Seth pulled out of her and stood, kicking his pants off the rest of the way. Reaching down he grabbed both of Jenna's hands and yanked her upright. "It may take me all night to get some relief as hard as I am right now. I hope you were planning on sticking around a bit because you're not leaving until I do."

Jenna lifted her chin at his bossy, arrogant tone. She wasn't sure what Seth's problem was, but she was the wronged person here. She had come here for his benefit more than hers, but that didn't mean he got to have it all his way. And she for damn sure didn't appreciate his attitude.

"If I wanted to leave, I damn well would," Jenna told Seth firmly. "So don't get bossy with me."

Seth had controlled her all Jenna intended to let him tonight.

"I am so not in the mood to argue this with you, Jenna. That stubborn chin of yours tempts me to clip you under it every time I see it come up in my face. I'm sorry I messed up your perfect seduction plans by being a thoughtful guy. If you want a fight, my inner Neanderthal is just looking for an excuse. Now lower your chin and come to bed with me," Seth told her.

"I'm not even sure I want to come to bed with you now," Jenna told him. "I don't like the way you're talking to me."

"Tough. I've learned you're not the type of woman who responds or even appreciates niceness. I'm warning you—this is the wrong time to get more stubborn with me," Seth told her, his gaze promising just as much retribution as his words.

When her glare got worse and she swore at him, Seth suddenly reached the limit of his patience. He snatched a sputtering, fuming Jenna up under her arms, lifted her several inches from the floor. Then he walked with her to his bedroom, her long legs dangling while she squealed and struggled in his arms.

Then Seth lifted her away from his body and threw Jenna backward on the bed where she screamed in alarm as she landed.

"Damn. That felt really good," Seth said, breathing heavily from carrying her that way. "There may be something to this caveman shit. That was a hell of a lot easier than trying to talk you into it."

"Listen you—you—I don't know what you are, but just because you're big enough and strong enough to put me here does not mean I'm going to stay," Jenna informed him. "I can still hurt you if I want to."

Seth shrugged off his dress shirt and let it drop unceremoniously on the floor. His cleaning bill was going to double with Jenna in his life. He was going to have to buy a lot more clothes.

Then he crawled onto the bed and followed her body even as Jenna was inching backward away from him. It only added to his desire for her, but he knew that was something that could never be said out loud to the strong-willed woman he craved.

"Yeah, if I were thinking clearly I would be worried about the damage you could do in my naked condition, but as you can see, all the blood has left my brain. It's my turn now, Jenna, and I'm picking the location. You're going to satisfy me in the bed, not on the damn floor."

"Stay the hell away from me, Seth Carter," Jenna commanded, even as she felt him pushing between her knees and edging forward up her thighs.

"That's simply impossible," Seth said firmly. He bent his mouth to her belly which rippled in apprehension as he kissed a trail from there to her breasts, wrestling the rest of her clothes up and off her as she complained and struggled against the pleasure of his mouth on her.

Damn it, damn it, Jenna thought, feeling her legs start to quiver in anticipation as Seth tugged the shirt off her. When he lowered his hips to hers, the rest of the fight in her simply left. All that remained was the need to have him inside her again. She didn't like her own capitulation, but didn't seem to be able to stop it from happening.

"I missed you insanely, Jenna. It's hard to go more than a few days without being with you now. This physical condition is just what happens to me when I have to wait so long. Now let me inside you," Seth demanded, forcing her hand to stroke him once before she jerked it away. "You can tell how bad off I am."

Jenna shook her head from side to side even as her hips loosened and her legs spread wider. It was like her body refused to obey her mind where Seth Carter was concerned.

Seth stopped as he studied her gaze on him. "Fine. I can stop now and go take care of things myself. I vowed I would never force you, but your stubbornness makes it difficult to be as nice to you as I'd like to be. This is your final chance. Are you going to help me out or not?"

His erection was smooth as silk resting against her thigh, and as hard as he'd ever been with her. She wanted him desperately, whether she was happy about the fact or not. Jenna gritted her teeth in disgust at both of them.

"Damn you—yes," she all but screamed at Seth. "Yes, I want you."

Seth didn't wait for Jenna to change her mind again. He sank inside her, trying to catch himself before he pushed too hard too fast. Just like the first time, he felt her wrapping herself around him, even as reluctant as she was. *Mine*, Seth thought again, not even understanding where the possessive feelings he had about her resided in him. He'd never known them before Jenna.

"I want to be with you so much sometimes that it drives me crazy. I can't believe I was so stupid about us sleeping together when I dated you. Maybe I instinctively knew that once I'd been with you I'd be this obsessed. I'm so damn glad I have you now," Seth informed her, moving her whole body with every stroke.

"This is just sex. *You don't have me*," Jenna denied, having to brace herself for every hard thrust.

"Like hell I don't," Seth said, sarcastically, the words pushing past his common sense. "You're mine, Jenna Ranger—at least for however long it takes to quiet this ache I have for you. Don't stay away so long the next time and it won't be this much effort for either of us."

"I was working! Damn you, Seth, I was working," she bit out angrily, pushing up against him.

Seth grabbed her wrists and held them at their sides as he continued his movements in and out of her. "If I'm just your damn booty call, you're mine too. You're all I want, all I can think about, and I fucking need you. Do you hear me, Jenna? *I. Need. You.*"

"I need you too. Why are you so mad at me?" Jenna asked, the plea torn from her, even as she let Seth hold her down and do what he wanted.

Seth closed his eyes and slowed his movements, but he didn't stop—couldn't stop.

"I'm mad because I dragged you to the hard, wooden floor, and you let me. Because I waited as long as I could to call you this week when you didn't call me, and it bothered me. Because I was damn afraid you might have talked yourself out of this being a good idea," Seth said, the words becoming more tortured the closer to the edge of panic he got. "I am trying like hell to honor our agreement, but worrying this week about whether or not you were coming back was *not* part of our bargain. I need to know where I

DONNA MCDONALD

stand with you. If you want out of the deal, just tell me. Don't just stay away and not call."

"I don't want out of our deal. Now let go of my hands," Jenna ordered softly.

When Seth released her, she clasped his head, kissed his neck, kissed the pulse at his throat, ran hands through his hair and over his shoulders. "I was just busy, Seth. I swear I was just busy. I was coming back. I need you, too. Look—this is me under you, me being your stress reliever. I want to be here."

Seth gathered her into his arms, turned and rolled them, and then rolled them back. He was not going to cry on her. No, he wasn't going to scare her away yet with confessing how much he loved her and how worried he had been, but damn—he had been more afraid than he'd realized. His profound relief to be connected to her did not bode well for him keeping to their agreement. He wanted her with him every night.

In fact, he wanted her in his life for as long as they both lived.

While need dictated that he couldn't completely stop moving inside her, Seth didn't want to abuse her body either. It was going to take awhile. That was just a physical reality for him in his current condition. He'd done nothing to ease his need for her in the days without her except miss her like hell. He didn't want to risk not giving her everything when she did show up.

"Am I hurting you?" he asked softly, not knowing what he would do if it were true.

"Yes, you're hurting me," Jenna laughed. "But it's okay. My whole body is getting used to being mauled like your personal stress ball. I'm starting to crave the torture, and I hate you for it."

"Thank God," Seth told her sincerely, the slide of their bodies together feeling like the only important thing in the world at the moment. "I think I would die if I had to stop now."

The phone on the nightstand started ringing. Without missing a beat, Seth reached over, looked at display, and promptly tossed the still ringing phone into the floor beside the bed. "I'm too fucking busy to talk, and I mean that in every sense of the word."

Jenna sputtered and laughed at his irritated tone. And then the more she thought about it, the more she laughed. The man was over the edge—and it seemed like he intended to take her with him to the point of madness.

"Hurry and finish. You know they'll expect a call back shortly," she taunted, letting her body give beneath his as the man above tried to drive her into his mattress.

"Shut up," Seth said in her ear, "I'm concentrating. This is hard enough without your snide commentary."

Jenna laughed and snorted at his choice of words, feeling Seth laughing on top of her now even as he was increasing his momentum. When the laughter died, a climax swept in to replace it. Her eyes rolled up when it went on for so long that Jenna found herself holding her breath as she writhed on the bed.

Seth thought it was like he had needed Jenna's release as a catalyst for his. His groan of relief echoed loudly in the bedroom as he finally found what he needed inside her at last.

"Kiss me," Jenna ordered, as she absorbed the last of his pleasure with her own. "I need you to kiss me."

Her demand surprised both of them.

"Jenna," Seth said, his tone softer, regretful, and calm at last. His body was practically comatose on top of hers now.

"Don't *Jenna* me in that regretful tone," she said, grabbing a handful of his hair and pulling his mouth down to hers. It was not her normal nature to be compliant or do what she was told. Seth Carter was the only exception she ever made, and he better damn well learn to appreciate it.

Jenna kissed Seth fiercely, feeling him let her make the kiss anything she needed it to be. When she finally released him, Jenna held Seth's head up where she could look him fully in the face. "I'll be lucky to walk straight tomorrow. And if you apologize, I swear I won't be the only one limping around."

Seth put his forehead on hers and laughed humorlessly. "I honestly don't mean to hurt you or be so rough. I'm supposed to be a metro man with you—sensitive and caring—not a damn caveman dragging you to the floor all the time."

"I'm coming to think you're both," Jenna said, laughing.

"Yes, you are—every time in fact—and I can almost always feel it happening for you," Seth said, snorting.

Jenna smacked him on the back of his head. "That was not a compliment on your sex skills, nor an innuendo," she exclaimed.

"Name one time you've ever been with me and had just one orgasm," Seth demanded softly, his hands rubbing her arms.

Jenna sighed beneath him. "You want to hear how great you are in bed? Fine. You're great in bed, Seth. You're the best ever."

Seth promptly bit her shoulder and felt gratified when Jenna yelped.

"What was that for?" Jenna said, smacking his head again. "I was paying you a damn compliment that time."

"No, you were being sarcastic," Seth corrected. "Besides it not me that's great. It's us. We are great together. It's always like this and I'm completely addicted."

"Finally something we can agree about tonight," Jenna said, yawning.

"Stay," Seth said. "It's late, and you're too tired to drive home."

"Don't be silly—I'm fine," Jenna said sleepily.

When she didn't speak for a couple of minutes, Seth looked down at her closed eyes and listened to her breathing. Sometimes being with her was like trying to pet a cactus. But when she finally gave in to herself and him, Jenna gave up everything no matter the cost. He loved her so much it hurt him to hold it all inside without saying it.

"You damn hard-hearted she-cat, I'm going to marry you one day and make you happy if it kills me." Seth whispered the threat and laughed when she hugged him close in her sleep.

He eased reluctantly out of her to remove his weight, and as he did he realized something that he hadn't before. They'd forgotten to use a condom. Jenna had come through the door smelling like her shower and he'd attacked her before he'd thought rationally. The condom he'd had ready was still in his damn pants pocket on the foyer floor.

Shit. Now what? Seth closed his eyes and sighed about how crazy they had both gotten tonight. If Jenna got pregnant, it would solve a lot for him, but he suspected Jenna would probably never forgive him for them conceiving their first child in the middle of a sex fight.

He lay on his side and watched her sleeping for a few minutes, wondering how Jenna was going to react to the news in the morning.

When the phone rang again, Seth picked it up from the floor and walked with it out of the bedroom to take the call. A half hour later he crawled back into bed beside Jenna's still sleeping body. He wanted to hold her, but she was already going to be upset when she woke in his bed. Seth sighed and settled for holding her hand in his as he fell asleep.

Chapter 11

When Seth woke the next morning, Jenna was already gone. He sighed and wondered how long she would make him wait this time before he saw her again.

After he had dressed, Seth checked his tie in the mirror and made sure his suit was free of lint. It was his second best choice of clothes, but the only suit available since his best slacks had spent the night on his foyer floor. That brought him back to thinking about the unused condom in the pocket of those slacks and he sighed in resignation.

Seth lectured himself for dwelling on what he couldn't change and for being too worried to call Jenna to talk with her about it. It wasn't that he was a coward about admitting his part of taking the risk. It was just that he was afraid to make Jenna mad again. She was the most angry, stubborn woman he'd ever been with in his life, but since he craved her like a drug, he didn't want to risk losing her completely. He would just do it in person. It wasn't the kind of thing to be discussed on the phone anyway.

Seth straightened his tie and told himself that he would just make sure he saw her today to talk about it. Making the decision to do so allowed him to move on to the next item on his list.

Pulling his mind reluctantly from Jenna, Seth thought instead about the woman he was heading to meet. It had taken him six months to arrange her visit and to lure her into talking to him. Today it was going to happen, and Seth was not going to let any other concern in his life mess up making a good first impression on her.

Too much of his future was riding on the outcome.

At the hotel where the exotic and talented Talia Martin was staying, there was a message waiting at the front desk for Seth, moving their meeting to her suite. Despite the intimacy of the situation, Seth didn't question the change of venue, just strode to the elevator like it was an everyday occurrence to meet a beautiful, successful woman in her hotel room.

Outside her suite, Seth knocked and waited. When the door finally opened, he smiled widely at the very polished woman in a business suit standing there with a still quietly sobbing baby falling asleep over one shoulder. Talia Martin was an elegant, attractive woman easily five foot ten in her heels with skin the color of a mocha latte and straight black hair to mid-back as shiny as Seth had ever seen. He had known what she looked like from pictures on her company's website, but she looked even better in person.

Whatever her genealogy, it served her very well, and the image she presented was both lovely and appealing. He could see why her sales were high.

"Mr. Carter, please come in," Talia said, smiling. "Thanks for coming to my room. Kendra and I are not having a great morning. She's one of those babies who misses home and her own bed."

"Not a problem," Seth said kindly. "We can even reschedule if you like."

"Not necessary. I think the worst is over," Talia told him. "Have a seat in the waiting area and let me see if I can put Kendra down now. Mason is already down for his nap. We should have at least an hour to talk."

Seth watched the efficient woman disappear into the large bedroom off the well-furnished sitting area. He was pleased that the accommodations he'd arranged had been so suitable for her situation.

She returned shortly and smoothed the skirt of her business suit as she sat on the small couch close to him.

"I guess you can see why I was intrigued enough with your offer to come here to meet with you," Talia said with a knowing smile. "Being a single parent is challenging even with the best support system. Mason needs to go to therapy several times a week, and it's important for me right now to be with him for his appointments."

Seth opened the portfolio he'd brought and pulled a sheet of paper out of it to hand to her.

"What's this?" she said, surprised, taking the paper and scanning the list of names and phone numbers it contained.

"A list of physical therapists in Falls Church and surrounding areas. I narrowed the list to the top ten, and put asterisks by the ones most highly recommended. They all work with children as young as your son. I checked," Seth told her.

The paper fell to her lap. "Why would you do all that research for my personal situation?" Talia asked, genuinely perplexed at the trouble he'd taken.

"That's how much I want you to consider my offer," Seth said sincerely. "You can only be happy here in Falls Church if you feel supported in what's important to you."

"But why go to this trouble for me specifically?" Talia demanded.

Seth Carter's thoughtfulness made Talia miss the man she'd married who had died and left her with a wounded child and a new baby. It also made her hopeful that there might one day be another man in her life who would be as thoughtful as Seth Carter was being—only for the right reasons.

Seth put the portfolio in his lap and his hands on top of it. "I thought as the potential employer I was supposed to get to ask the questions during our interview?"

Talia laughed softly. "I warned you I was looking for more control," she teased, smiling and making the soft lines at her eyes crinkle. At thirty-four, she was still mostly happy with the way she looked and never felt the need to hide her age. "I'm looking for an equal partnership—eventually."

Seth smiled broadly and leaned an arm on the back of the couch. "I'm looking for the same thing—eventually."

"Be careful, Mr. Carter. If you start flirting with me, I may take you up on *that offer* and not bother with the job," Talia warned, even though she was mostly teasing. "You have no idea what a challenge my life has been in the last year and a half. I can be mercenary when it suits me. Sometimes I think about marrying again just to get the help."

"Sorry if I came across that way. I'm extremely flattered because you are an appealing woman, but I'm taken," Seth said lightly, grinning at his hands. Then he met and held Talia Martin's teasing gaze, getting a great idea. "But if you do accept my job offer, I could probably help you out in that area as well. How would you feel about dating a weight lifter who's also a clothing designer? He's several years younger than you, but you seem just his type. Allen likes older women. He almost dated my girlfriend's mother, but my cousin got to her first. So he ended up dating my girlfriend instead, but they were never more than friends."

Talia laughed at his explanation. Laughing was impolite, but unavoidable given such a story. "Forgive me for saying this out loud, but I'm too honest not to speak my mind. Your personal life sounds like a soap opera, Mr. Carter. Now back to what you were saying—I want to get this straight—you're offering to fix me up with medical support for my son and a date with an eligible man if I move here and agree to work with you? That's the strangest set of incentives I've ever been offered during an interview," Talia said frankly, laughing and leaning back against the pillows.

"I work out of my home and I like it. I might one day have to become a brick and mortar business, but right now I'm not interested. In your contract, I'm not offering vacation or sick leave or a retirement plan, but I figured your needs were greater for other things the first year. I intend to offer you a place to stay and help with the medical support your family needs. Dating Allen would actually be helping me, so that's not technically an incentive for your benefit. If anything, it's just repayment of a debt I owe the man for stealing my girlfriend back," Seth said, laughing.

Talia Martin laughed at his explanation, and it felt really good. She hadn't had a lot to laugh about in a long time. "That is still totally bizarre, but okay. Now I'm going to ask my question again. Why are you convinced I'm the one you need to help you?"

"You speak eleven languages. Your sales record is unmatched at your company and no one has broken it the whole time you've been out on family medical leave, which has been almost a year now. Your company loves you and is holding your place with them. I think I can do better because I can give you flexibility to take care of your son like you want, and a chance to use your global sales skills in ways you haven't even thought of yet," Seth finished. "You would get a fairly small base salary to begin and ten percent commission on all orders placed and shipped. I would pay out commission net sixty days. The delay in payout time is to allow customers to receive the goods and make returns."

"How many other candidates are you considering?" Talia asked, wondering why her instincts were leaning toward the tall blonde man so strongly. There was just something so animated about him. He was engaged in his work and the excitement of it emanated from him.

"None," Seth told her honestly. "If you're not interested, I have to start my search all over again. That isn't going to work well for my personal life, but I'd just have to deal with it if you say no. You're the one I want. Now tell me Ms. Martin—what do you want?"

"What do I want? Well, frankly Mr. Carter, I want my secure life back," Talia told him. "I lost my husband and almost my son in a car accident. I found out about the baby a couple of weeks after the accident. I couldn't continue to work while I was busy struggling to just survive my life. If Ian hadn't been well insured, I don't know how I would have financially managed this last year and a half. A normal job is not a possibility unless I put my children with someone else all day. My son needs a special level of attention right now, and I am determined he will have it. Unfortunately, I can't be a stay-home mother all the time either. Even the best insurance plan eventually runs out of funds."

"You would have control of all your time, but you would also be making and taking calls all hours of the day and night," Seth warned, "but you could probably arrange them to end at midnight and not pick up again until after 5 a.m. our time. Maybe you'll find a way to conduct business that I haven't been able to manage. I speak Japanese, German, and a spattering of a couple Norwegian languages. I don't speak any Chinese, and China is where the next deal is going to be."

"I speak three dialects of Chinese," Talia said quietly.

"Yes, I know," Seth told her, smiling. "It's listed in your business profile on the Internet."

Talia looked at Seth. She was thinking, seriously thinking, about whether she could make this work. Something about his earnestness just made her believe. Plus it would be good to feel successful again, to know she was capable of supporting her children. And if Seth Carter didn't mind that she was dedicated to her son first, then it was probably worth a shot to her to see if she could do this.

"How about a test?" Talia offered. "Give me a month to make arrangements to move here temporarily, and I'll come back to stay for three months. We'll see how I do, and then you can decide. I will earn my own way with your company, or we'll part none the worse for our association."

"Unfortunately, I can't wait that long. I need you now," Seth said, extracting another paper from his portfolio. "This is a picture and the address of a spacious one-level duplex with a garage. It's available next week."

"That's a lot of turnaround to expect from a woman with children," Talia said, suddenly feeling too managed and too controlled for her comfort level. "I'm not used to someone else calling so many of the shots."

"Yeah—I hear that a lot lately, but I've become a desperate man in all areas of my life. If you get the deal for these replacement parts worked out, we will be the sole supplier for at least two large companies out west with wind turbines. The commission alone would buy you a house here in Falls Church and anything else you need for a couple of years," Seth told her. "The only thing I couldn't research for you is child care providers, but I thought the therapist might be able to offer some suggestions there."

"You're making it damn hard for me to say no to you," Talia commented.

"Good. What would make it impossible?" Seth asked.

Talia let the silence between them stretch. Seth's kind gaze while he waited pushed her over the edge of her decision-making. "Give me at least two weeks to get my Boston life in order," she said at last.

Seth opened the portfolio, took out open-ended one-way first-class plane tickets back to Falls Church for her and the kids, an employment contract for one year, and the work-up for the job he wanted her to do locating a manufacturer for the hard-to-find wind turbine replacement part. He handed the stack of documents to Talia, grinning at the utter shock on her face as she sifted through them.

He reached into his inner jacket pocket and pulled out a top-of-the-line cell phone and handed that to her as well.

"Here. If you have to take two weeks, you can start researching from where you are. Turn this on after you sign and date the contract. Your work can be done anywhere, but I don't want to be so far away from you during the first year. That's why I want you to move here."

"You were awfully sure I'd say yes," Talia told him, holding handfuls of her future and staring at the smiling man on her couch.

"My confidence helped me put two million through the bank last year," Seth said, smiling. "I want to double that this year. I would think ten percent of your two million in sales would be a good incentive for you."

Talia's eyes lit with excitement, and she laughed openly.

"My husband was my first boss. I am not opposed to mixing pleasure and business. Are you sure you wouldn't just rather date me?" Talia asked, laughing. "I'm an excellent wife. You're a bit overbearing in some ways, but after what I've been through, I have an open mind about helpful men."

"If you sign that contract, all I can offer is to let you call me Seth," he told her with a huge smile, "but that's as familiar as we will ever get. However, I am serious about getting you a date if you're interested. All joking aside, the guy is a friend of mine now. He says I owe him a woman to date since I stole Jenna back. You'd help me get out of his debt if you went out with him even once."

"Wow, is there anything you won't wheel and deal about?" Talia asked, laughing. "Are you completely legal?"

"I am a damn boy scout about everything, which you'll learn quickly enough. I'll expect the same level of ethical decision-making from you," Seth told her. "I'm sure I don't have to tell you about import and export rules and how strict they are now. I simply don't bend them. I've found it's not worth it."

"I don't bend them either. I've had my share of debates in the past over that," she mused.

"You're going to like what I do," Seth told her again. "You're going to like the work even if you decide I'm a pain in the ass most of the time. So you'll stay on and we'll work things out. My instincts about business are very good, even if they're not always spot on about personal matters."

"Hence the need to steal your girlfriend back from your new friend?" Talia asked, grinning at his sincerity and his honesty.

"Yes. But I'm quickly learning my lessons about her too," Seth said, smiling. "I intend to marry her as soon as she stops being stubborn and admits she's still in love with me."

Talia burst out laughing. "Well, I can see working for you will be entertaining if nothing else." She stuck out a hand for Seth to shake. "I'll let you know if I need contract changes, but for now let's just say I accept. I'll think about the date with your friend and let you know."

"Great," Seth told her. "Now I need to go track down my girlfriend to tell her something."

Before Seth could rise from the couch, a little boy of three limped out of the bedroom wearing leg braces and walked slowly to where his mother sat on the couch.

Seth looked over at the boy, who hadn't stopped staring. "Hello," he said, reaching out a hand for the boy to shake. "I'm Seth Carter. Nice to meet you, Mason."

"How do you know my name?" the boy asked quietly, but still reached out a tentative hand to Seth.

Grinning at the kid's self-possession, Seth shook the boy's hand briskly and dropped it gently.

"Your mother and I are going to be working together," Seth said.

He shifted his attention to Talia, who was looking at her son with love and concern.

"When you come back, I'll introduce you and your children to my cousin, Casey. He recently had a second hip replacement and has been doing physical therapy. He doesn't even have to use his cane anymore. Casey can tell you about his program and what he's learned."

"You are an unusually thoughtful employer, Seth Carter," Talia told him.

The more she found out about him; the more she liked him. Too bad he was taken. But when she got back Fall Church, Talia decided she would make it her business to find out just how taken Seth Carter was and make her own decision about it.

When Seth contacted Jenna's office looking for her, he was told she was out of the office on a job site. Seth knew exactly where she was and which site she was on, so he didn't bother leaving a message for her.

Pulling into the gravel area poured in the shape of the circular driveway it would contain, Seth instantly fell in love with what he saw. The front curved back around what would be a paved entrance. Each side of the house extended out the length of multiple rooms. What would save the house from looking colonial when it was finished were the stucco and stone materials and the modern sculpture fountain that would grace the front.

Jenna had explained it to him just recently, and now he could see what she meant.

In the open frame of the center of the house, Seth admired the picture the serious-working Jenna made in her jeans, steel-toed boots, hard-hat and standard white shirt, the ends of it flapping in the breeze. There was an incredible sense of pride watching her going toe-to-toe with men who were all much larger than her. Seth could tell Jenna was agitated by the way she waved one of her hands toward the building while the other pointed to the blueprints on the paper with a demanding finger.

Seth almost felt sorry for the big men with the pained looks on their faces. The empathetic feeling made him grin. She was not going to be an easy wife, but she was not going to be boring either.

He stuck his hands in his pockets and just stood there watching her work. It was almost ten minutes before any of the group noticed him leaning on his car. When they did, it was Jenna who separated from the group and came over to him.

"What are you doing here?" Jenna demanded, irritation at the argument she'd just had making her unreasonably sharp with Seth. She felt chastised when Seth grinned and bit the inside of his jaw to keep from laughing. "Sorry. Didn't mean to take your head off. Hi."

"Hi back," Seth said, reaching out to put a caressing finger in the opening of her shirt, stroking for a moment before pulling it back. "Having problems?"

"Nothing I can't handle. You know, just because something's never been done doesn't mean it's structurally impossible to do. Damn it, I'm the one with the architecture degree and I'm damn good with the math," Jenna said harshly. "When I want it done a certain way, that's what I expect."

Seth chuckled to see her all riled up about something other than him for once.

"You don't have to convince me. I trust your judgment. I happen to know you're damn good at a lot of things," he told her.

Jenna laughed at his teasing support, his words strangely calming to her despite the sarcasm lurking behind them. "I never knew you were a sweet talker, Seth. Want to look around while you're here?"

"Dying to—thought you would never ask," Seth told her.

"Let me get you a hard hat. It's required. Wait here," Jenna said, turning on her heel and stalking off.

Seth watched Jenna walk away from him, laughing because he knew she never questioned that he would do as she ordered. It dawned on him how much in control of herself and her surroundings Jenna had to be to work in a field where her primary interactions were convincing strong-minded men to do as she requested.

What he'd been reading as stubbornness in her was probably just a survival skill in her work. Not that he'd let her always order him around or have her way in everything, but Seth had to admit that he hadn't exactly been the best about letting Jenna have much say in their relationship since they had been sleeping together.

He was too used to controlling his environment as well.

When she walked back to him carrying a hard hat in her hand, his heart rolled over in his chest. The sense of her belonging to him and with him was strong.

"Here. Bend your head down," she ordered, putting the hat on him and fastening the chinstrap. "There—you're safe now. You're going to get sawdust and god knows what else on your clothes, but there's no protection from that. Come on."

Seth laughed and followed, letting Jenna walk him through the chaos of saws, air tools, and hammers. The plumbing was being installed and the back of the house was being covered in the framing that would act as support for the stucco and river stone finish. Beyond the foyer was a great room with a vaulted ceiling and a loft area framed around the edge. At one end was a floor-to-ceiling fireplace that was installed but not yet finished.

"So did the mystery man ever engage with you?" Seth asked when they had walked to the master bedroom wing of the house and away from the tools. They could almost talk without yelling there.

"I sent the final plans over along with video of me explaining my intentions. I had to make the video on my computer even though I felt like a complete dork talking about what would have taken me ten minutes to do in person, and I could have given him a tour," Jenna replied. "The lawyer called me personally to say his client was very pleased. If things keep going this well, I may even get this done a few weeks sooner than I thought."

"Well, even I can see how awesome it's going to be." Seth told her sincerely. "What's the master bedroom going to be like?"

"Huge," Jenna said, laughing, the one word saying everything from her perspective. "Room for a bed and a sitting area. I wanted it to be a true getaway from everything. I'm also adding a hidden mini-bar and invisible flat screen in the master bathroom. And I made the walk-in closet the same size as a small bedroom. It will have cherry shelving and a dressing area. He might not appreciate it, but his wife is going to love me for it one day."

"Oh, you never know. A man like Ben Kaiser would love it. Somebody with a dual life like Allen would enjoy it. Hell, even I would appreciate it. I'd probably buy more suits and find many ways to fill up the space. Evidently, two suits aren't enough anymore anyway, especially if I keep leaving my pants abandoned in the floor," Seth said, joking.

"I'm sure Sydney would just love to make you some suits," Jenna said, grinning.

"Yes, I'm sure he would. Do you know what the man charges for a suit? It's criminal," Seth complained. "Casey would never have bought one on his own if Alexa hadn't insisted. Neither of us is used to spending the kind of money Sydney charges on clothes."

"Well, get used to it, Seth. Think of buying Sydney's suits as a business investment," Jenna said seriously. "You work damn hard for your wealth. You deserve to look like it."

Seth smiled at her compliment. "Their cost wouldn't stop me from leaving them on the floor on the way to bed with you," he told her.

Jenna looked through the walls and across the rest of the lot without commenting back. She always got a little uncomfortable when Seth started talking about how things were between them.

"About last night, Jenna," Seth began, knowing there was never going to be a better segue into talking about what brought him to see her. "Did you realize we forgot to use a condom?"

Jenna sighed. "I realized it this morning when I woke up. It's okay. I'm using birth control. I meant to tell you before. We don't have to use the condoms, but I just figured they were a back-up precaution. I've been on birth control almost since the first day I met you."

"So the night of the engagement party, I wouldn't have made you pregnant?" Seth said, realizing the greater error of not following through now. And the even bigger one of just not talking to her about such things.

"Well, there's always a chance of pregnancy, even with the best birth control. If you hadn't insisted on stopping that day, I would have told you," Jenna said, shrugging. "I did try to tell you several times while we were dating because I thought knowing might make you feel better about sleeping with me. Eventually it became a moot point so I just shut up about it. I stayed on the birth control after we broke up because it didn't make sense to go off when I was actively dating. I have a lot of faults, but I'm not going to be careless about creating a child."

"So you were planning on eventually sleeping with Stedman," Seth said, not really upset about it, but he couldn't help feeling like he'd barely prevented the worst from happening.

"I prefer not to discuss the rest of my personal life," Jenna said quietly. "I'm not involved with anyone physically other than you at the moment. I do have a date for next weekend, but it's nothing major. I keep my word."

A date. Another man. *Again*, Seth thought. And he couldn't say anything because it was a violation of their agreement.

"So you're okay with how things are with us?" Seth asked instead, not liking where this conversation was going, but unable to avoid asking the questions that had been festering in him for a few weeks.

Jenna crossed her arms and looked up at him. "Yes. I guess I am. Are you?"

Seth looked down into her face, looking hard for signs that Jenna was not being completely honest. Dismayed when he found nothing but sincerity, Seth slowly nodded yes.

What other choice did he have?

"If that's all you're willing to give me of yourself, I guess it will have to do for now. I don't want out of our deal yet, but you probably need to know that I'm going to eventually want more from our relationship than just sex. If you're not going to, then I'm definitely going to want out one day," he said.

"Okay. Thanks for making that clear," Jenna said softly. "And thanks for caring enough to come tell me about last night."

"Well, at least you realize I care," Seth said, sarcasm getting the best of him at last when he realized she wasn't going to say anything more about her feelings for him. "I've got plans for this evening so I need to run. Thanks for the tour. I'd like to come back again when it gets closer to being finished."

"Sure," Jenna said, having to stretch her legs to keep up with Seth's long strides now that he seemed in a hurry to leave. "You working tonight?"

Seth looked sideways at Jenna as they walked through the chaos in the great room again. When they were out of the noise and at his car, he unsnapped the hard hat, removed it, and handed it to her.

"Thanks for tour. No, I'm not really working tonight," Seth said enigmatically. "A business acquaintance is in town. We got finished with the business part this morning. Tonight, we're going to dinner and touring the town while she's still here. This is her first time in Falls Church. She flies out tomorrow morning."

"So you have a date then?" Jenna asked.

Seth narrowed his eyes at Jenna and the snippy way she had asked the question. She seemed determined to call his business dinner a date, probably to justify her own date next weekend. Damn the woman. "Yes. I guess you could call it a date. I wasn't thinking in those terms, but what the hell."

"Look, you don't have to be so secretive about seeing other people. We have an agreement," Jenna told him, kicking gravel with the toe of her boot. "I'm not jealous."

"Great. Good to hear," Seth said, climbing into his car. He needed to leave before he lost his temper.

Jenna Ranger and her stubborn refusal to acknowledge the truth of their relationship were straining his patience to its limit.

Chapter 12

After dinner at the hotel, Seth arranged for a limo to take them all on a tour of the city. Talia seemed content as she took in the sights.

"Everything is very historic here," Talia said, hoping Seth Carter would see her comment was not a judgment. "Boston is like that too."

"Oh, the modern is here as well. You just have to know where to look for it. The locals don't want it making too much of an impression on the public at large," Seth said, laughing. "Still, Falls Church is a good place to live and work. I like the East Coast and the business community on this side of the US. However, I vacation in California a lot. The West Coast has its charms as well."

"Ian and I used to travel a lot before Mason was born," Talia said, putting her hand on her son's back where he was stretched out in the long seat beside her. Kendra was asleep in the car seat the limo service had provided. "I miss traveling at times. I tell myself the kids will be older soon, and then I'll get to travel again."

"I'm sure you could travel for our company all you like. I've managed to do all the business electronically up to now, but face-to-face is always better," Seth said.

"How about multi-media conferencing? Maybe we could set up video and audio in a room of one of our homes and use that for meetings," Talia suggested. "It would be the next best thing to being there. Then you can get in the bowing and so forth that many Asia cultures observe even in business. It's quite charming to follow their customs."

"You'd have to teach me," Seth told her. "I learned the languages but didn't study the culture. Believe it or not I made Cs in my French classes at college."

"But you speak several languages now?" Talia asked, laughing.

"Even *Français*, Madame Martin. *Avec la compétence passable*," Seth said, laughing in return. "Mind over matter. Never underestimate the power of determination."

"I think I never want to underestimate you," Talia said lightly. "This has been a great evening. I look forward to coming back now."

"I look forward to it also," Seth told her. "Tomorrow, I'm going to prepay three months rent on your condo and arrange for a six month lease. That will get you started. You can have your household items sent anytime. The rental company will let the movers inside."

"You make it all sound so easy," Talia said in wonder, climbing out of the limo at the hotel. "I'll be back as soon as I can."

"Good. Here—let me get Mason," Seth said, easily lifting the sleeping boy into his arms. "You can get the baby now."

Seth settled Talia and her children into their suite, said goodnight, and headed home to an emptiness greater than he had ever felt. Spending time with Talia Martin's family had forcibly reminded him of the life he truly wanted and how very different it was from the life he had.

For once, he didn't even long for Jenna to be with him. If she had come by, probably nothing would have prevented him from the fight Seth knew there were going to eventually have about the nature of their relationship. Maybe tomorrow night he would be back in control of himself again and able to keep to their stupid agreement.

But when the text message came moments later asking if he was home yet and could she come by, Seth sent back a yes without any hesitation at all.

Jenna arrived at his place at just about the same time he did. He was dressed in his suit and Jenna was still in her work clothes. She had come straight to him from another long day of battling to make her dream come true.

Damned stubborn woman, Seth thought, locking his car and walking to her where she stood by his door. She was jealous and had wanted to see if his "date" had meant anything. It was the first time he had ever been tempted to punish her for first accusing him of something that wasn't true, and then coming around to check on it.

"I probably need a shower, but if I went home first, it would have been too late to come, and I thought—I—well, I just wanted to see you," Jenna stopped. *Stupid, stupid to come here*. She could smell the other woman's perfume on his suit, and here she was ready to fling herself into his arms. Where was her pride now, she wondered?

Seth put his hand behind Jenna's head and pulled her mouth to his for a searing, mind-numbing kiss that he only hoped let Jenna know how welcome and wanted she was.

"I. Need. You. Just you." They were the only words he knew Jenna would hear and understand. He would have gladly added that he loved her, if there had been slightest chance of Jenna being ready to hear how he really felt. But she wasn't.

She had her own damn date next weekend, and if she had been ready to love him back, it would have been a date with him. Knowing she was going out with another guy hurt, but he'd let the jealousy she felt tonight reassure him that there was hope one day she'd forgive the past and let herself love him again.

So tonight, instead of hurting, or fighting the way he wanted to, Seth settled for kissing Jenna like she was the most necessary thing in the world to him.

It was exactly the truth of how it was between them, whether Jenna Ranger wanted to hear it or not.

It wasn't like Seth not to answer his phone even at ten-thirty at night, but Casey wasn't too concerned about stopping by unannounced on a weekday even as late as it was. He had wanted to retrieve his humidor from the kitchen pantry where he'd forgotten it. The latest job he and Ben were working on was close to Seth's condo, so it just made sense to stop by briefly while he was in the neighborhood.

He turned his key in the condo's lock and stepped silently into the foyer.

Then he heard voices coming from the obviously open door of Seth's bedroom. One man and one woman. The woman was moaning and calling Seth's name, and his cousin was groaning hoarsely in reply. Even though the rest of the dialog was muffled, it was pretty easy to figure out what they were doing.

At first the shock of Seth having a woman there was so great that Casey stood frozen in place.

Then he noticed the trail of clothes littering the hallway. He felt his eyebrows lift as he recognized the clothes even if he still had trouble believing it.

Humidor forgotten again, Casey slipped silently back out the door so neither Seth nor Jenna would ever know he'd been there and heard them.

"I'm sorry to wake you, honey. I couldn't help myself," Casey said in apology, his breathing still not back to normal yet. He lay on his side with one arm and one leg thrown possessively over his wife's relaxed body.

"I don't think a woman ever minds waking up to a hard, horny man begging to get inside her, especially one that knows how to really, really, really make it worth her while," Alexa told her husband, laughing.

Casey touched the smile lines beside her eyes. "I want a set just like these. Did I ever tell you that?"

Alexa reached out to touch the corner of his eyes in return. "You're getting them. If you want, I can get mine reduced until you catch up. At the rate you're laughing these days, it's not going to take many years."

"Don't iron out a single line or wrinkle for me ever," Casey whispered fiercely. "They're my favorite things about you. You're as perfect as a woman can get, Alexa. Please don't change anything."

"Good lord," Alexa said, heart swelling in her chest, her voice breathy and overwhelmed. "All this romance at midnight? I'm wide awake now. If you want to go another round, I'm game after all that sweet talk."

Casey laughed against Alexa's shoulder. "I just—I just wanted you to know how much I love you. I'm so damn glad I married you."

Alexa snorted. "Really? Didn't you slam the garage door as you left this morning, fuming about how I could make the coffee occasionally when you had to be somewhere so early in the day? I wasn't completely awake yet, but I believe the slammed door was accompanied by a symphony of creative swearing and further banging noises as you peeled out of the garage like a bat out of hell in the truck."

Casey's groan vibrated in his chest. "Yeah, okay. Maybe I was a bit cranky at crawling out of bed at 5 a.m. and took it out on you. I know you can't even see the coffee pot before seven."

"Well, next time you throw a tantrum over coffee I'm going to remind you that you think I'm the perfect woman. I swear I'm going to put a tape recorder by the bed to catch things like this in the future," Alexa said, giggling at his consternation. "And I'm buying a damn programmable coffee pot so you can have more control over the coffee situation. We will never repeat this morning. I almost took poor Allen's head off because I was mad at you."

"I'm sorry," Casey said, his laughter making it somewhat less than sincere. Alexa had gone from holding a grudge to holding him accountable. It was healthier communication, but he ended up apologizing more and more. Evidently, he had some faults he hadn't been totally aware of until her.

"Well, you should be sorry," Alexa said firmly, closing her eyes at his stroking hand, which found its way to her backside for a stroke and a loving pinch.

"Don't start," she warned.

Casey sighed in contentment and pulled her tightly into his arms. "I love you so much, Alexa."

"I love you too," Alexa said. "Where's all this humility coming from? What happened to you today?"

Casey ran a hand over her stomach and up to her breasts as he pondered how to best tell his story.

"Since I was in his neighborhood all day, I decided to go by Seth's on the way home and pick up the cigar humidor. It was around ten thirty and still early on the Seth Carter clock, but I didn't make it past the foyer. There was a line of discarded clothing down the hall and double moans coming out of his bedroom. I got the hell out before they heard me," Casey said, grinning in the dark.

Alexa looked at the ceiling and sighed. "Well, it was inevitable. Seth's a good-looking guy. Jenna is being stubborn about the attraction between them. Who could blame him for wanting some *companionship?*"

Alexa used the nicer term Casey had coined for sex because it helped her not be so disappointed in Seth for not waiting. Though Alexa would agree that the boy had waited longer than any other man would have to be with her daughter.

Casey chuckled at his wife's misunderstanding of a situation he knew was secretly breaking her heart. She had been doing all she could to encourage Jenna to give Seth another chance.

"You're being very pragmatic about this, Alexa. Where's your romantic soul hiding these days?"

Alexa turned to him. "I've lived too long to be completely romantic about everything and everyone. What Ben did to woo Regina, admittedly that was romantic. What you and I did to work out our relationship was practically a war. What Lauren and Jim did torturing each other would make a best selling drama novel, complete with a horrible ex and insensitive mother-in-law. Romance—genuine romance—is damn hard to come by these days."

"True enough," Casey replied. "I doubt what I heard coming out of the bedroom was romance either, but it was definitely Jenna's work boots, jeans, and other clothing strung with Seth's down the hall."

Alexa clutched his hand. "Casey—are you serious? You're sure it was Jenna's clothes?"

Casey nodded against her, feeling her excitement. "Those work boots look like they're a hundred years old. She needs new ones. Yes. I'm pretty damn sure."

"Oh, thank God," Alexa said, breathing a sigh of relief about her daughter's happiness at last. "That boy is all my daughter wants. She's just so hard-headed—like her father."

Casey laughed hard, shaking the bed and Alexa with it. "No, not really. Paul's a great guy. Jenna's hard-headed like *you*," he corrected.

Alexa snorted at his laughter. "I thought you said I was perfect."

Casey rolled over on Alexa and raised himself up on his hands to look down into her laughing gaze.

"You are. You're the perfect woman for me, but I'm sure those other twenty-five guys or so before me caught hell in their day. Of course, you are pretty addictive. Look at Paul— he just went out and found another person exactly like you in Sydney. Still, I kind of feel sorry for Seth having to contend with his version of Ranger perfection. It's great, but it ain't easy," Casey declared, grinning at the fire in her gaze.

Alexa reached around and slapped Casey hard on his rear, the sting lighting his eyes as he called out in pain, the slap echoing in the room.

"Well, that's new," Casey commented. "If we're going to play that way, I want a turn."

"That's was punishment, fool, not foreplay," Alexa said, laughing. "I'm not into pain."

"Are you sure it wasn't foreplay? Because I'm turned on now," Casey told her, sliding down between her legs, and then back up inside her. Her moan of pleasure washed over him.

My woman and my fire, Casey thought. *All mine.*

"Yep, that sounds exactly like the female moan I heard coming out of the bedroom. Had to be Jenna. She sounds just like you," Casey confirmed.

"Stop thinking about Seth and Jenna. Damn it. I can't believe I let a pervert like you inside me. Get out," Alexa ordered, even as she pressed all ten fingernails into Casey's backside to hold him in place, the pain making him hiss.

He laughed harshly. "Shut up, woman, and make love with me. I have leverage now. If you don't do everything I want, I'll call a reality show and tell them to come interview us. The headlines will announce to the masses how the Carter men bedded the Ranger women. Or I'll get Kaiser to have it announced on TV. That anchor woman still calls him."

"Oh dear. Does Regina know the anchor woman is calling Ben?" Alexa said, laughing but biting her lip.

Casey laughed and had to stop moving. He was pressing deeper into the woman he adored, trying to get her attention back on him. It was his own damn fault for talking too much in bed, and now he'd ratted out Kaiser.

"No, she doesn't know. Ben's afraid Regina would be convicted for murder if she gets wind of it. He handles it well. Besides, you know there's no one else for him but one woman. Kaiser's just like the rest of us."

"Yes, but you and Seth take that one-woman thing to a whole new level," Alexa said. "It's very inspiring to be the only one for a Carter man."

Casey pressed hard and held himself still inside his wife to ask his question. "How inspiring?"

Alexa rolled them over and showed her husband just how inspiring he was.

Chapter 13

The Vanguard fundraiser was black tie formal, so Jenna dressed in a sleek fitting black dress that hugged all curves and donned a pair of strappy black sandals that lifted her several inches to almost Lauren's height. She was a little worried about towering over Cristo's head, but the alternative was black ballet flats, and this was just not that kind of dress. Even she knew that much about clothes.

Jenna drew on a heavy gold jacket that brought out the highlights in her blonde-brown hair that was many shades lighter than her mother's, but just as lush. She looked at the clock on the wall and headed to the entry of her building.

The taxi she'd called was just pulling up as she got outside.

"Where to, miss?" the driver asked.

Jenna gave him the address and settled in for the ride. Her mind drifted to wondering what Seth was doing tonight, but she refused to dwell on it. She'd gotten her fix last night, several times in fact. It had been two in the morning before she'd gotten home, and nine before she'd made it to the job site. Seth had been in a strange mood, and she'd actually snuck out after he'd fallen asleep wrapped around her.

No more thinking about Seth, she told herself.

Tonight she was having a real date. The good-looking, very polite Cristo would be waiting for her at the end of her taxi ride. She'd dance and smile and enjoy his attention as she always did. The man had a way of looking at her like she was the only person in the world. It was flattering and soothed her ego. And he kissed well too—not that she'd be doing much of that tonight. It wasn't fair to kiss a man when your mind was on kissing someone else.

Jenna paid the taxi driver and thanked him, and then walked quickly up the steps of the majestic building where the dance was being held. With the fundraiser fully underway, the crowd of people was thick and the music loud. Jenna scanned the room and spotted her boss and his wife dancing intimately.

To her surprise, she also saw Jim and Lauren. They were standing at the food table, which was not a surprise, given Lauren's appetite. Seeing them laughing and talking brought a smile to Jenna's face, which faded into need curling in her belly when she smelled the distinct and alluring cologne that had become part of her recent addiction. She turned and saw the man she craved most in the world standing two feet away from her.

"Seth—what—what are you doing here?" Jenna asked, stammering out the question.

Seth shrugged. "Helping to sponsor a good cause. My company's on the list with yours."

"Oh, I—I didn't know that," Jenna said, her breath catching.

"Where's your date?" Seth asked softly, keeping his voice as neutral as possible, not giving away his true feelings on the matter.

"I don't know. I just got here," Jenna said. "Working late on the house again. I finally made everyone go home early. I didn't want them there without me."

Seth laughed. "Well, at least you're a beautiful control freak. I'm sure no one minded going home early after all the late hours they've been putting in on that job."

"Yeah, I'm sure. I've become so possessive about the house. It's awful. When I have to turn it over the owner, it's going to hurt a lot. I'm hoping he'll let me come visit now and again," she said, laughing softly. "I can't seem to help my attachment."

"Understandable I think, given the amount of sweat equity you're putting into it," Seth told her. "Want to dance while you wait on your date?"

Jenna looked around the room again, but saw no Spanish weightlifter. Cristo was distinctively handsome. He would have stood out in this crowd.

"Sure. I guess so," she said, letting Seth lead her to the dance floor by the hand.

"Lauren. I think Seth and Jenna are here together. Are they dating?" Jim asked.

Lauren narrowed her eyes and sought out the couple weaving close together on the dance floor. Seth's hand slid smoothly down the back of Jenna's dress and then even further to pull her hips closer to his. Lauren gasped in surprise and pleasure. That was a practiced move if she ever saw one.

"It sure looks that way. I'm also getting turned on just watching them," she said.

"Don't get too carried away. We are *not* sneaking off to a broom closet tonight. You're just going to have to wait until we get home," Jim told her, laughing.

"If I did something I needed to apologize for, would it change your mind about the broom closet?" Lauren asked.

"Not even then," Jim told her. "But I like how you're thinking."

"I knew something was happening. I just knew it. I wonder why they haven't said anything," Lauren said, picking up a canapé to pop it into her mouth.

"Oh—well we might be wrong. Look," Jim said, motioning discreetly with his shoulder.

Lauren's heart fell as she watched a very good-looking man butt in and Seth walk off with his hands in his pockets. *Probably keeping them there to keep from strangling the man who had broken in on his dance with Jenna,* Lauren thought.

"Jenna needs her head examined," Lauren said fiercely. "Sure the dark muscle guy looks great, but Seth is the one for her. It's so obvious."

Jim laughed. "So you think the new guy looks great?"

Lauren shrugged. "I suppose. Jenna doesn't date ugly men. I mean—with a father like hers, she's going to be drawn to the good-looking men every time."

"She didn't keep that Stedman fellow. Isn't he the ultimate female fantasy? Muscles, permanent tan, even white teeth, and lots of charm?" Jim asked.

Lauren stared at Jim in his new SydneyB suit, looking every inch the successful businessman he was. Her husband was smiling at her and her growing body with enough pride to satisfy the most demanding female ego.

"Stedman never did much for me," Lauren told him sincerely. "I married my fantasy. I don't know what other women want."

Jim put his plate down and pulled his wife into his arms for a kiss.

"Stay here by the food while I look for a broom closet. I need to apologize for turning you down earlier," Jim whispered seductively to his laughing wife.

Jenna swung around the floor in the arms of a handsome man who drew the admiring gazes of most of the women passing by them. She had lost sight of Seth after he'd surrendered her to Cristo.

Seth had certainly not looked happy when he walked away. His reaction made perfect sense to her because Jenna was not happy now either. She couldn't even enjoy the company of her date.

It was the dancing, Jenna thought. She'd let Seth touch her, stroke her, and now she could think only of him and what she knew he could do to her.

Misinterpreting the frown on her face, Cristo assumed Jenna was tired and suggested they get something to eat and drink. She was more than happy to get off the dance floor and out of Cristo's arms, so Jenna meekly let him lead her away.

Seth watched Jenna frown and walk off the dance floor with her head bowed as she trailed behind the man who had claimed her away from him. He didn't know which bothered him more, the existence of yet another good-looking man in her life or Jenna's meek behavior with him.

He took out his cell and typed furiously.

Does your date know you like to scream during sex? Want me to tell him how to make you? I could give him some friendly advice.

He pressed send and waited. From a distance, Seth watched Jenna pull out her cell and read his message. He laughed when she clasped the cell phone to her chest to hide the message when the man asked if everything was okay.

The hold he had on Jenna Ranger wasn't love yet, but Seth knew how to push the right buttons in some ways.

"We'll see which one of us she climbs into bed with tonight, you Spanish bastard. It's for damn sure not going to be you," Seth said under his breath.

"Why don't you dance with me and make her jealous?" a voice suggested near his elbow.

Seth turned to see a tall, gorgeous blonde smiling at him as she sipped a glass of champagne.

"Sorry," Seth said, apologizing. "Ex-girlfriend. I didn't mean anyone to hear that."

"Didn't look like ex-anything when you were dancing with her earlier," the woman said with a laugh. She put out a hand for him to shake. "My name is Linda Warren. My husband Todd is Jenna's boss. He sent me over here to dance with you and find out who you are. He thinks you're the one who's got Jenna smiling and being nice now at the office. Is that true?"

Now Seth laughed as he shook her hand. "I'm Seth Carter. If Jenna's being nice, you couldn't prove it by me. I only have part of her affections right now, but I'm damn possessive about my part. I don't like to share her attention with her—dates."

"My kind of man," Linda said, grinning and setting her champagne on a nearby table before taking his hand in hers again. "Jenna actually introduced me to Todd. I used to model for Alexa when I was younger. Jenna and I have always been good friends even though I'm a decade older. Once I got married, she ditched me to hang out with her single friends. Come on, let's dance."

Seth tucked his phone back into his pocket as they walked to the dance floor. "Are you sure your husband isn't going to come after me if I dance with you?"

"Only if you run your hand over my rear like you did Jenna earlier," Linda said, laughing when he blushed. "Look at you blushing, Seth Carter. You are the sweetest thing. Todd and I were looking hard. That's the only reason we noticed."

"I have little self-control where Jenna Ranger is concerned," Seth said contritely, "but I didn't mean to do anything to embarrass her in front of her boss."

"Like Jenna would care. Besides, you can't embarrass Todd. Not even on a good day. The man is outrageous. That's why I married him. He and Jenna get along great, and he's says you're the best thing to ever happen to her," Linda said, smiling up into his face. "I mean, that is—if you *are* the one happening to her. Todd says she's being very discreet about her love life. No bragging at all. He says she just smiles a lot."

Seth smiled at the thought of Jenna being happy because of him, and then laughed because there was no other choice in the face of Linda Warren's enthusiastic teasing. He wanted the whole world to know how he felt about Jenna. He certainly had no problems with her boss knowing. "Okay. I admit it. I'm the one—even if Jenna hasn't accepted it yet."

"Jenna is stubborn, but she's loyal, smart as hell, and has a heart of pure gold too. I wouldn't have married Todd if it hadn't been for her lecturing me on how he was the perfect man and that it was stupid to let our seven-year age difference be a factor," Linda said. "That's why I couldn't believe Jenna gave Alexa such grief over Casey. Hey, you're Casey's cousin, aren't you? No wonder you're such a nice guy. Casey is a great guy."

"Well, if you say anything nice about me to Jenna, you'll just make her more resistant," Seth warned. "I'm wearing her down. It's just taking a while."

And because he was smiling at the top of her head, Linda knew Seth didn't see the woman they were discussing glaring at them from across the room, but she did.

It made her laugh to know at her age someone as young and beautiful as Jenna could be so jealous of her.

Across the room, Jenna glared at Seth dancing with the lovely older woman. Not only was Linda lovely, but she was charming and funny as well. Todd adored her and usually never let other guys be around her for long. Jenna wondered what the man was thinking letting Linda dance with Seth.

"Cristo, will you excuse me a moment. I need to go say hello to my boss. Why don't you ask one of these pretty women to dance with you until I get back?" Jenna said, patting him on the arm and pushing him lightly in the direction of a smiling brunette giving him the eye.

Jenna stalked in her strappy sandals over to talk to Todd.

"Why is Linda dancing with Seth Carter?" she demanded.

"Who? Oh, is that his name?" Todd asked, keeping his face composed when he wanted to laugh outright at Jenna's jealousy. "I was just wondering who he was. Carter. Carter. Is he related to your stepfather?"

"Yes. Don't just stand there watching them, Todd. Go do something about it. Cut in and stop them," Jenna demanded.

"Why?" Todd asked, fascinated with the fury on Jenna's face. He'd never seen her this animated about anything but work, certainly not about a guy. "Linda is just dancing with the man. I've got an eye on them. The man seems to be keeping his hands where they belong."

"They're smiling and laughing, Todd," Jenna said furiously. "Don't you think they're being a little *too* friendly?"

"I trust my wife completely, Jenna. Besides, I saw you dancing with that man earlier. He seemed nice enough with you," Todd said, narrowing his gaze on her. "What's wrong with him? Isn't he your date?"

"Nothing's wrong with him. And no, he's not my date. I'm here with the dark sexy guy dancing with the short brunette over there by the window," Jenna said tightly.

"*Really? That's your date?* Well, you don't seem worried about him dancing with another woman. The blonde guy is the one you seem concerned about right now. What's the deal, Jenna? Why are you so upset about the Carter guy dancing with Linda?" Todd commented, sipping his soda and watching Jenna fume over the rim of his glass.

"I'm not upset. I'm just—" Jenna stopped, not knowing what to say. She watched Todd's wife smile and laugh at something Seth said. There was no reason for the situation to bother her. Really. She was overreacting. But did they have to dance so damn close together?

"Jenna, whoever that man is—the one that's not your date—he seems to really care about you," Todd stated. "It was obvious when you were dancing with him. You could see it in the way he looked at you and from the way he held you in his arms."

"You don't know the man, Todd. He spent four months dating me and just as long rejecting me. He's obsessed with his business and has a more intimate relationship with his cell phone than me. So it's not so obvious that he cares," Jenna said harshly.

"He makes you happy—at least in some ways," Todd said quietly, hoping to defuse the unexpected bomb he set off by asking his lovely wife to dance and spy. "If you seriously want me to, I'll go drag Linda away from the man who is not your date, but I'm guessing he'll just find another woman to dance with. He's a good-looking guy. If you're not dating him, someone else is going to come along and snap him up. It's only a matter of time."

"Fine. If you're not worried about your wife, then I'm not either," Jenna said, ignoring the rest of Todd's commentary about Seth being good-looking and getting snapped up. She

DATING A METRO MAN

couldn't think about Seth and another woman. It made her want to kill people.

Jenna went back to stand and wait politely for Cristo to finish his third dance in a row with the brunette. Jenna pulled out her cell phone while she waited and typed a reply to Seth's earlier message that was sure to get retaliation.

Maybe I scream because I like drama. Maybe it's nothing you're doing at all.

Then Jenna waited, but Seth never missed a step in his dancing or pulled his attention away from his partner. Normally, he would have stopped to take the message or the call. When had Seth suddenly become Mr. Attentive, she wondered? And why to Linda Warren?

The dance finally ended and Cristo came back to her side. She let him lead her out for the next dance even as Linda led Seth across the room to meet Todd.

Great, she thought. Now she'd have no peace at work. Seth was too honest to lie about the nature of their relationship no matter how embarrassing the circumstances of it were to her. Todd finding out was almost as bad as their family discovering what they were doing.

She watched Seth talk to Todd for two whole dances without checking his phone.

By the time the second dance ended, she was ready to leave—but not with Cristo.

"Cristo, I think I'm going to have to go," Jenna said. "I've been working very long days and they're catching up with me.

Cristo raised a hand to her face and smiled in sympathy. The short brunette tapped him on the shoulder again. He looked at Jenna.

"Stay. Enjoy your evening. I mean that," Jenna said, mentally saying goodbye to yet another good-looking guy because of Seth Carter. She leaned forward and dropped a kiss on his cheek in farewell.

When she turned, it was to find Seth staring hard at the man leading the brunette out to the dance floor again. He looked puzzled when his gaze came back to her.

Jenna lifted her chin and walked over to where Seth stood. She ignored Todd and Linda completely.

"I suddenly find myself without a way home. Can I get a lift?" she asked Seth.

"Sure," Seth said, surprised and not able to hide it completely. "I need to drop a check off with the hosts. Be back in a couple of minutes. Todd. Linda. Nice to meet you."

"I see you're still hooking up the guys you dump with other women," Linda said, when Seth had walked away. "Seth Carter is a very nice man—dances well too. I bet he's good at a lot of things."

"He is," Jenna said automatically before turning a frowning gaze on the older beautiful woman and catching the twinkle of amusement in her eyes as she laughed. "You don't know anything."

"I know Seth Carter is into you in a major way," Linda said, hearing her husband laugh in agreement. "He talked about you the whole time we were dancing."

"Damn it. Why can't the man be discreet instead of honest?" Jenna demanded.

"Well, Seth didn't tell me stories or anything. That's pretty discreet if you ask me. I was really pumping him for information," Linda said, laughing. "What's your problem Jenna? He's a perfectly pleasant man."

"No. He's not. Seth's a lot of things, but pleasant isn't one of them," Jenna said.

"You need to get over whatever you're mad about and reel Seth Carter in while he's still interested," Linda told her. "Don't be as hard-headed as your mother. She spent a lot years alone."

"Mama waited for love," Jenna said defensively. "And she found it."

"Yes, she certainly did, and it was with the older version of that perfect guy, right? You've found love too, girl," Linda told her. "Open your eyes and see it. Quick now. He's walking back your way."

"Ready to go?" Seth asked, looking into Jenna's face for her answer.

Jenna nodded and headed across the floor frowning harder as she walked several steps in front of Seth. Despite her reaction to Linda's teasing, she was not in love with Seth Carter. And Jenna did not believe he was in love with her. They had some sort of infatuation caused by their intense and very consuming sex life. They had lust. They did not have love.

"By the way, I just saw your message," Seth said easily, holding the door of his car open for her. "We'll test that theory when we get home."

"Fine," Jenna agreed, wanting to slam the door of Seth's car, but couldn't since he helped her inside and closed it gently behind her.

Seth climbed into the driver's seat and sat there for a few moments, keys hovering over the ignition.

"I'm really trying not to let this go to my head, but frankly I have to ask the question. Did you just dump your date for me?" Seth asked her.

"Just drive, Seth. Don't talk to me until I calm down," Jenna told him. "You didn't have to get so chummy talking to Linda."

"Oh. You were jealous again. Well, good—welcome to my world. One minute my hand is on your ass pulling you into me, and the next I'm handing you over to another guy who's a genuine date for you. So don't start bitching at me for innocently dancing with your boss's wife. You're going to lose this argument hands down," Seth warned.

"We shouldn't even be having any argument about either of us being jealous," Jenna hissed. "We are not dating—damn it."

"Oh, that's abundantly clear," Seth told her, new anger and hurt feeding his growing irritation with her. "If we were dating, I'd have kicked the weightlifter's ass tonight, or at least tried. He's a big step down from Stedman, by the way. That guy didn't care which woman he danced with. What's that all about? He was supposed to be your damn date, not that brunette's."

Jenna was quiet for a moment, and than she laughed at the ridiculousness of the conversation. "This is the kind of relationship drama I precisely did not want, but can't seem to avoid with you. What happened to our sex-only relationship? It was supposed to keep things simple."

"Don't be naïve, Jenna. Our sex life has never been simple. We go up in flames every time we get together," Seth told her. "That's not typical and you know it. You've just chosen to see it like you wanted to and I've let you get by with your illusion because I've been avoiding this fight."

"Why are we at my house?" Jenna asked when Seth pulled into her condo's parking lot. "I mean, it's fine, but why are we here?"

"Because I'm seeing you home safely instead of taking you home with me," Seth told her. "I want you, but I can't keep up my side of the deal tonight. I want more. I should have been the date on your arm tonight. I met your boss, who thinks you hung the moon, but I didn't get to share the moment, and you didn't get to hear me tell him how proud I am of you. Even friends have more than we have, and tonight made that really clear to me. So here you are, safe and sound at your house. Give me a couple of days to get over feeling used before you call me again for just sex."

Jenna sat in the car and didn't get out. "We are friends, Seth."

"Are we?" he asked, his sarcastic tone emphasizing the simple question. "You haven't asked anything about my work since we've been sleeping together. I've been out to your job site, and now I've met your boss and his wife. I'm tired of being your walking vibrator and nothing more."

Jenna laughed even though Seth had not meant the comment to be funny. Truly, if looks could kill, the one Seth gave her over laughing would have certainly done the job.

"If all I wanted was sexual release, I would have bought a real vibrator. But mechanical boyfriends have never been my thing. I like the human connection. That's why I was so mad at you for not sleeping with me before. I had the female equivalent of blue balls for four months and you didn't seem to care. I'm still mad. I can't seem to get over it," she admitted.

Seth didn't want to laugh, but he did at her "blue balls" analogy. Regina hadn't put it in those terms, but it was still the same thing. When he thought about how uninhibited Jenna was now in her response with him every time, Seth knew she wasn't exaggerating the level of her frustration. Having had many opportunities now to satisfy her physically, he had at least gone from feeling like shit about how he'd ignored her to just feeling sorry he'd been so stupid about sleeping with her.

But even his remorse over not sleeping with her then wasn't reason enough to let her keep their relationship from progressing to something more than just mutually gratifying sex now.

"Come inside, Seth," Jenna pleaded. "I'll let you make me scream. You know you want to."

The degree to which Seth was motivated to satisfy Jenna Ranger again and again was familiar to him now. He already knew he was going inside with her. Pride be damned, he was still going in. It was just a matter of deciding under what circumstances he would concede.

Stalling, Seth tried to think of an instance where he might say no when Jenna asked him to have sex with her. Seth couldn't think of even one. That's how much trouble he was in.

There were a lot of terms, Seth knew, that were often used to describe men in his condition, and he'd heard them all over time. Seth had always been one of those men who laughed at the poor guy being labeled, thinking that he would never have an obsessive sexual attachment to a woman, especially a woman like Jenna who knew and would use it against him.

Boy, how wrong he had been.

He could smell her perfume in the confines of the car, feel the heated excitement of her waiting to see what he would say or do, and had to fight the images he played like a movie in his head about ripping Jenna's clothes off before he did what he wanted to her while she screamed. It was very difficult to bargain for a better life while he wrestled with his conscience just to be civilized to her.

"I'll come inside with you on one condition," Seth told her quietly, keeping both hands on the steering wheel and off her until the deal had been made for sure. "I want to date you—really date you. We don't have to tell the family."

"Oh, damn—*family*," Jenna said, laying her head back on the seat as she remembered. "I saw Lauren and Jim there tonight. I meant to go over and say hi, but I forgot."

"Lauren and Jim were there? Why didn't I see them?" Seth demanded, truly surprised.

"Probably because you were dancing and flirting," Jenna said meanly, and then could have bitten out her tongue for sounding jealous again. She closed her eyes and swore. The f-word fell viciously from her lips and resonated in the car. Vicious swearing was a side effect of working around blunt men.

Seth laughed openly at her ugly swearing, pleased that Jenna was suffering, and pleased that she was at least marginally worried about him.

"I wonder how jealous you'd have been if I had brought a real damn date tonight like you did," Seth said, glaring at Jenna in the dark. "If I missed seeing Lauren and Jim, it was because I didn't see anyone else once you got there in that black seduction dress and those damn strappy heels I know you hate wearing. You looked like some fantasy come to life for me. After I held you in my arms, the rest of the crowd might as well have been invisible. All I could think about was carrying you off and burying myself inside you for a year or two."

Jenna's heart beat strongly in her chest and just as loudly in her ears. She certainly didn't like the knot in her stomach at the idea of Seth dating other women. When had the emotions of the situation gotten away from her?

It was the naked truth that Jenna liked being the woman Seth Carter wanted to carry off and ravish. He *was* a great ravisher.

But what was it worth to her? That was the question.

"Okay. Fine. If that's your condition for coming inside with me, I suppose we can try dating again," Jenna said, resigning herself to her fate.

No sense waffling about it, she decided. She had to give their relationship another real try. Maybe with enough fights like this one, they would get tired of each other in a short amount of time. Maybe the next breakup would really take.

"Well, gee, Jenna—try not to sound so excited about spending time with me outside of bed," Seth said meanly. "On that high note, I still don't think I'm coming inside tonight. Call me later in the weekend."

Jenna looked at Seth sitting quietly in the driver's seat. He had swiped his hand through his hair so many times it was standing on end. The contrast between his messy hair and his perfect suit had Jenna suddenly giggling hysterically. He drove her crazy, but apparently it worked both ways. For some insane reason, it pleased her enormously to see physical proof that she irritated him. It was awful of her to be so happy over something so petty, but she did have intentions of making up to Seth for her bad mood.

"Come in and let me smooth your hair for you, Seth. I know how to make all that tension you're feeling just melt away. I'll even do all the work tonight if you talk to me nicely," Jenna said, trying to sound breathy and sexy, but it was hard to do that when she was laughing. "I'll sit in your lap and let you tell me what to do again."

Seth looked in the rearview mirror and used a hand to smooth his hair down. "Tempting, but I'm not that easy. I'm tired of being your sex toy."

"No you're not. You're just mad. If you don't come inside, I'm just going to sext you until you're so frustrated you'll drag me to your wooden foyer floor next time you see me. So save yourself the technological torture of the next few days and just come inside with me," Jenna said, smiling at Seth in the dark.

"You are a confusing, frustrating woman with a moody temperament like an angry purse dog," Seth told her. "You yap and bark and snip at me, but you still want to climb into my lap and be petted when you're in the damn mood. Do you even care what I think or feel?"

Jenna snickered over the analogy. It was more fair than she wanted to admit, but she wasn't about to confirm it for him. Yes okay—maybe she was high maintenance, but thanks to Seth, Jenna was starting to think she was worth it. It was his praising of her lovemaking, and how sexy Seth seemed to find her, and how no matter how mad Seth was he still sent her flying over the edge with him.

"Sometimes I take the time to care and sometimes I don't. I'm working on getting better about it. I'm trying hard to be as fair to you as I can. Even if what you say is true about me being a moody purse dog, you sure seem to like petting me well enough, Seth Carter. So I don't think that argument is going to take you very far in convincing either of us that you don't want to come inside with me," Jenna said logically.

Then she watched Seth morph from metro man into caveman with something very close to—what she wondered? As she pondered the strange feeling of satisfaction, Seth pushed open his car door and climbed out, viciously swearing the whole way around the car.

Jenna climbed out and stood by the car door while Seth came the rest of the way around to her.

He stepped into her firmly and pressed her hard against the car, but stopped short of kissing her. "I'm not going to give a damn if I'm hurting you or not tonight. Still want me to come in?"

Jenna closed her eyes. She could already feel it happening.

"You have no idea how much I want you in my bed. I've been dreaming about it for weeks," she said, her voice a quivering whisper between them.

Swearing again, Seth's mouth sought hers in a blaze of sweeping heat that set both of them instantly on fire. His hands slid down behind her hips and he bent his knees so he could better rock the evidence of his frustration against her.

"I'm tempted to do this right here in the parking lot against my car like some rutting sixteen-year-old," he threatened.

"Well, I'm wearing garters and my underwear is the unsnapping kind again. So it's technically feasible," Jenna said easily, using her business voice. "But if we go inside you can enjoy the show more, and I can do some of what I've been thinking about on the ride home."

Seth moved off Jenna but clamped a hand around one of her wrists as they walked up the sidewalk to her condo. He was practically dragging her as she stumbled in her heels.

"I'm going to have you now no matter what, so if your mood does one of those mercurial shifts again in ten minutes, tough shit for you. I'm beyond nice and just determined to get what I want tonight," he informed her.

"I have no problem with that," Jenna told him. "Is this make-up sex? Or punishment?"

Seth laughed at the excitement in her voice as they walked in the dark. "I'll know for sure in the morning." He looked down at Jenna when they stepped into her lighted entrance. "You got a problem waiting that long to find out which it is?"

Jenna felt Seth release her wrist so she could dig inside her small purse for her house key. She found it and handed it over. The symbolism of the action wasn't lost on either of them. It was more than her home she was surrendering.

Still Seth hesitated, waiting for her reply. He wanted the words.

"No. I have no problem with finding out in the morning," Jenna said, reluctant but resigned to him spending the night as well. "I have to make an early run out to the site. You might wake up alone."

"Wake me before you go and say goodbye," Seth ordered.

Jenna nodded as she walked ahead of him inside, wondering how her relationship with Seth Carter had gotten out of control again so fast.

Chapter 14

Allen Stedman stood outside the door of the luxury duplex thinking that letting Seth Carter talk him into meeting a woman he refused to tell him anything about was a bit like unwrapping a present from your grandmother at Christmas. It could be an ugly sweater she made for you or something she knew you really, really wanted. He savored the anticipation a few moments more, took a final deep breath, and then rang the doorbell.

While he waited, Allen moved the clipboard to a single arm where it covered the discreet company name on his polo. He fished his security badge out of his wallet for identification as he heard someone on the other side of the door. When the door opened, Allen stood almost nose-to-nose with an exotic fantasy.

She had straight black hair drawn up into a long ponytail, a tight fitted T-shirt that stretched taut across both breasts, and short yoga pants that barely covered her knees. The clothing revealed curvy hips and long legs, which drew so much of his attention that he had a hard time meeting her gaze again. When he did, he saw dark lashes and brows framing dark chocolate eyes, which looked surprisingly relieved to see him.

"Talia Martin?" Allen asked, hoping like hell the woman said yes.

"Yes. Thank you for coming quickly. The condo office said you left several boxes against the building. They're throwing a bloody fit. I can't go get the boxes myself right now, so please retrieve them for me. I'll leave the door unlocked for you," Talia said, waving a hand at the ID in his hand. "I don't need that anymore. You look enough like a mover to me. I trust my instincts."

"Well, actually—I...," Allen stopped. She just blinked at him, looking impatient, and he found himself getting turned on at the idea of arguing with her. Then he saw a little boy in braces walking toward them. His attention swiftly shifted.

"Hey," Mason told Allen, "you guys forgot stuff and Mom was talking ugly on the phone. You're not s'posed to make her mad. Seth said you were to be nice to us."

Allen smiled at the mention of Seth's name. It had been sneaky of Carter not to tell him anything about the woman in advance.

"I'm sorry," Allen said, apologizing for the missing movers, who he promptly decided needed their asses kicked for not treating this family right. "Will you watch my clipboard until I get back?"

Allen held out the clipboard to the boy, who took it eagerly, studying the writing on it intently like it was secret code. Allen supposed that was what it was like when you couldn't yet read.

"These words are all too big," Mason said sadly. "You should use small words."

"I'll tell my boss you said that," Allen said. "Let me get the boxes and I'll be right back."

After he left, Talia took the clipboard from Mason and read the paper it contained.

"Security checklist," Talia read, biting her lip even as she laughed at herself. "Uh-oh Mason. He wasn't a mover after all."

Mason laughed at her tone, even though he didn't fully understand what his mother meant.

Talia sighed at what she'd done. One day, she was going to learn to ask more questions before she jumped to conclusions. Sometimes instincts could be a little wrong.

Allen walked in and set down the first two of six boxes.

"Going to take a couple more trips," Allen said, smiling at the clipboard in Talia Martin's hand and her flushed face. It hadn't taken her long to figure out her mistake he noticed.

"You're not a mover, are you?" Talia asked.

"No. I'm from the security company, but I don't mind moving a few boxes for you. I don't want Seth mad at me too," Allen said, joking.

Talia laughed at his niceness. "I'm really sorry. Moving is a crazy time. There's a cold beer in it for you after you finish what Seth really sent you here to do."

"I'm doing the biggest part of it even as we speak," Allen said, declining to mention that the security inspection was an excuse. Meeting her was actually what he had come for. He trained people to do the residential inspections, but rarely did them himself. "Be right back."

He headed out the door again and came back moments later with two more boxes.

"The other men only carried one box," Mason informed the big man as he set the boxes on the floor next to the other ones. "Are you strong?"

Allen shrugged. "I like to think so. I work hard at keeping in shape."

"I want to be big like you," Mason said wistfully.

Allen closed his eyes in pleasure as he fell instantly in love with the kid. It was a heady thing to be admired for something you loved to do.

"I can probably help you with that," Allen told him. "I work at a gym. When you get a little older, your mom can bring you by to work out with me."

"Really?" Mason asked, smiling genuinely.

"Really," Allen told him sincerely, putting a hand on the top of his head. "Let me get those last two boxes."

"Did you hear that, mom?" Mason asked, as the man headed out again.

"Yes. I heard," Talia said softly, smiling at her son's enthusiasm. The man had an excellent body, and his heart seemed to be just as prime as the rest of him.

Allen came back with the last two boxes to find Mason waiting for him. The boy slammed the door shut after Allen got across the threshold.

"Mason! Close the door gently, son. Don't slam it off the hinges," Talia said firmly.

Mason rolled his eyes, but mumbled "Sorry."

Allen couldn't hold the laugh in anymore. Mason's gaze swung to Allen's laughing one.

"I get a little a carried away in my 'thusisam," Mason explained.

Allen laughed more because the kid was obviously trying to quote his well-spoken mother.

"I completely understand. Happens to me all the time," Allen told him, getting a laugh from the boy in return.

He walked over to stand in front of Talia Martin again. "I'm going to need my clipboard back to finish the security inspection. Seth is having us install a modest alarm system for you. The neighborhood is pretty good, but he was concerned about you and the kids being alone here."

"Do you know Seth well?" Talia asked.

"I work for his cousin—well, at least part-time. I'm also Seth's personal trainer at the gym," Allen told her, liking the way her look took all of him in thoroughly before returning to his face.

"Explains the muscles," Talia said, sweeping his body with one more interested gaze. She liked what she saw. A woman would never grow tired of admiring all that physical perfection.

Then Kendra started complaining as she awoke. Talia walked over to scoop her up from the playpen.

"Hey, sleepy girl. I wish I had had time for a nap today." She kissed her daughter's cheek and grabbed the body wrap infant carrier from the side of the playpen. Walking to the small dining room table, she laid her daughter on it, and then wrapped the yards of material around her in loose loops before scooping the now cooing baby into it.

Allen was mesmerized by the whole process. He walked to where Talia Martin stood with her daughter facing out and tied securely to her body by the wrap.

"Fascinating. May I?" he asked, tracing the material and the intricate way she had wrapped it around her with his fingers. "I've never been a fan of women's fashion, but this is amazing. Imagine if clothing was made this way."

Talia laughed at the man's genuine appraisal of the baby wrap. "Well, some clothes are made like this, if you're a supermodel walking down an Italian runway. I don't quite shop in those markets."

"You have a body that would look good in anything," Allen said sincerely, meeting her surprised chocolate gaze with his startled blue one. "Uh—sorry. I didn't mean that as anything but a fashion observation—I don't think."

Talia snorted and laughed, making Kendra laugh too.

Allen looked down at the little girl happily hanging from her mother's front. "How old is she?"

"Ten months," Mason answered.

Allen looked down to see Mason standing next to his leg.

"Wow. Your sister is young," Allen told him. "How about you?"

"Five or six," Mason answered enigmatically, making Allen laugh again. The kid was as fascinating as his mother.

"Which is it?" Allen asked.

"I don't know for sure," Mason said seriously. "Progidees are smart for their age."

Allen laughed. "How do you know you're a prodigy?"

"Grandpa Henry says I'm terrible smart," he answered, doing his best to imitate his grandparents. "Grandma Lily says I'm just terrible."

Allen looked at Talia, who was turning all sorts of interesting colors. The smile he gave her was automatic, genuine, and he hoped just a little bit revealing of his interest.

"Can I come back tonight and bring pizza? I really like you all, and I haven't had this much fun in a long time," Allen told her.

Talia blinked a couple of times trying to absorb that he wanted to spend more time with them. "Sure. I guess that would be okay."

"Okay. Well, I need to get this check done and the results back to my boss before the day ends. Rain check on the beer? I'll have it tonight." Allen started to walk away, but then stopped. "There isn't a husband or boyfriend I need to worry about is there?"

How amazing is this? Talia thought, as she shook her head in reply, smiling at the man over her daughter's head. She wasn't going to need Seth Carter to hook her up. Mason was doing the job for her by charming this really great one.

"Come around six-thirty or seven. These two go to sleep around eight-thirty. Make at least a quarter of the pizza plain cheese. Mason doesn't eat anything interesting."

"Unhealthy food will kill you," Mason said, wisely, "but I like pizza."

"Mason quotes more miscellaneous facts than Seth," Allen said, grinning. "If you ever give that kid access to the Internet, he'll take over the world."

"He's five and half. I think Mason is growing a super brain to compensate for other things," Talia said, liking Allen's husky laugh.

"Well, let me get this check done so I can get out of your way," Allen said kindly, walking off to the bedrooms.

Behind him, Allen heard the clink-clink of metal leg braces as Mason tagged slowly along wherever he went in the house. It made him smile and think of when Casey used to walk with a cane. Allen made conversation with the boy while he made quick work of checking where sensors would need to go.

"So what will happen next is that some very nice men will come by to install your security alarms sometime next week," Allen said to Talia, smiling. "Now I'll just leave you to your settling in and come back later."

Talia walked him to the door. "Thanks for bringing in the boxes. I really do appreciate it."

"Glad to help," Allen said, winking. "What do you like on your pizza?"

Talia shrugged and smiled. "I'm pretty easy to please. I like everything."

"I tend to like a lot of variety myself," Allen said, watching indecision flash in her gaze as she tried to decide if he was flirting with her or not. Deciding he liked her off-balance, Allen left it as it was, not bothering to confirm or deny. "Well—see you later."

"Wait," Talia called after him, hearing her daughter giggle at the tone of her voice as she yelled. "What's your name? I never got it. I should have looked at your badge when I had the chance."

"Sorry. It's Stedman," Allen called, lifting a hand to wave. "Allen Stedman."

Talia stood open-mouthed and gaping as the man and his shapely rear end disappeared down her sidewalk on his way to the visitor's parking area.

The man bringing her pizza tonight, and who had been charmed by her son, was the twenty-six-year-old weight lifter slash clothing designer Seth had mentioned to her. The laugh bubbled up inside her as she realized how smoothly she'd been maneuvered.

Well, the man was as nice as he was nice-looking, she conceded. Talia could definitely see why he'd been able to lure Seth's girlfriend away. Truth was that Allen Stedman could lure any woman. If a woman wasn't hot for his muscled good looks, the niceness alone made him good enough to eat with a spoon.

Her mind raced, wondering if she could put her hands on anything other than exercise clothes and mom-wear for this evening. Stedman was a little younger than Talia preferred, but then a pizza and beer wasn't really dating anyway. And with two kids as a chaperone, it wasn't likely to get very far.

Still, it would be nice to make a decent impression on the first man she'd agreed to spend any time with in quite a while. Besides, you could never tell what kind of connections a person would bring to you.

One thing for sure, Stedman had just helped her learn a valuable lesson about her employer. Talia would never underestimate Seth Carter in any of her future dealings with him.

If Seth made a serious comment about anything, it was now blatantly obvious to her that he meant it.

With the sheetrock in most of the house finished, Jenna was now able to see her creation really coming to life. There had been fewer compromises to be made than she had anticipated and the job was still three weeks ahead of schedule.

Jenna had intentionally remained behind when everyone else had left for the day. Needing some time alone to think, the mostly finished house provided the safest, most solitary place she had available at the moment. So she sat on the hearth of the stacked stone fireplace in the family room and sighed in contentment to be sitting still for a change.

If she had a pillow and blanket, she would have stretched out on the hearth and been fast asleep in minutes. The long days and long nights were rapidly catching up to her. Not that she minded the long nights; she just needed some sleep to better enjoy them.

She opened her eyes when she heard a car crunching on the gravel. Moments later, Seth walked in carrying a picnic basket.

"What are you doing here?" she demanded.

"Look, try this greeting—*Hi Seth. It's nice to see you*," he suggested, sarcasm dripping from every word.

Jenna laughed. "Sorry. I swear I'm never this bitchy with anyone else. I don't know why I do it with you. It's like an automatic response to your presence."

Seth shook his head. "I don't know why you do it either, but it's getting old."

He set the picnic basket down on the hearth beside Jenna. "This place is seriously looking like a house now. Love the double office spaces on each side of the loft. You really are designing this space for a couple, aren't you?"

"Yeah, I guess I am. The office spaces offer privacy, but don't cut the person in them off from the rest of what is going on," Jenna said. "And I put skylights above those spaces instead of the center of the room, so the workspaces will be well lit during the day. The light filters down into the great room enough. That was the argument I was having the first time you visited."

"Glad you won. Fireplace is nice too," Seth commented, looking at the stacked stone that went all the way to the ceiling. "It's like a piece of art in the room."

"I spent more on the stacked stone than I should have, but it makes a strong visual statement in the space. I hope like hell the client likes it. His answers about materials were too vague to know, so I did what I liked," Jenna complained with a shrug. "I end up sitting on this hearth now a good part of the day. It's wide enough to nap on, and I can't tell you how tempted I've been."

"The client will love it," Seth said with confidence. "It's the first thing you see when you walk through the door. The fireplace visually screams *you're home* so loud that even the busiest brain would have to register it."

Jenna looked at Seth in open-mouth shock. "That's exactly what I wanted it to do."

"Congratulations," Seth said sincerely. "You're as talented as you are beautiful."

"Under other circumstances, I'd physically reward you for your moral support, but I'm too damn tired today to even offer a hug," Jenna told him with a weak smile.

Seth laughed. "Glad to hear I finally wore you out. It only took sleeping with me and this huge project to find the limits of Jenna Ranger's inexhaustible energy."

He put one hand in the pocket of his dress slacks as he looked down at her sitting on the hearth, doubly glad he'd followed his instincts. "I brought dinner with me. I was going to chase you down wherever you were and convince you to eat whether you wanted to or not. I'm calling this a date, but you can call it being a friend if it makes you feel more comfortable. We'll argue the semantics of this out-of-bed time together when you're less tired. I don't want to take advantage."

Jenna looked away from Seth's gaze. She could feel tears threatening. "It's like we've switched places. You spent the whole time we were dating before ignoring me. It bothered me much more than I ever told you. Now it's like I want to keep my emotional distance, and in the process I end up being just as bad to you as you ever were to me."

Jenna sniffed a little when she felt Seth moving her work things and sitting down beside her. "When you're nice to me, Seth, it's hard to remember that I'm still seeking retribution."

"Don't worry—I'm sure to make you mad at me again within a few days," Seth said softly. "Right now I just want to take care of you a little. I'm trying to be more attentive to what's going on in your life than I was before. I can't undo the past, Jenna. I can only be nice to you now."

"Congratulations," she said, sniffing as tears rolled down her cheeks. "You're doing a great job of being nice to me at this very moment. It has the same impact on me that this fireplace has on the house."

"I know you're too tired for a hug. Can I kiss you instead?" he asked, dipping his head even as she nodded.

Seth lifted her into his lap and kissed her softly, lovingly, uncaring that the truth of his heart was in every move. "Whatever our problems, I have always cared for you. I was just really bad at showing you before. But I'm learning. I'm sorry it took me so long to figure it out."

The phone rang in his jacket pocket, buzzing silently against Jenna's breast that was pressed against the same spot. She kissed him again as it continued to buzz between their bodies. "Lauren informed me there are a lot better places to put a portable vibrator. She offered to share her secrets with me. I'm sure it applies to guys too."

Seth laughed and hugged her closer. They sat quietly for a minute, and then his phone rang again. She kissed him, surprised to find herself wanting for the first time in months to be as genuinely supportive to Seth as he was being to her.

"Take the call. I'll set up our picnic here on the hearth. I think I have some rug samples we can sit on to keep the sheetrock dust off your pants." She rose from his lap and walked to the area that would house the kitchen. Not finding what she wanted there, she strode back through the great room and on to the other end of the house toward the master bedroom.

Seth didn't take his eyes from her as he talked on the phone. She looked damn good walking around in the impressive house she'd built.

"Talia! Good to hear from you. Are you and the kids settling in okay? I'm sorry I haven't been by to visit again. Oh, you liked him? Glad to hear it. Bringing pizza, huh?" Seth laughed, listening to her stories of Allen and Mason discussing him today. He laughed and smiled broadly. "My cousin and his wife have offered to host a welcome bash for you in a couple of weeks. They have a great place on the edge of town. Yes. Bring the children. Okay. Talk to you in a day or so."

He slid the phone back into his jacket and rose to follow Jenna's trail down the hall where he'd watched her disappear. Spinning around in the massive area of the master bedroom, he admired the wall sconces which would flank a king size bed. Then he swiveled to the doorway of a master bath where he could see the beginnings of a large, tiled steam shower. Jenna's tastes in everything suited him perfectly, and he wanted to share that fact with her.

If he could only find her.

He wandered until he found Jenna inside a room that could have easily been a small bedroom, except that the walls were lined with cherry shelving and racks for hanging clothes. In the center of the room was a large dresser with drawers on both sides and a tie rack on one end. A leather bench still in its wrapper was on the other side.

"This room is flat amazing," Seth said in wonder.

"I think this and the fireplace are my favorite things in this house," Jenna said, bending back to her task. "Oh, here they are." She stood up finally, lifting and brandishing two carpet pieces in the air.

"The master bathroom looks amazing too," Seth told her. "Is that a steam shower?"

"Yes. One day I'll build a house this nice for you. You work hard Seth. You deserve a wonderful house. Then you can fill the closet with SydneyB suits. Ben will be jealous," Jenna said, grinning.

"It's interesting to see what you like and what you have chosen. I wouldn't have made all these same decisions, but the final outcome is damn impressive. I can't wait to see it finished now." Seth reached out a hand to her and she took it as they walked back to the great room. "This place feels as big as Gallagher's house."

"It is as big," Jenna said. "I was exploring the day of Lauren's product launch when you followed me. There were a lot of great features in his house that I liked. I guess you could say this house is sort of an amalgamation of other houses. I just combined them in a more modern way."

"I think you're in line for a magazine cover. The entrance alone is enough for that, I would think," Seth said, setting the food out on the hearth. "So I don't cook, but I got take-out from a catering place. The entrée should still be hot."

"It's better than the bowl of cereal I've had every night for the last week," Jenna said honestly.

Seth looked at her with deep concern. "No wonder you're so tired. You're not eating right."

"Well, I am tonight," Jenna said, shrugging. "Let me enjoy this moment without guilt. I'm going to pretend this is my first meal in my new house. Thinking of this place as mine is a fantasy that I let myself indulge in now and again. You're welcome to join me in it."

Seth swallowed hard as the first bite he took had some trouble going down. "You have no idea how much knowing that makes me want this for you. I am definitely in metro man mode tonight. I want to take care of you so bad that I ache with it. It's as bad as wanting you sexually."

Jenna laughed and dug into her food with both enthusiasm and sincere enjoyment. "Better watch that tendency around me. Growing up a spoiled only child of two indulging parents, I'm completely an opportunist," she warned. "I will get used to this treatment and be petulant when I don't get it."

Seth leaned over and licked a line of pasta sauce from her bottom lip. "Get used to it. I intend to get better at it. It's a win-win for both us. I want to keep you."

"Seth, I—I," Jenna stopped trying to talk, because she no idea what to say. She had no idea what she wanted long term from him. She hadn't been able to contemplate it without a getting a massive headache.

Seeing the conflicted emotions warring in her gaze, Seth gave her an out this time and dropped the subject.

"Is your food still hot?" he asked, watching her nod.

"It's delicious," Jenna replied honestly. "Did you bring dessert?"

"Chocolate mousse with raspberries," he said, wanting to laugh when she sighed.

"I may have to call a taxi to take me home, unless— unless you want to come spend the night again, and drop me off in the morning."

Seth let the suggestion hang in the air between them while he savored it, her, and the food. "I'd love to spend the night. It will be the first time we actually just sleep together."

Jenna leaned over for a kiss. "Think we'll make it?"

"I promise to try," Seth told her, grinning. "Maybe we'll do a shower together and wash each other's backs. We'll just carry the nurturing theme through the rest of the evening."

Jenna rolled her eyes and laughed.

Chapter 15

"I like cheese," Mason announced, taking another healthy bite out of his pizza slice.

"Me too," Allen said. "You and I have a lot in common."

"What else do I like?" Mason asked, having fun with the game. He liked the big guy with the nice eyes. He was funny.

"Let's see. Do you like your mother?" Allen asked, tilting his head as he bit into another slice of pizza.

Mason laughed. "Yes," he answered cautiously, sneaking a look at his mother to see her smiling at him.

"Well that's another thing we have in common," Allen told him easily. "I like your mother too."

And he did.

Allen looked at Talia, who had fed the baby and rocked her to sleep as efficiently as most women put their shoes on. If anyone had told him that he'd be this incredibly attracted to a single mother of two, he'd have said they were crazy.

But he was attracted.

He watched Talia bite her lip to keep from laughing at his flirty comment as she stood and walked to the baby's room to lay her daughter down. Allen wanted to bite her lip too. In fact, he was already wondering how long it would be until she let him.

"Will you tuck me in?" Mason asked. "You don't have to carry me. I can walk."

"I've never tucked anyone in before. What would I have to do?" Allen asked, keeping his gaze on Mason's to listen closely to the boy's answer.

"I know. I can *teach* you," Mason suggested, pleased with himself for having the idea.

"Allen, you can go in and say goodnight once Mason has finished his bathroom routine, which will include brushing teeth. Right, Mason?" Talia interjected, walking back into the room.

"Yes. I will brush my teeth. *Assolutely*," Mason said.

"*Absolutely*," his mother corrected, fighting back the giggle of mirth made worse by the grinning giant who seemed to be enjoying every minute of her son's company. Talia was jealous and trying really hard not to be. It was rare for Mason to take a liking to a man so quickly.

Seeing Allen cover his mouth with his hand and unsuccessfully hold back a laugh, Mason felt elated that the man thought he was funny. He smiled at his mother, who smiled back.

"May I go get ready for bed now?" Mason asked.

"Yes," Talia answered. "Use toothpaste this time."

Mason nodded, climbed down from the chair, and walked as quickly as his braces would let him down the hall toward his bedroom.

"Sorry. I didn't mean to laugh at his mispronunciation. Mason is just so earnest in everything he says," Allen said, letting his humor show.

"Mason has a large vocabulary for a child his age, but his diction needs some more work," Talia said lightly, rubbing the bridge of her nose.

Allen got up from the table and walked to stand in front of Talia Martin. He was very pleased when she held her ground and didn't move away as he purposely invaded her personal space.

Talia was both mother extraordinaire and exotic goddess from his point of view. He wanted to get to know her.

"You know—I happen to have a large vocabulary myself. Maybe we can get together sometime and have a long discussion so I can prove it to you," Allen told her, holding her gaze as the smile lines crinkled beside her eyes. "Lady, you are incredibly beautiful when you smile. You've got the kind of face poets write about."

Talia stopped smiling to stare at Allen in shock. She'd never heard such heartfelt praise in her entire life. "Thank you. Sorry for my reaction. Been a while since I heard a personal compliment."

"Now I'm sorry. You should hear that every day of your life because it's *absolutely* true," Allen told her sincerely, teasing because his heart was starting to beat a rapid staccato in his chest from the way Talia was looking at him.

Talia's mouth went dry at Allen's teasing even as the opposite effect was happening elsewhere. The man was joking with her and turning her on. She straightened, licked her lips, and cleared her throat in order to drum up her best business voice.

"Well, I certainly believe you have a large vocabulary. You just look like the type. But how's your diction, Mr. Stedman?"

Allen grinned so hard he thought his face was going to crack. "I'll let you decide that for yourself sometime. If you're interested in talking to me that long, that is."

"I am *absolutely* interested," Talia answered clearly, blinking at the sudden blaze of blue fire in Allen's gaze warring with the humor there.

Laughing, Allen leaned forward, and put his lips on Talia Martin's, surprising both of them with the boldness of the move. His tongue had just swept along her very lush bottom lip when Allen heard Mason call out from the bedroom that he was ready to be tucked in.

He pulled away from her mouth reluctantly.

"Excuse me. I have something I have to do. Can I get back to you on our discussion in a few minutes?" Allen asked. He lifted a few strands of silky black hair from her shoulder and stroked his fingers down it. "I like your hair down by the way. I've been wanting to get my hands in it since I got here."

Knowing he was on dangerous ground indulging himself in one area when he wanted to indulge in a hell of a lot more, Allen let go of her hair and walked away.

"Allen?" Talia called, as he strode down the hall toward her son. "You may need to remind Mason to take his braces off. He's not supposed to sleep in them. Sometimes he forgets. When you come back we'll talk some more."

Allen smiled, nodded, and walked down the hall.

"Don't make me do any more work. I'm just going to stand here in the hot water and hope I get clean," Jenna said, closing her eyes in bliss as the hot water worked a miracle on her exhausted muscles. "I'm too tired to wash off."

Seth laughed. He'd already washed himself, but put more of the fruity body wash on the washcloth he used. When he had a sufficient lather, Seth lifted one of Jenna's hands to brace on his chest while he washed her arm. He sighed as he ran the washcloth over her breasts and the ends got perky when he did so.

Jenna opened her eyes at his sigh and snickered at the pained look on Seth's face.

"Stop laughing and turn around," Seth ordered, turning her when she just continued to laugh softly at him. "I can't believe you're laughing at me when I'm trying to be noble and take care of you. Your father and mother need to be punished for raising you with a complete lack of appreciation."

Jenna groaned as Seth ran the washcloth over her back, to her waist, and did an even slower thorough job running over her rear.

"I'm not laughing because I'm enjoying your discomfort," Jenna told him sincerely. "I'm not that heartless. I'm laughing at how hard it is to not think of sex with you sighing over me."

She reached out to stroke his obvious reaction to her to prove her point.

"Now we're both thinking how hard it is," Seth complained, leaning into her strokes. "I love your hands on me. Have I ever told you that?"

"No. I don't think you have, at least not in this particular way," Jenna said, giggling, keeping her strokes long, but making them a little more aggressive.

Seth put his hands on her wet shoulders for balance since he was weaving on his feet because of what she was doing.

"I can tell you like this, and I so want to finish it. How close are you?" Jenna asked, closing her eyes in pleasure as she listened to Seth's rapid breathing and the many tiny groans he couldn't hold back. Seth was easy to read because he was so vocal in his response. It was one of the things she liked most about him as a lover.

"Don't know—but please don't stop yet," Seth begged, stepping into the next stroke to get closer to her.

For once obeying him without comment, Jenna's hand continued to move between them.

Seth could feel Jenna's knuckles grazing his taut abdomen with each stroke. He bent his upper body and shoulders to minimize the distance down to her so he could kiss her temple and put his hands in her hair.

"Jenna, I—I—*oh God, baby*," Seth said roughly, almost falling against her as the release he hadn't even tried to slow from happening swept over him sooner than he'd anticipated.

He wrapped Jenna in his arms, with her hand still gripped tightly on him, stroking the last of his climax away. Seth ran his hands over Jenna's back and shoulders, stroking and massaging as the water beat down on them like warm rain.

Jenna kissed Seth's chest and cuddled against it. After a couple of minutes of Seth rubbing her back, she was practically asleep on her feet.

Seth turned them until the warm water could flow between them. He felt Jenna's hands busy at work again, but this time moving slowly and carefully over him, washing him and her. Love was in her touch and in every slide of her hands. Seth wondered how much longer he was going to have to wait until Jenna could admit what was between them was so much more than just great sex.

When the water started to cool, Seth reached and turned the shower off.

Taking one of the large towels hanging just outside the shower, he wrapped it around his waist. Then he took the other and wrapped it around Jenna's body, which was now slumping with fatigue.

"Easy," he said, scooping Jenna up in his arms.

"If you're still strong enough to carry me after what I did for you, I must not have done it right," Jenna said, letting her weary head drop to his shoulder.

"You were perfect, and what you did was wonderful. I'm just feeling my inner caveman for a moment. I'm carrying you off to have my way with you," Seth said, setting her down on the bed.

"Well, all I ask is that you don't wake me," Jenna said tiredly, keeping her eyes closed as Seth dried her with the edges of the towel. "Do whatever you want, but if you care about me at all—let me sleep through it."

Seth laughed and coaxed her into lying down. He unrolled her out of the rest of the towel and pulled a series of covers over her before trotting back to the bathroom. A few minutes later Seth came back out and crawled into bed to scoop Jenna close.

"Are you asleep?" Seth asked, rubbing Jenna's arms to warm her as he curved his body around the back of her.

She mumbled something incoherent because the words were all jumbled in her head.

"Sleep, baby," Seth said, his heart full of unexpressed emotion. "I'm just going to hold you while you sleep. One of these days I'm finally going to love you enough to get through that stubbornness of yours."

"Love you, too," Jenna said, sleepily. "I'll have marshmallows with mine, please."

Seth froze at her words of love, and then shook in laughter at the crazy sleep talk that followed her declaration. He looked at the clock and was amazed to see it was barely after eight-thirty. He was tired too, especially after what she'd done for him in the shower, so sleep was not going to be a problem—even this early.

"Marshmallows? Jenna, you drive me crazy. Do you know that? Is that why you do it?" he asked her sleeping form, sighing and putting his head next to hers on the pillow. He was really glad Jenna was finally letting him spend the night. Leaving her would have been impossible with her words of love ringing in his ears.

It was only a couple of minutes later that Seth fell deeply and contentedly asleep at her side.

"So is it true?" Talia asked, watching Allen sip his beer. "Did Seth steal his girlfriend back from you?"

"Carter also tell you what kind of underwear he wears?" Allen asked, laughing. "You better read the fine print of that contract you're about to sign with him. No telling what he put in it."

Talia laughed, delighted with how witty and fun Allen was.

"I have to confess—Seth offered to fix me with up with you. I hadn't made up my mind about him or you when you showed up today," Talia said, eyes twinkling.

"*Him?* You were thinking about dating Carter? But he's your boss," Allen said, a bit shocked, but then what did he know about most of the real world? He'd spent the years between eighteen and twenty-four in the military. He'd spent the last two in school trying to figure out his life. Women had been few and far between, especially the ones in the last two years since most thought he was nuts for wanting to design clothes for a living.

"I married my boss once and got ten wonderful years of marriage and two great kids out of it. It worked out pretty well for me. Seth Carter is a kind and caring guy. I figured any woman dumb enough to trade up on him ought to have some competition. Of course, that was before I saw you today," Talia said firmly, watching Allen dip his head and grin. "Now I'm wondering how the girlfriend ever left you for him. What's your side of the soap opera?"

Allen laughed at the soap opera comment, but he guessed it was fairly close to being the truth about the situation.

"Jenna Ranger was in love with Seth Carter even when I was dating her," Allen admitted with a shrug. "Hell, on some level I think I knew it. But she was beautiful and pretty convincing about being over Seth. It took me awhile to see she was just lying to herself. And for the record, I broke it off with her, not the other way around. Don't let her or Carter tell you differently."

Talia snorted, her sense of humor sharpened by the beer and pleasant male company.

"I believe you, but mostly because I can't imagine you losing a woman to Seth. I mean Seth is nice and caring, but you're—well, maybe we should discuss my theory about your appeal some other time," Talia said, laughing at herself and her loose tongue. She hadn't had beer in ages either. She'd bought it for her father when he came to visit.

"Honestly, I never got to know Jenna that well. I work for both Jenna's mother and stepfather. I had to be very honorable where she was concerned. Fortunately, I hadn't used my best moves on her yet, so there was no permanent damage done by our brief stint of mostly platonic dating," Allen said, grinning at Talia's snorts and laughter.

"Really? Platonic dating, eh? Well, lucky her then. I'm sure she was saved from a sordid life of sexual guilt for not getting to see your best moves," Talia said, rolling her eyes. "How old are you again? You brag like a teenage boy."

Allen certainly knew a challenge when he heard one. He leaned forward and put his still half full beer on the coffee table. Then he leaned back on the couch and put one arm up along the back of it.

Allen slowly turned his massive body to face Talia's where she was curled up on the other end of her couch, feet tucked under her.

"Want to see one of the moves that I never used on Seth's girlfriend? It might be risky though. You're older and have already admitted you don't date often. If you're worried about what might happen to your self-control, I totally respect that. We can try it some other time," Allen said sincerely, finding it difficult to keep his composure and not to give in to his amusement when he was flirting with Talia.

Talia just laughed at Allen's warning. "I think you're very attractive, but I can't imagine anything you could do that would make me lose my self-control. My dear boy, you are practically a stranger. I just met you."

Allen laughed. "*Boy?* You're only eight years older than me. That doesn't make you an old lady or me a boy. And I can already tell you're interested in me physically from the way you've been checking me out. We aren't going to stay strangers, Ms. Martin. I'm just a little apprehensive about changing the situation between us tonight. As you said, we just met today."

Talia did burst out laughing then. "How you do love to brag. Fine, Mr. Stedman. Show me this amazing move of yours. Give me your best shot. I've lived a very full and interesting life. I spent most of the eight years difference in our ages having sex with some very interesting men before the one I married, who was quite proficient in that area. I must warn you that I've seen a lot of very good moves."

"Okay," Allen said softly, shrugging his massive shoulders as elegantly as someone his size could. "Don't say I didn't warn you. Here it is."

Hooking one large hand over both her feet, Allen pulled Talia down the couch, threw one of her legs off the front of it, and moved his massive body over hers landing his growing interest squarely in her crotch. He could only be grateful that his tactic had worked as well as it had. Of course, he'd been mentally rehearsing it and other potential moves for the better part of an hour as they talked.

"Hey," Talia said, surprised at Allen's aggressiveness, which was a tad out of character with his niceness.

"So are you ready to see the move now?" Allen asked politely, whispering the question in her ear and feeling her laughter even as the heat of her called to him. Allen instinctively knew he would find the woman wet and willing if he checked. Lord, how he wanted to check, but he didn't dare. It had been too long and she was too, too intoxicating.

"Sure," Talia said, laughing at his playful teasing, but reluctantly admitting he did have some good moves. "Bring it. Show me this irresistible move of yours." She stared up into Allen's eyes as he stared down into hers.

For all her brave talk, Talia felt her heart beating rapidly in excitement and her body going up in flames with Allen's massive form hovering over her. He smelled like spicy men's cologne and hot aroused male. What they were doing was a dangerous game to play with a man she had only met a few hours ago. But now Talia wanted badly to know what it was that Allen thought he did that was so extraordinary.

Allen bent to her mouth so slowly that Talia wondered if the man was going to kiss her or not. Then just millimeters above her mouth, Allen started to whisper endearments in French as he licked the seam of her partially opened lips. Her surprise at his reserved actions was quickly snuffed out by a sigh from her that echoed in the mostly quiet living room.

Talia closed her eyes and let herself enjoy what he was doing. It had been so long—so very, very long since she had been kissed so thoroughly and with such attention to detail.

Allen felt her surrender, but fought the urge to take what he knew he could. All the while he whispered, nipped, and nibbled, he also continuously pressed down between Talia's legs little by little until he was deftly stroking the hard evidence of his own desire against her. Once full contact was made, he bit and sucked Talia's bottom lip, absorbing the moan of building arousal that erupted from her throat. He laughed and stroked even harder as both her legs lifted along his sides.

Then Allen felt her heels digging into his flexing glutes and knew beyond doubt he had gone a lot farther in arousing her than he had intended. He was going to stop until Talia's hips shifted to show him just the place she needed attention most.

Suddenly, the game they were playing took Allen to a serious place he hadn't been expecting to visit so soon. It had been quite some time since he'd known this level of arousal himself. And he'd never known a woman who had handed over the key to her pleasure quite so willingly.

There was a time to be noble, Allen decided, and a time to take a gift when it was being offered. His body was informing him with every surge of her hips that the woman beneath him was a gift for him. That's when he realized what he wanted to do with Talia Martin and what he was going to do were the same thing. The realization sent the rest of the blood in his brain rushing to another more useful area.

Against Talia's mouth, Allen whispered succinctly in French that he understood what she needed, even as he used one hand to rub her thigh and knee in approval as it bracketed his hips. A couple minutes later he had to cover her mouth totally with his so neither of them would call out and wake the children as they sweetly, thoroughly rubbed and climaxed together on her couch. His bluff had been called in a major way and Talia's vibrations under him were both torture and reward. He hadn't done this much lovemaking with clothes on since high school, but didn't regret a second of it.

If Talia had asked him, he would have started all over and done it again.

When their breathing finally returned to something almost normal, Talia brought a trembling hand to Allen's face even though her eyes were too heavy yet to open. Still, she could feel Allen hovering over her, supporting his weight on his arms, not resting his body on hers completely. She finally forced herself to open her eyes and look at the man who had given her physical happiness for the first time in a long while.

"Thank God you never used that move on Seth's girlfriend," Talia whispered hoarsely. "You were right. It was *assolutely* irresistible. Best move I ever had used on me."

Allen laughed at the awestruck sincerity in her voice, even as his heart beat frantically in his chest at her teasing. He kissed her hard because he simply had to. He liked this woman. Lord, he really, really liked this woman.

And he wanted to do this with her again. He wanted to do it better. He wanted to do it over and over until he found her limits, until she begged him to stop.

"It's going to be even better when I show you without the clothes," Allen said finally, touching his forehead to hers.

"Lie down on me," Talia commanded, closing her eyes again. "I just want to feel your full weight. I need to after we—after you—hell, just do it. Okay?"

Allen eased himself down until he rested his full weight on her. Talia wrapped her arms around him in pleasure. She whispered sexy praise in French in his ear as she stroked his back and ran hands through his hair.

He shivered at the touch of her hands, fighting the urge to press down harder on her. Allen knew he was probably crushing her with his weight, despite her healthy size. Jenna had been the smallest woman he'd ever dated, and he hadn't gotten nearly this far with her, for which he was now incredibly thankful. Carter would never have felt beholden and he wouldn't now be lounging, relaxed and content between Talia Martin's wonderful legs.

Allen shifted in Talia's arms and rolled them to their sides until they were nose-to-nose on the couch. She looked at him with nothing but adoration.

"Is there any other woman in your life that I have to worry about?" Talia asked finally in English.

"No. But one look at you and I would have forgotten about her anyway," Allen told her honestly, running strands of her silky hair through his fingers.

Talia sighed as she toyed with the collar of his T-shirt. They hadn't even touched skin yet. She barely knew the man and yet they had already made love once. But his jaw was relaxed and his eyes were kind as they studied her in the growing dark of her new living room. She didn't feel a shred of regret. All she felt was grateful.

"You're in big trouble for admitting that to me," Talia said, tracing fingertips up to his mouth, and over his careful, but not too careful lips. "I have a few moves of my own. Since I speak many languages, I can make a man think he's with a different woman every time."

Allen groaned. He felt himself twitching and getting hard again, wanting her again. "Are you going to date me? Say yes, please."

Talia nodded as she embraced him. "I'm going to do a whole lot more than that, but sure—let's start with dating. Some of what I have in mind isn't as tame as what we did tonight. I like a lot of variety too."

Allen groaned again. "On second thought, let's skip the preliminaries. Just marry me so I can be with you every night," he said, tucking his head between her neck and shoulder. "I'll carry boxes for you and teach Mason to be as strong as me. I'll do anything you want."

"Mr. Stedman, we hardly know each other. I am an excellent wife, but still—some decorum must be maintained in every courtship. What if I can't keep up with you? What if you get bored with me? There is our age difference to consider." Talia started giggling as Allen shook his head against her shoulder. "Well, it could happen. We are still strangers, you know."

"Just remember six months from now when you finally say yes that I asked you to marry me the first day I knew you," Allen told her. "The only downside is that Carter is never going to let me forget that he found the perfect woman for me."

"You? I signed a bloody contract with the man. I'm supposed to be making him two million dollars. Now that I'm shagging you, no telling what the man is going to expect," Talia teased. "Once you accept an incentive from an employer, there's really no turning back."

"I think I like being your incentive. Are you English?" Allen asked, laughing at her words. "I've never *shagged* before. I like the way it sounds though."

"Looking like you do? Like hell," Talia said, laughing. "You know too much for me to ever believe you haven't had your fair share of sex. And yes, I'm from England, but haven't been there in ages. I only sound like it now and again. Really I'm a mutt. I lived in Boston most of my life. My parents live in London and Boston. I guess I keep the language because of them."

"Talia," Allen said, leaning up on one elbow. "I like you. I really would like to date you. I like your children also."

"I like you, too, Allen Stedman," Talia said. "Come back Friday night and we'll order in Chinese food. Then when the kids go to bed I can practice my dialects on you. I have to make some phone calls to China next week."

"Okay. Maybe I can correct your diction," Allen suggested, teasing again.

"You speak Chinese?" Talia asked, surprised.

"No, I only speak French. My mother taught it to me. It's almost solely responsible for my *shagging* experience," Allen joked, rising up and kissing her lips once more. "I was talking about something else, trying to tease you. Now I need to go quickly before I forget that we're still strangers."

"Oh. *Diction.* Yes, come back and correct me anytime," Talia sighed as he climbed over her and off the couch. "Why do I feel like I've always known you? Is that just good sex? I had no idea how much I had missed it."

Allen stopped as he stood, shocked. "I'm sorry for whatever happened to you in your life that kept a lovely, loving woman like you from having all the sex she wants and needs."

"See—that niceness of yours. It makes me doubly glad about what happened tonight. I should be ashamed of what I did with someone practically a stranger. Instead, I'm already thinking it's too many days until Friday," Talia told him honestly.

Allen reached down a hand and helped her to stand up. "Come. Lock the door behind me."

Talia weaved on weakened legs, but laughed again when Allen steadied her.

"I'm fine. Totally normal now, except for the brilliant bliss going on all over me," Talia said, padding softly behind him to the door.

Allen opened the door, but turned back to her before he left. "I *absolutely* can't wait until Friday. I know there is supposed to be some decorum about all this, but—"

Talia's hot mouth on his shut down the rest of what he was going to say. All he could think about was coming back to her the first chance he got.

"Hell, woman. I need to go before I drag you back to the couch to try my move without clothes. Take care of yourself," Allen said roughly, leaning in to kiss her one last time.

"*Absolutely*," Talia assured him, letting his tongue invade her mouth, shivering as one of his hands cupped her breast as he kissed her. That was another thing they hadn't done.

Allen practically ran down the sidewalk to his car in order to escape his urge to stay forever with the bewitching, sexy-as-hell Talia Martin.

Chapter 16

On Thursday, Alexa walked from her office briskly heading to the marketing conference room before she left for her lunch with Casey. When she got to the desk in the front, she put on the brakes and stopped in front of Allen, who was typing a letter for her.

"Allen? You look very different this week. Why is that?" Alexa asked, narrowing her gaze as she studied the pink climbing his neck to his face.

"I got a haircut," Allen said easily, trying to distract her.

"No, that's not it," Alexa said, laughing. "You're relaxed and smiling—every day. Who's the woman?"

"What—what woman?" he asked, lifting his chin and staring at Alexa. Could she really tell from just looking at him?

When the door to the office opened, Allen almost sighed in relief at the reprieve the visitor offered from his employer's sharp scrutiny. It lasted about two seconds until the tall, light brown woman walked through the door and smiled at him in pleasure. Talia Martin was dressed in a suit that fit her well and made her look like a worldlier version of business Barbie. Allen stood and stared, his gaze taking in all of her. His heart was all but leaping out of his chest at the way she was looking at him.

DONNA MCDONALD

Alexa laughed as her gaze took in both of them smiling at each other like they'd won the lottery.

"Allen? Was there a lunch appointment on my calendar that I forgot today?" she asked coyly.

Allen finally tore his gaze away from Talia back to Alexa. "No. Alexa, this is my friend, Talia Martin. Talia, this is my employer—Alexa Ranger."

"Pleasure to meet you, Ms. Martin. Allen and I were just discussing you," Alexa jokingly informed the smiling woman, her gaze now unabashedly taking her in. "You are amazingly beautiful. Have you ever done any modeling?"

"Modeling?" Talia said, laughing at the gorgeous older woman, hoping she looked as good when she aged. "As in clothes? No, not me. I'm a mother of two. I don't have the body for it, but thank you for the lovely compliment."

"Like hell you don't," Allen said firmly, then blushed when both women swung their gazes in his direction. "I mean. You have obviously kept yourself in shape, Talia."

Talia smiled at him for the compliment and dipped her head, fighting a blush. She had come to try to talk Allen into lunch because she couldn't wait one more day to see him. It was an unexpected treat to hear what he thought about her body.

Alexa laughed at her assistant's now obvious intimate knowledge of the gorgeous woman. "Well, you can trust Allen's opinion, Ms. Martin. He's got quite the eye for a perfect female body. He's brought me several new lingerie models since he's come to work for me."

Talia lifted an eyebrow. "Lingerie models, eh? Allen brings you new ones. Fascinating."

The flush Allen had been fighting completely took over. The door opened again, and Allen let out a breath when he saw the Marines had arrived to save him.

Casey walked in, taking in the beautiful women and Allen's flushed face. He walked to his wife and kissed her cheek.

"Hi. Are you teasing Allen again? He's looking ready to bolt any second. You promised me you were going to stop that," Casey said, admonishing her.

"I am perfectly innocent of any shenanigans today, darling. This is Talia Martin. She appears to be a friend of Allen's," Alexa said, eyes twinkling. "She's the reason for his blush, not me."

Casey put out his hand to Talia. "Casey Carter. Pleasure to finally meet you, Ms. Martin. My crew will be out to see you next week and get that security system installed for you."

Allen cleared his throat, drawing everyone's gaze to him again. He sighed heavily, growing more and more resigned to his new relationship with Talia becoming gossip fodder at the company before the day was done.

"Actually, I'm doing the installation myself this weekend, Casey." Allen stated, and met Casey's amused gaze with his own daring one.

"Oh, right. Forgot about you mentioning that," Casey lied smoothly, shifting his still laughing gaze to Talia Martin. "So are you settling in well? Seth treating you okay?"

"You're Seth's cousin. The one who raised him," Talia stated, figuring it out and smiling broadly. "You did well, sir. Seth is a very nice man. He speaks very highly of you."

"Seth is his own person. I can't take credit for much of anything except his determination. I did drill persistence into him when he was a teenager, which is why he pursued you so hard," Casey said easily. "And please call me Casey. Alexa and I are delighted to be hosting your welcome party next week. We're looking forward to meeting your children."

"Oh, *you're* Seth's new right hand," Alexa said, Allen's unexpected connection to the woman momentarily forgotten. "Silly me. And to think I was trying to hire you to model lingerie. It would be fun for you, but not a great use of a mind like yours. Seth has been bragging about your talents and hiring you away from your former company."

"Seth made me an excellent business offer with some incentives that were absolutely impossible to refuse," Talia said truthfully, smiling as Allen rolled his eyes and turned his back to the three to them, suddenly pretending to be very busy.

"Would it be okay if I brought some extra guests along? I have some family in town visiting," Talia said. She looked at Allen, her gaze communicating that she'd explain when they were alone. He nodded once to let her know he understood.

Casey and Alex watched the silent communication with growing interest. There were only a few conditions that created that type of connection between a couple. They exchanged a glance that said they were both thinking the same thing about what had caused it in this case.

"Bring whoever you want," Casey said easily. He looked at his wife. "Ready for lunch? I thought we'd walk to that deli you love down the street."

"Yes. I'm starved," Alexa told him, slipping her hand in her husband's. "Allen, this would be a good time for you to take lunch too. I'll probably be gone a while. Casey and I have some things to talk about. Take your time getting back."

Alexa winked at him when Talia looked at him with curiosity in her gaze. Allen sighed.

"Talia. That's an interesting name for an interesting woman," Alexa said, extending her hand to the woman again. "Looking forward to getting to know you better."

"Likewise," Talia said, smiling and shaking Alexa's hand.

Talia watched until the office door had closed behind the older couple before turning a questioning gaze back to Allen. "Lingerie models? You work for a lingerie company and see women in their underwear all day?"

Allen walked around the desk to her. "It's not as cushy as it sounds. Models are such prima donnas about it. Most of them insist on wearing robes despite how much you beg."

Talia snorted at his answer. "Why aren't you using your moves on them? I assure you getting them out of their robes would not be a problem if you did."

Allen lifted her long hair with both his hands and pulled it down her shoulders to the front of her, letting his large knuckles graze her breasts through her lightweight suit. When she shuddered against his hands, Allen leaned into her and kissed her fiercely, his tongue dancing along hers. Her hands went to his waist and he stepped into her, thrilled when she gripped him tighter.

"Allen, do you know when—oh God, sorry. My bad. I'll just—check back later," Jeannine said, walking quickly back the way she'd come.

Allen released Talia, his frustrated groan audible to both of them. "Great. I just seriously frenched you in front of the biggest gossip that works here. I may have to resign after today."

Talia's hands came up to grab Allen's hands that were still knuckled against the front of her. If he palmed her breasts, she was going to attack the man in his office even if the woman came back to watch.

"I can actually feel my normal sense of decorum going straight out the window every time you put your hands on me," Talia told him softly. "My parents are in town. The good news is I have a sitter. The bad news is that they're here for at least two weeks."

"I have an apartment with a roommate. He brings women home all the time. I usually stay late at the gym when he's entertaining. It's not the best of situations, but I do have my own room," Allen said, making himself remove his hands from her. "On the other hand, Alexa's office floor is available right now. I know it has a door that locks. Casey locks it all the time when he goes in there."

Talia laughed as his hands caught hers. "They look really happy together.

"Want to go to lunch? I'm meeting Seth this afternoon at his attorney's office to finalize the contract and do some other paperwork. I went over it fairly closely and didn't see anything I didn't like. You weren't in it—in case you were wondering."

"Oh, I'm in it," Allen said. He walked around to his desk and tapped the keyboard to lock his screen. Then he walked back to take Talia's hand again. "Just in case you didn't get my innuendo, I'm planning to be in more than just your contract."

"Stop that this instant," Talia pleaded, closing her eyes against the desire in his. "The office floor is sounding better and better. Can we still do Chinese food tomorrow night? My treat. You bought pizza the other day."

"Deal. I'll be home after seven. Lunch sounds good now. I know a couple of places nearby. One is a Greek deli. The other is a bistro with organic food," Allen said, taking her hand in his again. The feeling of tugging her along with him was both pleasurable and frustrating.

"I could go for a pita. I haven't had good lamb in a long time," Talia said, trying to make any sort of conversation to get her mind off her hand tingling in Allen's.

When the elevator door closed behind them, Allen looked up at the camera and judged the angles at which it was capturing images. He tugged and then pushed Talia into a far corner.

"I needed to get you out of camera range," he told her.

"Why?" she asked. Her question was answered thoroughly by the invasion of his tongue in her mouth. Allen lifted her until her toes barely touched the floor of the elevator. His hands gripped and held her tightly.

"Tomorrow night, I'm going to hold you against the wall of my bedroom and show you just how strong I really am," Allen promised.

"Show me now. Press the emergency button on the elevator and you can hang my jacket over the camera," Talia said, trying to stifle her giggles.

"No. I can wait one more damn day, and so can you. I like spicy beef and steamed rice. Skip the egg roll. Don't forget the fortune cookies. I'll make green tea for us. I have my own condoms. Don't wear too many clothes," Allen ordered.

"Sir, yes, sir. You just love to give orders, don't you? Were you in the military?" she asked, blinking as he pulled her from the corner to exit the elevator.

"Army," Allen answered. "I was a military policeman."

"I can really see you doing that," Talia said.

"Well, I'm a clothing designer now. Or at least, I'm trying to be," Allen said, watching her eyes as her face crinkled into a smile.

"Yes, that makes sense too. I don't know why I didn't figure out who you were when you were so closely inspecting the wrap I use to carry Kendra. I let my physical attraction to you cloud my normal ability to size up a person," Talia said as she strolled along with her hand in his. "Though you seem quite full of surprises. You're a lot more complex than you appear at first glance. Your physique is quite distracting."

"I hope that was a compliment," Allen said, rubbing his face and holding the restaurant door for her.

She rattled off a string of French that included a crude, sexy suggestion about using other impressive muscles she assumed he had. He answered her with a French oath and a hard kiss just inside the restaurant door. The man behind the deli counter stopped to stare at them.

When they stepped up to the counter, the man spoke to them in flawless French to take their order.

Talia blushed when she realized the deli worker had heard and understood everything suggestive she had just said to Allen.

Allen spoke back to the man in French, explaining they had been fighting about his neglect of her. The man said something insulting to Allen, who just bared his teeth in a wicked smile. He didn't bother answering the insult, just stared at the man until he turned his gaze away. Eventually, Allen told the man he was intending to make it up to Talia as soon as he got the chance.

The man looked interestedly at Talia as he served their pitas to them. He told Talia to come back if Allen failed to please her.

Talia assured the man that she had no doubt Allen would please her as he had already done so earlier in the week.

"The other night was just a preview," Allen said to her in English, as they found a table in a mostly empty restaurant.

They had missed the lunch rush and seemed to have the place to themselves.

"Stop flirting with me, or I will not get a bite of this food down. I'm starved," Talia hissed, her eyes darkening with irritation. Allen's breath caught. It was the same look of impatience she'd given him when she thought he'd been a mover. Allen wanted so badly to see it under other circumstances that he was just further convinced he was a goner. He must have fallen for her the first moment he saw her.

"I hope this gets better after tomorrow. Everything you say and do tortures me too," Allen complained, taking a big bite of his pita. "I will never make fun of another guy in this condition again."

Talia laughed, sighed at what was simmering between them, and dug into her food.

Late that afternoon, Regina was sitting in her office jotting down the notes for her last session when her office manager knocked on her door.

"You have time for a visitor?" Ann asked. "Jenna Ranger is asking to see you."

"Sure. Send her back," Regina said, not letting herself wonder about why Jenna had sought her out. Regina knew the why. She was just busy trying to think how to explain to Jenna that she couldn't talk about Seth with her.

"Hey," Jenna said, coming in with dusty work clothes and work boots still on. "Sorry I'm a mess. I came straight here from work. I didn't know who else to talk with about this."

Regina motioned a hand to the chair in front of her desk.

"I'm not here to talk about Seth," Jenna announced. "I already know he came to see you. He told me he had gone to therapy. He didn't say you were his doctor specifically, but I guessed that much. Still, I didn't come about that. I came to ask you some questions because I know you will answer me honestly whether I want to hear it or not."

Regina raised an eyebrow. "Well, all I can say is I will try."

Jenna took a deep breath. "Am I an awful, selfish person, Regina? I mean, I can see that I'm spoiled in some ways, but am I truly selfish?"

Regina's eyes widened. "That's a strange question, honey. Why would you think you're an awful person?"

"Because I can't seem to stop myself from treating Seth badly. It's like no matter how nice he is to me, I still tense up and want to protect myself whenever I see him. He's commented a couple of times about how unappreciative I am of his efforts to be nice. I think he's right, Regina. Something is either wrong with me or I'm as bad as he keeps saying I am. I don't want to be that way. I figured if anyone would tell me the truth about myself—you would," Jenna finished, studying her hands.

"Jenna," Regina began. "Those things you mention are subjective. One person could view you as selfish and spoiled. Another person could view you as kind and selfless. We view others through the filter of our expectations and experiences of them."

"I don't want to be the kind of person who would hurt someone who's only being good to them," Jenna said, frowning.

"You were kind in giving Casey your approval when you didn't really want your mother to date him. Then you were selfless in standing by your mother, Casey, and even Seth when Casey was in that accident. We're all just human, honey. We develop character by the actions we take—what we do to serve ourselves and others," Regina said, studying Jenna's pensive expression. "Do good. That will be reflected in how you feel about yourself and how others feel about you."

"Mama and Daddy are both good. Aren't they?" she asked.

"Yes," Regina said firmly. "They are both amazing people—for the love they gave each other and what they have given to others since. You were unconditionally loved by two of the best people I've ever met. You have that in you as well."

"I don't know if I do, Regina. Every time I see Seth, I immediately say something ugly to him. It's like I can't help myself," Jenna said, hating to admit it, but knowing her confession was as sacred to Regina as it would have been with any priest.

"Jenna, have you forgiven Seth for hurting you before?" Regina asked.

Jenna looked at her hands. Her nails were deplorable. Her mother would have a fit if she saw how awful they looked. And she hadn't shaved her legs in a week or gotten a pedicure in a couple of months. Lately, a shower seemed like a luxury.

Pulling her attention back to Regina, she felt burning tears threatening. If she couldn't bring herself to shave her legs for him regularly, how in the hell was she going to forgive Seth? Even the idea scared the hell out of her.

"What will I do if he hurts me again?" she said quietly. "I never completely got over him before. It would be worse now. We've been seeing each other—dating again—and— well more. We haven't told anyone."

"Well, I hate to be the one to tell you this, but the people you love will definitely hurt you again at some point. Sometimes it's nothing but aggravating habits. It might even be another big thing you find out about. Emotional risk is just part of being in love with someone," Regina said softly.

"I am in love with him," Jenna admitted, tears making muddy tracks in her dusty face. "Even if I don't want to be."

Regina passed her a tissue box. "You've been in love with Seth Carter since you met him. I know what I told you before, and I would still stand by that if you tell me he's treating you the same."

Jenna was already shaking her head from side to side. "No. Seth has been great to me this time around. I mean, he's still busy as hell and tends to stay connected to his electronics 24/7. But he tossed his ringing cell phone on the floor once to be with me. And he tries to limit his calls to when I'm not there. He's either more complex than I noticed before, or he really has changed. I can't tell which."

"We can all turn into technosexuals sometimes. You looked pretty occupied by your cell phone the day of Lauren's wedding," Regina commented, grinning when Jenna laughed.

"I was sexting with Seth—not sending pictures, but sending sexy text messages," Jenna confessed. "Don't tell Lauren. I wouldn't want her to know. When I left, it was to sneak off with Seth, not to take a business call. We had only been together a few times at that point. You know how it is when you're new to each other."

"Indeed I do. Ben and I text each other like that all the time. Of course, we were doing it before it went mainstream. It was just that we missed each other so badly when we couldn't be together as much as we wanted," Regina said, smiling. "My attachment to Ben was pretty intense once he got me in bed."

"Has Ben ever done anything you've been really mad at him for?" Jenna asked.

"Yes. He gave up his job in his company as CEO," Regina said, her mouth tightening in a line. "I know Ben is happy in his new work, but knowing he sacrificed a lifetime of achieving for me still hurts. But that's about me more than him."

"What do you mean?" Jenna asked, finally stemming the flow. "I mean it's good that Ben loved you that much, isn't it?"

"My being upset is not about what Ben did. He's a grown man and has a right to make his own decisions about his life and his work. It's about the fact that to this day I still feel unworthy of that level of sacrifice. He should never have had to give up a top-level job he'd sweated and sacrificed for just to be with me and make my life better. I can't get over it because I haven't healed how I feel about myself. No one ever loved me like that before Ben, so I have a hard time believing he could. The net result is that it turns into anger at him, even though I know that's wrong. Therapists have issues like everybody else," Regina said easily.

"I'm not my mother, no matter how much I look like her. I get absorbed in my work and I have never cared much about looking like the perfect woman. Part of me still feels like I'm not interesting enough to hold Seth's attention for the long haul. I keep thinking he'll go back to not paying attention like he did before. He's enamored of me now, but I wonder what will happen when the lust wears off. I hear it does eventually," Jenna said, sniffing.

"Well, it changes," Regina corrected. "I hope like hell it never wears off. Ben Kaiser is like a drug I'm addicted to, and I need my fix to feel like life is worth living."

"I feel exactly the same way about Seth," Jenna said. "I guess it's the same no matter how old you are or how smart. When Mama went to the hospital to make up with Casey, I asked her if she was afraid of getting hurt by him again. She said yes she was, but that she was more afraid of trying to live without him. She said being with Casey was worth any emotional risk."

"Your mother is a very smart woman," Regina said. "And so are you. You're the only one who can decide if Seth Carter is worth the risk for you."

Jenna nodded. "Well, thanks for talking to me. I've been feeling like shit all day and just needed to talk to someone. Now I'm going home to clean up so I can go get my fix from him," Jenna told her. "It's been a few days now and I'm climbing the walls."

Regina laughed as Jenna walked out the door. She got out her cell phone and typed, which was never easy for her on the tiny keyboard the size of a credit card. Five minutes later she finally pressed send.

Feeling extremely grateful for you today. You can have anything you want tonight.

The phone buzzed a short time later. She laughed as she read Ben's reply.

Teach me something new.

"Something new," Regina said to the walls of her office as she pondered the possibilities.

She stood and walked to an early book she had published when she was in her late thirties. It had been hard as hell to get through all that sex advice then without a partner to practice on. Well, she had one now. She could only hope Ben's heart was up to the challenge.

She sat down and typed again.

What do ice cubes, hot fudge, and my mouth have in common? Only Ben Kaiser gets to find out.

The phone buzzed back at her within seconds.

I'll bring the fudge sauce, but I get to go first. I'm feeling pretty appreciative myself. Love you.

Regina set her phone down on the desk and sighed again for how lucky she was.

Chapter 17

Allen ran his roommate off Friday evening and told him to spend the night at his girlfriend's house. He had plans for once, and they included using the whole apartment. The woman coming to see him deserved to eat at the dining table and not in his room. He lit a couple of candles on the table and turned on some smooth jazz music, trying to calm himself as he waited.

When the doorbell rang, Allen nearly jumped out of his skin. He couldn't remember the last time he'd been with a woman he wanted this much. He opened the door to find Talia dressed in jeans and a T-shirt, and chastised himself for being even mildly disappointed. Even denim wasn't going to slow him down much, so there was no reason to be anything other than happy she had actually shown up.

Then Allen noticed Talia carried a bag with their food and another small tote bag over her shoulder.

"Hand me a set of chop sticks," Talia ordered, leaning in to quickly kiss him and pressing the bag of food into his hands. "Put the food in the microwave for a few minutes while I change. I need ten minutes. It will be worth the wait. If you have a pair of loose exercise pants, why don't you change, too?"

Allen handed her the chopsticks. "The bathroom is in the middle of the hall."

"Thanks," she said smiling. "Are we alone?"

"*Assolutely*," Allen said, teasing to help him handle the tension and dispel the urge he had to grab her and carry her off to his room immediately.

"Right then. I'll be back shortly," Talia said, for once not returning the tease. It was all she could do not to launch herself at him. *Not yet*, she cautioned herself. *Not yet.* She wanted him to remember this first time with her.

Allen carried the food to the microwave and started hunting up plates and silverware. Finally, he looked at his pants and wondered if he dared be in anything looser than his jeans around her. There was no way around showing her how anxious he was in sweatpants, but she had practically ordered him to change too. And though he wasn't used to letting a woman call the shots, Allen figured there was always a first time and a first woman to relinquish his control to.

He walked quickly to his bedroom and put on a pair of black sweats that didn't look too bad. They hung low on his hips but were comfortable. When Talia came out of the bathroom, she was dressed in a short, red, Asian style dress that went half way up her thighs and was held closed by a line of buttons from throat to hem. Her hair was wound and twisted on the top and back of her head, held in place with the two chopsticks she'd taken from the dinner she'd brought.

Allen put his hands on his hips and sighed at what was too quickly happening below his waist. This evening was already out of hand and it had barely begun. They would be lucky if they managed to even eat dinner first.

Talia spoke to him in some dialect of Chinese that sounded very harsh and demanding to his ears. Her words were softened only by the shy smile she gave him and her hand taking his to lead him to the nearest bedroom, which fortunately happened to be his. She stopped at his queen size bed with the thick, brown comforter. She was still talking in Chinese even as she patted the space beside her for him to sit.

Making sure the condom was still on the nightstand where he'd put it, Allen sat and then waited to see what she would do.

He couldn't stop the groan when Talia pulled the chopsticks slowly from her hair and let it cascade over her shoulders. Allen meekly let her pull his shirt off as he studied the long dark strands, and then felt her push him backwards with one hand until he was flat on the bed. She grabbed his shoulders and tried to turn him. Allen complied and rolled to his stomach.

With evidence of his need pressing into the bed now instead of saluting her, Allen felt a little braver about things. He felt Talia straddle his hips and lower herself to sit on his backside. The heat from her was even noticeable through his sweats. She leaned forward and used her hands to knead his shoulders and then his back. It wasn't long before Allen figured out that the woman actually knew what she was doing in massaging his tension away.

"*Arry che*," Allen said, his voice muffled against the cover as his large weight sunk further into the bed, his muscles actually unwinding under her talented hands.

Surprising him with her aggression, Talia grabbed the back of his head by his hair and lifted it from the cover. Again she said something that sounded challenging and harsh in Chinese.

"Ouch. Damn—woman. I was mostly joking. *Marry me.* That's all I said," Allen told her. His head was suddenly released and he felt a slap on the back of it that stung a little. It hurt his pride more than anything.

Talia went back to kneading his back muscles with a vengeance, her Chinese getting more and more agitated. Or at least it sounded that way to Allen.

He groaned under her hands, and flinched when she bent and slipped them under his stomach and down to grab and stroke him. She stretched her long body out on the back of him fully then, her busy hand doing what it could between him and the cover he lay on.

"You're killing me," Allen said harshly, flipping her off him deftly. "Speak English and tell me this is what you want because I'm about ten seconds away from being inside you."

"I was trying to take the edge off so we could enjoy the evening more," Talia finally said.

"I'm all about taking the edge off, but we're doing it my way this first time. You can be in control when I know you better," Allen said, laughing. "I'm too far gone to be as nice to you as I had planned. I hope you're ready for this."

Talia reached out a long arm and snagged the condom off the nightstand. "Here. I'd offer to do it, but you'd probably have a meltdown on me."

"No, keep it. I want you to do it. Get on your knees," Allen ordered, swallowing hard when she did as he asked. He kneeled in front of her, pushed all her hair to the back and wrapped it around his hand. He tugged to see if he had a hold he could control, and then started opening the buttons that ran the length of her dress.

"Better put that on me if you want to be safe when it happens. I'm coming inside you shortly no matter what," Allen told her, honestly not caring if they had unprotected sex or not. He was ready for just about anything with Talia Martin.

Her hands quivered as they tore at the packet. Allen smiled into her gaze. "Am I tugging too hard?" he asked.

"No," Talia said hoarsely, her breasts now bared to the air as his hand dropped to the lower buttons. Two or three more and he would know that she didn't have anything at all on under the dress.

Talia reached out with her hands, slid his sweats down and found him. Fumbling and out of practice for this sort of thing, she finally did manage to roll the condom into place. By the time the task was accomplished, her hands were shaking from touching and stroking his impressive length.

"I swear I want you more than I've ever wanted a woman," Allen told her.

He released her hair and the last two buttons, taking a moment to sigh at what was about to be his for real.

Then Allen lifted Talia up and over him, sliding up into her as he lowered her breasts within reaching distance of his mouth. Talia called out only once when he had to push up hard to get completely inside her. Allen had to clamp his jaw tightly to keep from calling out himself at how tight she was, further evidence to him about how long it had been for her. It made him unreasonably happy for both of them.

Then his mouth moved from breast to breast until Talia was breathing as hard as a marathon runner and murmuring please to him.

"You are absolutely the most beautiful woman I have ever come across. Now that I finally have you in bed with me, I may never let you out of it." He held Talia in the air by her hips, in front of his body, moving in and out of her without letting her do more than drag her toes on the bed and clutch his shoulders for support. The red dress billowed like a robe around her, but Talia was opened to him and Allen intended to take everything she let him have.

"Allen," Talia called. "Allen, you must slow down. Let me down on you. I need—I need."

"Baby, I know exactly what you need," he said roughly "And I'm happy as hell to be the one giving it to you. Let's go over now. We need to rest up for next time."

"What?" Talia asked hoarsely, not sure she had heard him correctly. Did he just announce her orgasm to her?

Fireworks burst inside her as Allen let her entire weight slide down on him. He pulled her against him as tightly as he could. He rocked back on his knees with her in his arms until his hips hit his heels, then he surged back up with her hard and strong, lifting her in the air again as he rose to his knees once more.

Unable to do anything but enjoy the ride, Talia slid back down toward him on the down stroke and shattered on him as he repeated the process one more time.

When Talia's legs wrapped around him, Allen could feel the earthquake taking place inside her depths. He promptly decided to add a volcano to their attempts to move both heaven and earth on their first night together.

Using his weight to propel both them both downward, her back and head hit the pillows of the bed even as he moved hard into her with several long, claiming strokes. Allen couldn't remember a woman ever feeling so good or so right to him when he did this. It was like his sex life started for real when he had rocked them both to climax on her couch earlier in the week.

When the eruption occurred moments later for him, Allen screamed his satisfaction in her ear and scared her into screaming in return. Her scream was promptly followed by equally loud, unrestrained laughter as Talia realized what she'd done and what Allen had done.

"Oh, dear God. We're going to need sound-proofing in the bedroom," Talia said sharply against his jaw.

"Or lots of duct tape and pillows," Allen said against her shoulder in return.

"You bloody screamed in my ear," Talia informed him, unsuccessfully fighting the laughter that continued to bubble up. "I have to say that you're quite the most demonstrative man I've ever known."

"I have to say that I love how you get more English sounding after you have an orgasm," Allen said, mocking her tone. "For the future, I hate Chinese during sex."

"Why?" Talia said, surprised and laughing at his comment. "It's a very expressive language." She began to sing in Chinese, stroking his hair and kissing his cheek.

Allen laughed against her as she sang to him. "Okay. Maybe I could get used to it. How many languages do you speak?"

"Eleven proficiently, I believe. Smatterings of several others. It's a gift," Talia told him.

"Yes it is. Now tell me what heritage makes you so beautiful," Allen ordered softly, running a hand down her arm as he shifted off her and to her side. He wrapped a leg over her so she would know he wasn't going very far.

Talia lay mostly on her back, head turned and smiling at the now rumpled, relaxed, blond giant lying at her side in the dimly lit bedroom. "My grandmother on my mother's side was Balinese. My grandmother on my father's side was a mixed race South African—I forget which tribe. My very English and very Caucasian parents were both quite surprised when the recessive genes from both sides all coalesced into my DNA. I understand there was quite the genealogy search during the first five years of my life," she said, unoffended. "I have always loved that I have a permanent tan and yet my hair is straight as any Asian. I love being unique. I think I have passed my unusual genetics along to my son."

"I think you have too," Allen said, remembering Mason's dark looks. "By the way, that was a pretty amazing first time. I wanted to let you have control, but I just couldn't. I'd spent too many days planning what I wanted to do to you."

"Well, good show, Mr. Steadman," Talia said lightly, giggling again. "Got any more plans tonight? I don't have to be home for hours yet."

Allen leaned over her and fastened his mouth to hers, finding it just as lush and welcoming as the other times. "Yes. Can we eat now? I'm starved. Aren't you?"

"Absolutely," Talia said, lifting up to meet his mouth as he started to move away. "I'm starved for you. But I guess I could eat Chinese food now too."

"Talia," Allen said, rolling to a sitting position. "I refuse to let this relationship be just about sex. I want more than that from you. I want that to be clear before I end up taking you like a madman against the wall later."

Talia sat up and crawled down the bed to climb across his knees and sit on his legs just above them. "I hope you don't think that sex is all I want. I genuinely do like you, Allen Stedman. You're truly one of the nicest men I have ever met, even if you are way too controlling in bed. This will have to be amended over time—but not tonight. I'm far too excited at the prospect of going up against the wall with you."

"Marry me and we can play every night," Allen stated boldly, loving the way she laughed when he joked with her.

But the trouble was, Allen knew he was no longer joking. Talia was smart, exciting, fun, loving, and sexy. God, was she sexy. He also knew he was going to love going home to her and the kids every night. Mason would make him laugh and teach him how to tuck him in. He would learn to carry Kendra in the baby wrap.

He could see it all as clearly as if it were already a reality.

Had he really only known this woman a week? If so, it didn't seem to matter. Allen wanted to be a permanent fixture in Talia's life.

"So which poets do you like?" Allen asked, trying to distract himself from doing and saying more than was wise at the moment.

"Be still my fainting heart. You read poetry too?" Talia asked, voice squeaking in surprise.

"Actually, I quote it." Allen softly recited some lines from his favorite love poems as he kissed his way across her shoulder and down her arm. He laughed loudly when he realized Talia had completely frozen on his lap and was holding her breath.

"I guess I've been saving all my best lovemaking just for you," Allen told her, running a hand down her glossy hair.

"I think we'll have a small wedding just before the holidays. Six months should satisfy propriety. Do you know any Lord Byron?" Talia asked, bending to bite his bottom lip as she pushed him backward on the bed.

Chapter 18

"What do you mean the client won't be interviewed?" Jenna shouted. "His house is worthy of a magazine cover. He ought to be kissing my ass, not kicking it."

"No need to convince me," Todd said, holding up both hands in an attempt to quiet Jenna's tirade. Construction workers had scattered for break the moment she'd raised her voice. Any other time he would have laughed. Today, Jenna's temper tantrum was justified.

"Look, you know I agree with you. This place is phenomenal. The fireplace is a freaking work of art. It takes your breath away when you walk through the door. I can't believe he hasn't come by here dying to see what you've done," Todd said.

"I want to talk to him," Jenna demanded. "Give me five minutes alone with him. I'll get him to change his mind."

"You can do the story without him, Jenna. It may even look better for you as architect," Todd said, watching her pace and fume. "*Architecture Digest* said they would focus solely on you instead. That's what they mostly would have done anyway."

"Todd, the man hasn't even seen the house. Hell, it's more my house than his. I picked the tile and flooring and the color scheme. I picked the cabinets in the kitchen and all the damn appliances. I chose cherry for the walk-in closet. What if he hates cherry? Not that I'm going to give a rat's ass if his check cashes for you, but it's the damn principal of it all. He needs to be appreciative. That's his job as the client. It's not going to look very good if all I've done is built a perfect damn ghost house," Jenna declared. "This place was meant to be enjoyed by people."

"Look, why don't you take the afternoon off and rest. You've been working non-stop since this project started. You need a break. Maybe after you have an afternoon to yourself, things will be clearer. There's really nothing we can do to force a client to agree to a magazine interview," Todd said easily.

"Maybe there's nothing more you can do, but that doesn't mean *I'm* out of options. My mother raised me to get what I wanted out of life and I plan to do it," Jenna said. "The afternoon off sounds like a great idea."

Jenna stomped off toward her SUV with thoughts of murder on her mind. Since it was illegal to kill clients in the state of Virginia, she was going to have him investigated instead.

And she knew exactly who to contact about it.

"Hey, Jenna," Allen said, seeing her come stomping into the office in her beat-up work boots that looked in worse condition than any pair he'd seen in the military, no matter how long or hard the march. But while the boots were awful, what struck Allen most as Jenna came through the door was how little girl there was in her today.

Her clothes were dusty and stained. The standard jeans and white shirt she usually wore looked as bad as her boots. The current outfit said she was a person reduced to wearing the oldest clothes in her closet. Jenna's eyes were the color of storm clouds, and her demeanor was tense.

In that moment, Allen couldn't even remember what he'd ever been attracted to in Jenna Ranger. She cleaned up nicely, but this was her nature most of the time. She was a handful under the best of conditions, and he couldn't fathom why a calm guy like Carter was so hung up on such a surly woman.

There must have been something he had liked as well, but all Allen could do now was be thankful he had found a laughing, sexy, girlie-girl like Talia. Shaking his head to move his thoughts away from Talia Martin and the effect she always caused in him, Allen gave Jenna a tentative smile.

"Alexa is out this afternoon. She and Lauren are meeting with a local organic farm about supplying the ingredients for Lauren's scents," Allen said easily.

"I didn't come to see Mama. I came to see you," Jenna said, running a hand through her hair. "Do you have time to visit with me?"

"Always," Allen said, his stomach dropping. He hoped this wasn't about Jenna and him, or about her relationship to Seth. He was done with the soap opera and just wanted his own happy ending now.

"I need to have someone investigated," Jenna began.

"Investigated? Why? Carter's an open book. If you want more information from him, I'll just sit on his skinny ass and bend him backward while you ask him questions. What's up? Do you think he's keeping something from you?" Allen joked.

Jenna's temper lifted a few notches because of Allen's humor. The mental image of Allen sitting on Seth was funny, but having lost her fair share of physical altercations with Seth, she well knew the man was a lot stronger than he looked. Allen might be surprised at how hard restraining Seth would be.

"It's not Seth. If I wanted more information from him, I have my own means of extracting it," Jenna said without thinking. Then she started to blush realizing who she'd said it to.

The comment only got a snort of laughter out of Allen. "Well, I guess you aren't pining away for me."

Jenna did laugh at his rebuttal. "Sorry. No. I'm—I'm mostly happy with Seth."

Allen grinned, his relief larger than he'd imagined it could be. "Good to hear, babe."

"Thanks. I need to investigate a client. I just built a local Taj Mahal for a man that won't reveal himself. The house is supposed to be featured in a magazine, and I want him standing beside me on the cover. I worked my ass off for the man. He owes me that much," Jenna said furiously, and then she took a deep breath and calmed herself. "I just want five minutes alone with him to discuss the matter. The problem is that I don't know who he is."

"Intriguing," Allen said, considering her words. "Why the secrecy?"

"I have no idea," Jenna said harshly. "That's one of the many questions I'd like to ask him. Can you help me find out who he is? I can't ask Casey. He'd tell Seth, and Seth—well, he'd try to talk me out of it. Seth would tell me it didn't matter. But it does matter—it matters to me."

"I'm all about helping you because it sounds interesting and fun, but I don't like the idea of keeping it from Gunny or Seth," Allen told her. "That sort of makes me nervous."

"I'll pay you three thousand dollars to find out for me, expenses included. You can keep how ever much of that you don't spend on finding out," Jenna told him.

"All the money up front?" Allen asked.

"Yes. So you'll do it?" Jenna asked, feeling righteous in her quest.

"I'll try my best. I could use the money, and it sounds like fun. But just in case, let's keep this between us and very quiet. I don't want Gunny to know I'm taking more work on the side. I like the work he gives me," Allen said easily.

"I am the soul of discretion," Jenna promised. "No one will know but us. Here." She whipped a check out of her shirt pocket, along with another sheet of paper listing the few things she knew. "Just write in your name and cash it."

"Jenna," Allen began as she headed to the door to leave. "Are you really okay with Carter?"

Jenna paused, considered, and sighed as she stood staring at the door. "I've finally learned that no one is perfect. I know now that I'm not an easy woman to be involved with.

Seth works hard to be nice to me, and I am trying to learn to be nice in return. I'm working on putting the past behind us."

She looked at Allen.

"He's done a lot to treat me better this time around. So I have to give this a real chance, Allen. I—I can't stay away from him anyway. I guess I'd rather be struggling with Seth than trying to live without him. That's as close as I've gotten to being okay."

"That's not exactly a declaration of love, honey," Allen said, smiling softly.

"I know," Jenna said sadly, closing her eyes at the thought of the love she sought and how what she had with Seth didn't look like anything she had wanted. "I'm working on it."

"Good. Keep working," Allen told her. "There is nothing else like it."

"You are such a romantic," Jenna said, chuckling. "I hope you find that one great love you've been searching for, Allen Stedman."

"Thanks," Allen said, grinning and thinking of the last time he'd made love to Talia. She had spent the whole hour whispering praise to him in Russian, and then had literally wept in his arms with the climax that had gone on forever for both of them.

Days later, he still got aroused just thinking about it. Damn she was fun. It *was* a little like having a different woman every time, except at the end when she gave herself over to him to do as he pleased with her. Then it was exactly like it was the first time—so perfect and right that he just knew she was the one.

By the time Allen left his daydream, Jenna had already disappeared. He looked at the check in his hand and pondered where to start his investigation.

With the check, Jenna had provided the name of the lawyer who had been representing the client.

He'd have to start there. It was his only lead.

In the middle of a late night phone call, Talia heard the doorbell ring. Never missing a syllable in her Chinese, she peered through the security port and felt her heartbeat speed up. It was after 10 p.m. Her parents were still sleeping in her room, the kids were in their rooms, and the man she wanted was on her doorstep with nary a bed available.

She let him in anyway and tugged on his hand to pull him to the couch with her. Holding up one hand when they were seated, she opened and closed it twice, signaling ten more minutes. Allen nodded and headed to the kitchen, bringing a beer back out of the refrigerator.

Finally, Talia noticed Allen looking worried. There was a heartbeat or two of personal concern, but then he reached out and linked their fingers as he drank his beer. The tension inside her unwound. Boy, did she ever have it bad for this one. She had already given him the power to unnerve her.

Some fifteen minutes later, she clicked the phone shut and squeezed his fingers.

"What's wrong?" she asked. There was never any choice for her but the most direct path between any two points of connection.

"I got involved in the soap opera again," Allen said sadly.

"I see," Talia, easing her fingers away from his. "And you came to tell me that you stole the girlfriend back again?"

Allen looked at Talia in complete shock. Did she really not know there was no competition for her in his world? "Hell no. I let Jenna hire me to investigate something for her."

Talia's eyebrows shot up into her hair. "Okay. On the surface, that doesn't sound so bad. In fact, I'm almost over wanting to kill her now. What's the soap opera part?"

"Your employer is involved," Allen said dryly, tilting the bottle and draining the last of his beer.

"I see," Talia said, but she didn't. "So what was the soap opera part again? Did I miss the explanation?"

"Jenna's an architect building a house for a mystery client. She wants to talk to this client about doing a magazine cover. She just built a six-hundred-thousand-dollar house for the man. This is the next rung on her career ladder on the line. In short, she paid me three thousand dollars to discover the mystery guy. And I did."

Talia's eyes widened. "Seth?"

"You are one sharp cookie," Allen told her. He met her gaze directly. "You're my cookie. My fortune. My everything. Yeah, I know. It's too soon. Screw that. There's no other woman. So don't go there anymore. It's just going to piss me off."

Talia leaned back with her elbows on the couch. "Are you this bossy with anyone else in your life?"

"I am almost always the nicest man you will ever meet. I just get insane at the thought of anything coming between us, except the hard length of me when I'm aroused," Allen told her. "Right now I'm severely pissed at Jenna and Seth and their problems communicating, even though I understand why Carter never told her that he sunk his life savings into letting her build the house of her dreams. I just don't want to be the one in the middle of it. So use that amazing brain of yours and tell me how in the hell I can get out of this. Say it in English, please."

Talia giggled at his anger, and Allen sent her a furious glare. She bit her lip and tried for a serious, yet sympathetic look.

"First, Seth did not sink his life savings into the house, just a healthy portion of it. Second, I'm your fortune cookie? How sweet—I like it. I don't think any man has ever called me his fortune cookie before. And last, your dilemma, my love, is quite easily solved."

Allen snorted as he met her laughing gaze. "Yeah? How?"

"Stall—until Seth comes out with the truth himself. This is not the sort of secret one divulges willy-nilly," Talia said, laughter in her voice. "You will get more devious as you age. Children help a lot with that."

"*Willy-nilly*," Allen repeated, smiling for the first time since he walked through the door. "Is that really a word? Did Mason make that up?"

Talia buried her face in her hands and rocked the laughter away against her knees to keep from waking her entire family. "Stop making me laugh, Allen. I really am trying to help you."

"I'm falling in love with you, Talia Martin," Allen told her. "Don't tell me it's too soon."

Talia shrugged. "What's too soon? I'm already in love with you."

Allen grabbed her feet and slid her down the couch to him, hoisting her to straddle his lap. "Stall, huh? In all your great wisdom of those extra eight years of life you have on me, that's best you can come up with?"

"Well, I might have suggested pretending to fail, but I just didn't see your male ego handling that well. I might also have suggested lying to a different sort of person, but dishonesty would probably be a huge burden for someone as level as you appear to be. So yes, I vote for stalling," Talia said, linking her hands around his neck.

"Stalling it is then. Thanks," Allen said, closing his eyes as she massaged the back of his neck. "You have magic hands."

"So do you," she told him, rocking herself against the palms that covered her rear.

"When can I have you—I mean, see you again," Allen teased, leaning forward and kissing the laugh off her lips.

"Mason is missing you, and mother would like you to come to dinner tomorrow night," Talia told him. "My parents like you and would probably watch the children tomorrow night after dinner while we go out."

"I like your parents too. I hear their accent sometimes, and it makes me smile. Not the Bostonian, but the British one," Allen told her.

"Lovely. I'm sorry though that it will have to be just a quick shag at your place tomorrow night," Talia said regretfully, feeling him lift her off his lap. "I can't stay long."

"No more talk about shagging until tomorrow. I'm not that strong. I love that word," Allen said. "I may one day write a poem about shagging you."

"Lovely," Talia said dryly this time, letting Allen pull her from the couch to walk him to the door. "I'll sext you tomorrow. I'll do it in French in case your employer picks up your phone accidentally. "

"Not wise," Allen told her. "I'm a beast when aroused too much. I'd hate to drag you to your bedroom before dinner tomorrow night. It would be embarrassing for all of us. I really don't want to have to explain to the children why their mother was screaming my name while I screamed hers. Mason is too smart for his age already. Save the sexting for after your parents leave. By the way, I'm working on the sound proofing part."

"Sir, yes, sir." Talia said quietly, mocking him even though she intended to comply.

At the door, Allen pressed her against the jam and kissed her in a way that was going to keep her up longer tonight than she wanted.

"Will you send me a text when you get home?" she asked. "I just want to make sure—well, don't make me explain this. I'm not just keeping tabs."

"Of course not," Allen said, leaning into her and hugging tightly. He couldn't remember the last time someone wanted to check on him to make sure he was okay. Uncle Sam had kept tabs. Before that, it was his mother. He had never had a girlfriend even act concerned. Now there was Talia asking for a text. Talia—a sexy woman who wanted to shag him. God he was lucky.

"I'll send a text. See you tomorrow, honey. Lock up behind me," Allen said, kissing her hard one last time and walking quickly away.

Chapter 19

"Behind the lawyer is a business. Behind the business is two more businesses. If I didn't know it was a residential house, I'd say it was a business building he was requesting. It's going to take a while to figure this out," Allen said, rolling his eyes to the ceiling and hoping his small lies would not come back on him later. "Give me a few days and I'll check in again. I've got other commitments for the next four days."

After saying goodbye to Jenna, Allen hung up the phone with great relief. He had managed to stall for four more days. Part of him toyed with the idea of confronting Seth about what he knew, but he discarded it. What would that accomplish? Nothing probably.

He just hoped that Carter intended to tell Jenna, and soon. For the life of him, he couldn't imagine what Seth was waiting on. He just hoped Talia was right about stalling being the right thing to do.

Fully dressed in his best suit and required hard hat, Seth stepped around the clear water shield and inside the steam shower where the hardware gleamed. There was a tiled seat for sitting, a rain head above him in the ceiling, nine power jets in the walls for water, and four for steam. The tan colored tiles were soothing, but interesting.

It was a dream shower. The only other fixture it needed was a smiling, sexy woman in it.

Seth could definitely see Jenna and him in this shower together. The picture of it was clear in his mind. When she walked into the master bathroom to retrieve him, Seth pulled her around the clear shield and into the recessed area where he stood.

"I love this shower," Seth said, his enthusiasm showing. "There is so much room in here.

Jenna laughed at his excitement. "Right. Steam shower. I'll keep that in mind for the house I build for you. Who knew you'd be so excited about a shower? Most guys want man caves and pool tables."

"I love sharing a shower with you. We need to buy a teak stool for you to stand on so we can be the same height. Don't worry though. I would never let you fall no matter how carried away we might get," Seth told her.

"Don't get too attached to the shower, Seth. It's time for me to give the house up to the owner. As gut wrenching as it's going to be, I have no choice," Jenna said, letting out a breath. "I still don't understand how a man could not even want to come see his own house. The lawyer said he wasn't intending to occupy it for some time yet."

Seth put a reassuring arm around her. "Well, maybe he has good reasons. So, Jenna, when are you going to be available to build another house?"

"Depends on Todd, I guess. I haven't even talked to him about what's next," Jenna said with a shrug. "Why?"

Seth took her hand and led her out of the bathroom and back to the great room.

Jenna walked along with him, subdued by her melancholy over giving up the house. The workers were done. The cleaning crew was coming tomorrow. Then after that the keys would be given to the lawyer. It was all but a done deal.

She closed her eyes as they got to the center of the house. Jenna opened them after a few moments to see the fireplace, the single thing she would miss most.

When Jenna turned her head, Seth was looking at her with such concern that she dropped her gaze to the floor. "I'm going to be fine. Really. It's just that I put a lot of myself in this one. I've never really done that before," she said.

"When are you doing the magazine interview and photo shoot?" Seth asked.

"Next week—maybe. When the cleaning crew gets finished. They're waiting on me to give them a call and schedule it," she replied.

"Jenna?" Seth said, stopping to swallow hard before he continued. "I love you. I want to marry you. I want to live with you in a house that you build for us. I want to fill the rooms with children we make together. You're the only dream I have left in the world. Will you marry me?"

Jenna weaved with emotion. She shut her eyes tight. "Seth—I—I don't know. I haven't—haven't thought about this. You're ahead of me on this."

Seth closed his eyes too, turning to look at the fireplace instead of her. "I love you. Do you love me?" He reached up and unclipped his hard hat, setting it on the hearth.

"I don't know," Jenna said, her voice tight. "Maybe. Sometimes I think I do. Sometimes I—I'm afraid you're going to reach some point of ticking me off your to-do list, and then you'll go back to your plans, and I—I will be ignored again. If we had children and that happened, I don't think I could bear it."

Seth nodded. "So all the love and support I've given you in the last two months hasn't made up for what happened the first time we dated? Is that what you're saying? You can't forgive me and will never trust me."

"I don't know what I'm saying. I haven't had time to think about it," Jenna said again, unclipping her own hard hat and setting it on the hearth beside the one Seth had worn. They weren't really needed anymore anyway.

"If you were wondering if I understood how it feels to be rejected, you've done a great job of teaching me that lesson all the months after we broke up until now. I've watched you with other men, worried myself ill thinking you were going to sleep with Stedman, and I ruined our first time together because I was insane to prevent you being anyone's but mine. We have belonged to each other since we met, but it's clear to me today that I'm the only one of us that feels that way about it." Seth turned to face her, made himself meet her tortured gaze. "You can't even tell me you love me. Can you?"

"Seth, I care about you. I do. I like being with you now. Can't that be enough for a while?" Jenna asked, not understanding why it was so important to him to get a commitment from her today. "I'm trying to figure things out."

"How long until you're ready to discuss getting married? When will our sex-only relationship not be enough for you? The sex has never been enough for me, Jenna, not even at the beginning. I've wanted to marry you since the day I met you. I've been waiting and waiting these last couple of months for you to catch up. I thought you had. I thought I had finally gotten through that stubbornness of yours," Seth said harshly.

"I'm not being stubborn. I'm being practical. How am I supposed to be as sure as you are that things will work out with us?" Jenna asked.

"If you loved me the way I love you, having faith wouldn't be difficult at all. You'd just know how much you mean to me," Seth said, walking across the room.

He stopped at the archway to the foyer and turned back to see Jenna framed by hearth, the fireplace at her back. He swept an arm up and indicated the room and the house.

"Even this house, as big as it is, can't hold the amount of love and faith I have in you—in us. There isn't anything I wouldn't give you, but if the love I have isn't enough. . .We're done, baby. We're just done."

Seth walked away. The ring box carrying the promise he'd wanted to give Jenna felt like a weight on his chest. His wedding present to her seemed like a silly idea to him now, regardless of how expensive it had been.

When his phone rang, he answered it, grateful for the distraction. It might just keep him from going back and shaking Jenna Ranger until her teeth rattled.

Jenna took the wad of tissues Regina pulled from her purse and dabbed at her eyes.

Eddy's was crowded as usual. Her mother squeezed her hand tightly and looked at her with great concern, which made Jenna's eyes burn and water even more.

"Seth's not even answering my texts. I know he's home, but he won't come to the door. I handled things badly. I did. But he just surprised me. I was giving a final house tour, not expecting a—a—a—damn marriage proposal," Jenna complained, wiping her red-rimmed eyes.

She was still in her work clothes and had barged in on their evening. It reminded her of the last time she'd coming running to these three women for support. Seth had rejected her then. Now it was the other way around. Or maybe they had rejected each other this time. She was ill trying to sort it out.

"Seth and I have been sexually involved for over two months. Just a couple of weeks ago we decided to start dating again. I thought we were taking things slowly, then suddenly today he decides that we need to get married. He has never, not once, even talked about marriage to me before today," Jenna wailed, tears flowing and leaving her face streaked with them. "Was he just assuming it was what I would want? Damn. I'm a mess."

"Happens to all of us," Regina said, waving a hand. "You should have seen me wailing over Ben."

"I never cried over Casey until he was hurt," Alexa said. "That doesn't count as wailing. I guess I did cry over Paul, but I was way younger than Jenna at the time. I had a baby too. Hell, it might have been baby hormones making me bawl."

"I never cried over Jim—well except that time I thought I hurt him," Lauren said, rubbing Jenna's arm. "Jim just makes me mad a lot, but not as much as he used to. It's hard to stay mad at a man who feeds you cannoli while he—oops, never mind. I guess that's a different conversation."

Regina laughed but rolled her eyes at them. "Fine. *I'm* admittedly the emotional wienie in the group. I cry at weddings. I cry when I'm sad. I cry when I'm happy. I cry over everything. The point is that panic and tears are just the sort of things that happen to a passionate woman."

"I'm usually not that passionate," Jenna said, almost laughing at their bickering. It was a constant in her life. The friendship they offered each other was bolstering, and they had offered it to her since she had gotten old enough to appreciate them.

"Seth makes me passionate," Jenna admitted. "He makes me be a lot of things. Then he calls me bossy if I try to exercise any control and stubborn if I disagree with him. He's the most frustrating man that ever walked. How could I possibly love a man like that? We can't even get along most of the time."

The snorts and snickering started out being stifled, then grew into giggling that all three older women tried to control. But as they looked at each other, they broke out in loud laughter that drew every eye in the place to their table.

"I came for sympathy, not to be laughed at," Jenna said, sniffing back another round of tears threatening to fall any second.

Alexa held on to her hand, and Lauren gripped her arm hard to keep her in place until they could control themselves enough to talk.

"Casey used his cane to hold me against the wall in my office and lectured me on what a bad woman I was," Alexa said, one eyebrow arched at her daughter. "Don't get me started on how pissed I was. I didn't talk to him for a week, and then I made him grovel."

"He put his hand on your leg to comfort you at breakfast the morning he met Daddy," Jenna told her. "That's what I want. That's love."

"Sure. It all goes together, honey. Casey also likes to control our entire sex life—when, how often, where. Pretty much everything. It's annoying as hell," Alexa said.

"That must run in the family. What do you do about it?" Jenna asked.

DATING A METRO MAN

"Let him—most of the time," Alex said sagely. "I'm not stupid. The man is good in bed."

Jenna closed her eyes and shook her head. She was never going to stop being shocked at some of what her outrageous mother said.

"Ben gets his way with me by using sex," Regina confessed, sipping her mineral water. "Don't ask me for details. I'm taking his secrets to my grave or putting them in my next book. I haven't decided yet."

Jenna laughed, dried her eyes, and threw the used tissue on the table. Her gaze swung to Lauren expectantly.

Lauren shrugged. "I'm the bad one in my relationship. I get my way using sex. I'm better than Jim in bed, but he's catching up nicely. He thinks he's in competition with Ben."

Jenna laughed out loud, her strong throaty release easing the pain in her chest. "That certainly explains why Jim wouldn't let you have a stripper when I asked."

Alexa and Regina looked at Lauren with knowing grins.

"It's not what you think. Jim just didn't want me to get over stimulated," Lauren said, shrugging again.

That sent the four of them laughing for another round.

Jenna closed her eyes. "So how dumb am I being? You're all telling me that it's never going to be any better than this with Seth, aren't you? He's going to drive me crazy forever."

They all just shrugged and looked at her with great empathy.

"It's the great mystery," Regina said wisely. "You never know what love is going to bring."

"Well I just kicked Cupid's ass and sent him home with his bows and arrows between his legs. The man isn't talking to me," Jenna said sadly. "This is going to be a problem for the making up part."

"Well, you know where he's going to be Saturday night," Alexa said, giving her a daughter a haughty look. "Put on a great dress and come seduce him."

"Where is he going to be?" Jenna asked, perplexed at her mother's comment.

"At Talia Martin's welcome party, where else?" Alexa answered. "Casey and I are hosting."

"Who's Talia Martin?" Jenna asked, even more perplexed. "And why are you two hosting?"

Alexa blinked at Jenna several times in disbelief. Jenna was sleeping with Seth. How could she not know?

Lauren and Regina sat up straighter and leaned back in their chairs. If Jenna got mad and starting throwing things, they were both going to be making a run for it. They had both witnessed her temper tantrums before and they were never pretty.

Alexa cleared her throat. "Well—I assumed you knew this, and don't know why you don't, but Talia Martin is the woman Seth is hiring to help him with his business. She's a single mother with two kids, and she's terribly smart. I really liked her when I met her. Seth asked Casey and me to host a party to welcome her to Falls Church. Didn't—didn't Seth say anything to you about her at all?"

Jenna was in shock—utter shock. What else didn't she know? She had been so caught up in the house, and all the work of it, that she had never surfaced to visit with anyone for literally two months now. Outside of Lauren's wedding, all she had done was crawl into bed with Seth every chance she got.

Then she remembered the fight they had. Seth had said that she hadn't asked him about his work since they had been sleeping together. He was right. It hurt even more to realize that he was right then and still right. Everyone knew what was going on in his life, but her. Her lack of knowing couldn't have been more humiliating.

She had no one to blame but herself. She hadn't even bothered to ask.

Jenna laid her head down on the table in the crowded bar and cried for how selfish and stupid she had been. The women at the table looked on in shock, but Regina grabbed Alexa and Lauren's hands before they could touch her. Regina shook her head. "This is good," she mouthed silently.

DATING A METRO MAN

Alexa raised her hand to Eddy and motioned for him to send over another round of drinks. Jenna was going to need some serious lubrication for her ego until she could find enough pride to make this right with the man she so obviously loved.

As the drinks hit the table, Jenna raised her head and grabbed a mangled tissue to wipe her eyes.

"Mama?" she said.

"Yes, honey." Alexa looked at her daughter with deep understanding of how much it was going to take for her to set this right.

"I'm going to marry Seth Carter and make you a grandmother soon. I hope this is okay with you and Daddy," Jenna said, blowing her nose. She picked up her beer. "I've been an idiot. He's the only one for me. He's always been the only one for me. I couldn't replace him and I couldn't get over him. I'm addicted to his lovemaking. I have no choice. I have to marry him. I'm never going to be able to love anybody else."

"Now you just need to find a way to tell him that," Lauren said, smiling softly.

Jenna sniffed. "Not a problem. I'm crashing a party I wasn't invited to Saturday night. I hear he's going to be there. God help the person if he brings a date. Seth Carter is mine."

Alex patted her hand. "Woman up, sweetie. Come looking your best. You don't want him getting any ideas about making you compete."

Jenna stood and walked to the woman who bore her, a woman who was also becoming a steadfast friend. "I love you, Mama. You're the best mother in the whole world."

"Damn straight," Alexa said. "Now get rid of those man clothes and spend some money on yourself. I swear Sydney and his globe-trotting is hard to get used to. Every time we have a fashion crisis, the man is out of town."

"It's okay," Jenna told her, trying her damnedest to stop crying, "I know exactly what Seth likes most."

"What's that, honey?" Lauren asked.

"Me," Jenna said. "Me. It's always been me."

She turned on her heel and marched out of the bar.

"Do you think she's sober enough to drive?" Lauren said, concerned.

Alexa shrugged. "I would say my daughter has never been more sober. It was like I got to watch her grow up five or six years in the last hour. I've never felt so old."

"Well there's where you're in luck," Regina said, smiling over her mineral water. "You got a younger man at home who can fix that for you. You'll be back to your young self in no time."

"Or after two or three times at least," Lauren said, sipping her second glass of malted milk. She loved the way Regina laughed at her every comment these days. "What did I say? You know it takes more than once sometimes."

Alexa shook her head. "All it takes is for Casey to smile at me. I'm glad Jenna's getting a man Casey helped train. I just hope my daughter lets herself love him. The boy is crazy about her."

"You don't know the half of it," Regina said, laughing, then caught what she had revealed. "And I can't tell you either. Sorry. I was just trying to say something equally validating."

Lauren lifted her glass of milk. "Here's to Jenna and Seth. May they find the love we have."

"Here's to my future grandchildren for whom I will also be an aunt. Please never tell the press," Alexa said, holding up her wine. "At least Lauren's child will have someone to grow up with."

"You're the only woman who ever toasted with malted milk. I'm not even sure your toast counts," Regina said wryly, laughing as Lauren stuck out her tongue at her. "Here's to true love, all the bumps, grinds, and g-strings."

Lauren cracked up. "What kind of toast was that, Regina?"

"Sue me. I'm horny," Regina said, gathering up her purse. "I'm going home to my man."

"Here. Here." Lauren and Alexa said in agreement.

Chapter 20

"Talia, that's the third dress you've tried on. They all look good on you, darling. Pick one," her mother said smiling.

Talia chided herself for being brave enough to take on companies but still scared to share her true feelings with her mother.

"Tonight's very important. I want to look my best," Talia said.

Her mother met her gaze in her mirror. "Because many of Allen's friends will be there?"

Talia flushed and glanced away from her mother, but she heard the woman laugh.

"Do you think I'm being foolish with him?" Talia asked, looking on in wonderment as her mother just laughed harder.

"If you are, darling, you picked a hell of a man to do with it. Allen Stedman is prime," her mother said, running a hand down her hair. "Besides that, the kids love him, and he likes them too. That doesn't happen often. I don't blame you for hoping it works out. I say go for it."

"Go for it," Talia repeated. "That's very American."

"Well, we have been here for several decades now. Your Allen was an American soldier, right?"

Talia nodded. "A military policeman, actually."

"Well, I can certainly see him doing that," her mother said. "What does he do now—besides put a relaxed smile on your face a few times a week."

"He speaks French fluently, and recites poetry during— odd moments," Talia finished, catching herself before telling a little too much. She lifted her chin to say the rest, hoping to communicate that she didn't give a flip in case her mother did. "He works as the executive assistant for a beautiful older woman who designs lingerie. Alexa and Casey will be our hosts tonight. He also works for Casey in his security business. I'm not sure of everything he does there. I believe he works as a trainer at a gym as well, or so he's told Mason. Then he also has a dream."

"Seems to me things are getting serious if you're wanting to help him with his dreams already," her mother said, teasing.

"He's a clothing designer," Talia said baldly. "He trained for it for two years. He sews. He draws. He—I'm being obvious, aren't I?"

"It's quite okay, dear. I like your renaissance man. Your father likes Allen too. He said he was glad if you and the children had to be so far away from us that at least you had a real man to watch over you," her mother said, watching relief pour into her daughter's eyes. "Do try to plan an early fall wedding if it comes to that. Your Aunt Margaret is wanting us to come to Kent for the holidays this year."

"We thought we needed to wait six months for the sake of propriety," Talia said meekly.

"Who knows you here well enough to judge? Screw propriety. Be happy, darling," her mother said boldly. "You know it's more fun shagging in your own bed. You've been married before."

Talia spun on her mother and hugged her close. "Have I ever thanked you for blessing me with your wicked sense of humor and your happy outlook on life? I am the luckiest woman in the world. And I am also one phone call away from being wealthy enough to buy a home. I may get the call tonight. I am so looking forward to it."

"Well, that's splendid, Talia. You've put that amazing mind of yours to great use for you and your family. Now put on the red dress with the black trim and those monstrously tall skinny heels that make you look like a super model. You'll wow everyone tonight."

"Thank you," Talia said, kissing her mother's cheek.

"You're welcome, darling," her mother replied.

Mason appeared in the doorway. "Mom, it is two hands together on the clock and you said we needed to leave by then. I told Allen I would help you keep to the sedule," Mason said.

"Schedule," Talia corrected.

"That's what I said, sedule," he said, serious. "You need clothes."

Talia looked down at her slip that looked like a nightgown. Allen would love it, but she needed to stop stalling and start dressing. "Oh my goodness, look at me. I'm still in my underwear. Thank you, Mason. I won't be a moment putting my dress on."

"You mother is nervous, Mason. Women get a little silly. Be kind and supportive, sweetheart," his grandmother said.

"Always, Grandma Lily," he said.

"You are a wonder, Mason Martin," she told him.

"Assolutely," Mason agreed, walking off down the hall.

Talia looked at her mother. "Allen cracks up every time Mason says that. I'm going to have the devil of a time trying to get him to pronounce it correctly now. He knows it makes Allen laugh."

"You know how males are when they bond. I'm sure that's assolutely true," her mother stated. "I'm going to go wake your father now. He was napping on the couch with Kendra on his chest a few minutes ago," she said.

"I love you, mother," Talia said, smiling.

"I love you too, darling," her mother said. "Be happy. You've suffered enough in your life."

Talia zipped up the fitted dress and stepped into the heels. When she removed the clip from her hair, she brushed it to the front just the way Allen liked. She knew he would approve of what she saw in the mirror. It was amazing how much that was enough for her.

"Talia Martin," she said to her reflection. "You have it so bad."

Seth paced the sitting room in Casey and Alexa's house, wishing for the millionth time that he'd given in and told Jenna about this. He'd whacked her over the head with a marriage proposal, and then reacted poorly when she had asked for more time. Now he was here without her, feeling guilty and sorry for himself. He had only himself to blame.

When the doorbell rang, he dashed to answer it. It was Talia, the children, and her parents. He ushered them in and shook hands. Mason immediately attached himself to his side, making Seth grin again. He introduced him to Casey who asked him about his leg braces. Remembering what Seth had said, he asked Casey where his cane was. It wasn't long before Casey was walking off with Mason following close behind to retrieve his cane.

Alexa was giving Talia's parents a tour of the house.

"Casey and Alexa are just as wonderful as they were the other day," Talia commented.

"You met them already?" Seth asked.

"Yes—well, I went by the office to ask Allen to lunch," Talia said, flushing.

"If I'd known how well you were going to like the man, I would have put Allen in the contract instead of three months rent. He's always looking for ways to make extra money," Seth said, teasing. "He's worse than me."

"Nobody is worse than you," Allen said, walking in with Kendra strapped to the front of him.

Seth looked at Allen, who met his gaze defiantly, then looked down at the smiling, laughing baby who kept giggling and cooing at Seth.

"Stedman, there's a baby strapped to your chest," Seth told him, stating the obvious.

"Yes, and I put her there all by myself. That's what took me so long to get in here. Wrapping three yards of cloth around yourself is not easy. I'm just glad Kendra is a good sport," Allen said.

Hearing her name, Kendra flexed and jumped in the baby wrap.

"Are you sure you want to carry her tonight?" Talia asked, chewing her lip, worrying that Allen might feel awkward packing the baby around all night on his person. She didn't expect him to do that.

"Assolutely," Allen told her, giving Seth a sideways look when he choked on a drink of his beer. "Carter, if you can't hold your liquor—don't drink."

He looked back at Talia. "Walk around, look beautiful, and let Carter here introduce you to people. If any of the guys try anything funny, just nod in my direction and I'll come break some fingers or something. In the meantime, Kendra and I are going to mingle and watch the crowd for suspicious people. It's what we do for fun at these things."

Allen gave Seth one hard look, and then tugged Talia to him for a kiss before striding off.

"A month ago I wanted him dead because I thought he was going to sleep with my girlfriend before I could. Now he's packing a baby and making me laugh hard enough to spew beer out of my nose. He constantly surprises me," Seth said to Talia.

Talia watched Allen's very nice rear now encased in dress slacks move easily through the crowd. "My mother calls Allen a renaissance man."

"That fits," Seth said easily.

"So which one of these alluring women mulling about is the leading lady of your soap opera," Talia asked with a smile. "I'm simply dying to meet her."

Seth's smile dropped away. "She's not here. We had a fight and I—I didn't invite her."

"Oooh, not good, Mr. Carter. That's definitely going to be a bugger come make-up time," Talia said on a laugh. "None for you, sir."

"Assolutely not," Seth said, making Talia laugh in return.

Jenna slipped in the door of her mother's house and heard the party in full swing. She adjusted the blue dress it had taken her three days to find, not to mention locating the matching three-inch heels on her feet.

Nerves had taken over, and she now wondered how she was ever going to pull off crashing in on him without melting. She had no idea what she was going to say to Seth. It had taken all her bravery just to find clothes to wear. Actually following through on crashing now seemed almost impossible.

But her feet took her forward down the hallway, and the next thing she knew she was merging with the crowd.

Talia felt the phone ringing in the bodice of her dress. She turned from common view and slipped the phone out of her bra. Seeing who it was, she walked quickly to the nearest room off to the right, ducked in, and closed the door.

Five minutes later, she emerged with a smile that was brilliant. She searched for the man she needed to share it with until she saw him in the middle of the room. Talia parted the crowd before her, striding confidently to his side like the conquering warrior that she now considered herself.

"Mr. Carter," she began when she had his full attention. She crossed her arms across her chest. "I just made you a very rich man. It's going to cost you."

"You got it worked out?" Seth asked. "Seriously. Two mil?"

"No," Talia said, watching him closely for signs of disappointment. "I couldn't stick with the two mil number. It just wasn't going to work."

"Well, anything is good. We can always work on the rest of it later," Seth said.

"No need," Talia said, waving a hand. "Three point five, Seth. Three. Point. Five. That would be million. I added two extra wind turbine companies who needed the part. Production will start in a month. Parts will be delivered in two. You're going to owe me commission before summer is over."

Seth blinked a couple moments in shock. "Seriously? You exceeded my original order? Can I hug you and do a dance?"

"Well the number is in the millions," Talia said, grinning and raising her arms. "Definitely hug and dance worthy."

Seth scooped up the brilliant woman he hired from the floor and spun Talia Martin around while she laughed.

Mason walked up with Casey close by. "Do me," he demanded to Seth.

"Certainly," said Seth, releasing the smiling Talia. "Spinning and dancing for everyone tonight." He scooped up the laughing boy and spun him in a circle while his braces jingled.

"Do it again," Mason demanded.

Seth laughed and did just that.

Jenna watched in stupefied horror as Seth first spun the beautiful laughing woman, and then the child.

I'm too late, Jenna thought, as dizziness engulfed her. She knew she had hurt Seth and more than once. How could she blame him for wanting to move on?

The irony of the situation wasn't lost on her as she stood watching him. She was wearing her new clothes and shoes that she'd bought to impress him—to seduce him, and fighting not to cry. If she had ever been unsure of her feelings for Seth, seeing him happy with someone other than her cleared everything up completely and immediately.

Lesson finally learned, Jenna decided, just a little too late.

She was absolutely and totally in love with Seth Carter.

The competition of the beautiful woman Jenna could have handled, but the kid with the braces on his legs and Seth's obvious affection for him made Jenna feel ashamed for not appreciating the good heart Seth possessed. Even now Seth held the boy in his arms, still hugging the child and smiling. Seth looked happy and carefree with the woman and little boy, not irritated and frustrated, like he usually was with her.

And then there was Casey laughing and talking, as if the woman was already one of them—one of their family.

When realization came this time, Jenna accepted that what she was seeing was the family Seth could have without her. She thought of all the men she had dated. Seth had hated her dating, but he'd never really gotten in the way. How could she not get out of the way now and give Seth a chance to find a better happiness than she'd been able to offer?

Jenna turned to escape before anyone saw her, and ran straight into Allen Stedman.

"Don't you have more faith in Carter than that?" Allen chastised, seeing the shattered look on her face.

"I disappointed him one too many times, Allen. You don't understand," Jenna said, the confession choking her.

"I understand perfectly. Sydney isn't here to point out the obvious, so I'll do the honors for him. You're wearing the dress and the kick-ass shoes, honey, but you got to do them justice. I've seen you charge into much worse situations with both guns firing. Don't you have the guts to go find out what's really going on with Seth?" Allen chided.

Jenna lifted her chin in anger, and Allen laughed. He was glad Carter was the one who was going to have to live with this so easily angered female and not him. The thought made him smile.

The headache brought on by a thwarted temper tantrum descended on Jenna viciously, but thankfully the giant flood of tears that threatened receded.

Then Kendra jumped and giggled as Allen's chest rumbled against her back. He wrapped a hand around the baby, making her squeal in delight as she grabbed the fingers splayed across her. He looked down at the top of her head, marveling at how much it thrilled him to be the cause of her amusement.

Jenna was marshalling the nerve to order Allen to get out of her way when she finally noticed the yards of material Allen was wearing and what it contained.

"Allen? Why is there a baby strapped to your chest?" Jenna asked, trying not to sound shocked, but finding it hard not to laugh at the squealing pixie.

"Now that's the right kind of question to be asking," Allen said wisely. "Man, I thought for sure you'd bolt before you stopped to think rationally. Jenna Ranger, meet Kendra Martin. She's a very excitable cutie who likes to hang out with muscle guys—just like her mother does."

Kendra cackled and squealed again when she heard Allen say her name. It made the ends of Jenna's mouth twitch. Allen? With a baby?

"That baby is not yours," Jenna stated firmly, but looked at Allen with questioning eyes. "What are you doing with her?"

Allen looked so—well, so normal with the baby that it almost spooked her. It was like Jenna was slowly waking up in an alternate reality.

"Well, I'm hoping Kendra will be mine soon," Allen said enigmatically. "I guess it's not totally your fault for being in the dark. I saw Carter coming out of a storage closet after you the day of Lauren and Jim's wedding. You both were so dazed with lust, you looked high. What's Carter doing? Keeping you chained to the bed?"

Only her raw emotions kept her from blushing.

"Chained, no. I was working too much to handle anything kinky," Jenna said, smirking at Allen's low laughter despite the fact she was still fighting the urge to cry a little. "But the combination of Seth and sixteen-hour work days made a normal life impossible for a while. I've been building a house, remember?"

"Yeah—speaking of work, I've got a hunch about your mystery client. I think the man is planning to give the house to his future wife for a surprise. That's why he's been so secretive about it all. Want me to keep digging to see if I'm right?" Allen asked, watching her face to see if she had a clue, laughing at the irony when he saw she didn't.

"No," Jenna said, shaking her head. "I'm over that too. Stop where you are and keep the rest of the money. It does make me feel better to think that the man is intending the house for a couple. I just had a feeling about it the whole time I was designing it."

"Good. Now follow your instincts about Carter, even when your eyes are seeing things you can't understand," Allen told her. "Now turn around and go get your man away from my woman before he hugs her again and I have to hurt him. Their damn business deal probably came through."

Jenna's eyebrows rose at Allen's orders and his pronouncement. "Your woman? You're dating the tall Asian woman Seth was hugging? That was quick."

"Yeah, it was. Talia and I are much less stubborn than you and Carter," Allen told her. "We're both optimists and just want to be happy."

The jab was fair, but it smarted.

"Seth is an optimist too. I guess I'm the pessimist. I've wasted months being too mad to give him a real second chance," Jenna said, feeling the last of the unshed tears ebb away. "You were right to break up with me. Seth had to practically chain me to the bed to make me admit I wanted him. You were right about me being stubborn too, but I'm over it now."

"Great. I love being right," Allen said. "Now go ask Carter the right questions while you're still feeling humble. I know you. Humble moods never last long."

Jenna snorted at the insult. "You don't know me all that well."

Allen tilted his head. "Damn straight I don't. Make sure you validate that if you're ever asked by a tall, exotic woman. I need her to trust me. I'd like to marry her one day."

Jenna did laugh then and put her hand out to stroke the baby's cheek. "Is Kendra always this happy?"

"Yes. Wait till you meet her brother, Mason. Kid's as sharp as a whip and doesn't mind telling you about it. He cracks me up," Allen said sincerely, motioning Jenna to walk back to the crowd.

A few minutes later, Allen walked up to Talia and laced his fingers with hers, leaning in to whisper in her ear. "Run away with me for a few minutes. Carter has some unfinished business to take care of soon," he said.

Trusting the serious look in Allen's eyes more than his words, Talia nodded and slipped quietly away from Seth as he was talking to someone other than her.

When the phone in Seth's pocket buzzed, he stopped talking and excused himself to check the message, eyes widening as he read it.

Meet me in my room. Please.

Seth looked around, looking to see if Jenna was actually here. Across the living room, he saw Allen and Talia talking to Jim and Lauren. Casey and Mason had bonded when they met and had been inseparable for the evening. Mason was packing Casey's cane and hanging with him everywhere he went.

Seth turned and walked quickly down the hallway and padded softly up the carpeted stairs to a room at the top. He stopped to peer through the partially closed door. Inside he could see Jenna standing by the bed, arms crossed in her typical defensive gesture. She looked guarded and upset, but also wonderfully sexy. Not an easy woman to love, Seth decided, but his—all his now.

He wondered how many years they would be together before they could have a serious conversation without her crossing her arms. His wishful thinking only made him laugh.

Pushing the door open, Seth entered the room, and then closed and locked the door softly behind him. Jenna didn't move when she saw him, just waited for him to come to her, which was what he'd been doing the whole time he'd known her.

Her lack of warm welcome didn't matter to him, Seth thought, walking across to her. He would always keep coming back, no matter how long it took or how she greeted him. Eventually, Jenna would open her arms to him, and Seth was just going to have to work harder to get her to open her heart. Jenna was all he wanted. There was no other choice.

He walked over to where Jenna stood and looked down at her, noting the distance wasn't as far as usual. His gaze dropped to her feet and enjoyed the journey back up to her face. "You're very tall tonight."

"My mother made me buy new clothes," Jenna said, knowing she sounded a bit like a pouting twelve year old.

"Well, it's a very nice dress," Seth told her, taking in every nuance of her appearance. "The shoes are sexy as hell. You can wear them to bed next time."

"Don't get too used to seeing me in girl stuff. Being this womanly isn't easy for me. It seems to always turn into slutty instead of glamorous. Just so you how serious I am though, I'm not wearing any underwear," Jenna replied, liking the way sweat beaded on Seth's forehead almost immediately.

"Marry me," Seth ordered. "I'm not going to bother asking this time around. Consider it a damn demand, and let's fight about it. And when I win this round, I'm going to want the wedding to be soon. Don't think I'm going to give you time to change your mind when your mood shifts. I know better than that."

Jenna sniffed. Damn it. She was going to cry. "Just like that? I thought we were done, Seth. You said we were and I believed you. I thought you were never going to talk to me again," she said.

"I changed my mind about talking, but I'm not touching you until I get the answer I want," Seth said, crossing his own arms and giving up all plans he had for a peaceful life.

"I guess I can understand that. So here it is—I love you. I've always loved you. I—I was afraid to talk about marrying you when you asked me the first time, and I'm still afraid. But I've decided not to let my fear of being hurt stop me," Jenna said softly. "Just know if you ever start to ignore me too much, I'm going to give you hell until you pay attention."

Seth took in steadying breaths, in and out, in and out. Was she saying yes? It was hard to tell with Jenna.

"I know you love me. You tell me all the time with your body. Once you even said the words in your sleep," Seth told her, more confident sounding than he actually was about her.

Usually he never knew where he stood with Jenna. He had just taught himself to live with the insecurity.

Jenna closed her eyes, willing herself to just tell Seth exactly how she felt—to risk it all—commit and let the rest work itself out as they went along. They would build their life together, one compromise at a time as they debated everything under the sun.

"Well, I'm not asleep now," Jenna said firmly, forcing her eyes to open and her gaze to focus on his. "And I know how I feel. I love you, Seth Carter."

"Good. Progress at last," Seth said, his heart beating in his ears. "Now say you'll marry me, Jenna Ranger. Be my wife."

Jenna nodded yes and closed her eyes. "Okay," she said.

"No, too wimpy an answer. Try again," Seth said firmly, shaking his head, biting his lip not to laugh at the frustration on her face. "Marry me, Jenna Ranger. Have my children. Make love to me every night. Keep giving me a reason to throw my cell phone on the floor. I need you, but I want it all."

"I need you too. So—yes," Jenna said, her arms uncrossing, tears running down her cheeks.

Seth hands went to Jenna's face then, his thumbs wiping the tears away as fast as they fell. "I've been waiting forever to hear you say yes to me," Seth said, his voice breaking.

"Yes, Seth Carter. I will marry you. I will be your wife," Jenna said, sobbing her agreement, grateful that he hadn't changed his mind about her after all.

"I hope like hell you were being truthful about your underwear," Seth said, laughing harshly against her mouth. "We're consummating this agreement right now before you change your mind."

Jenna was openly crying now. Seth's mouth was hot and on hers again. She was back in his arms. He was shedding his pants and pulling her down onto him, sliding home. The relief of being connected again was so profound they both just held tight to make sure it was real.

"I was coming after you again. I was mad and hurt, but I wasn't giving up," Seth said quietly, his voice rough with emotion and lust.

"Thank God," Jenna said. "I'm trying to become a nice person, but at the rate I'm going, it's going to take years. In the meantime, I need a man as stubborn as me."

"I know what you need, and I'm more than happy to give it you," Seth said, smiling. "I'm the one, Jenna."

"Yes. You're the one. You've always been the one," Jenna agreed, rocking in his lap, happy again for another chance. She was going to be smart about it this time.

"Wait," Seth said, stilling her all too talented hips. "We don't last long in this position. I have one more thing to say first."

"What?" Jenna said, frustrated. She was close, so close. "Say it fast then and stop making me wait."

"This is worth waiting for and then we'll celebrate," Seth said laughing.

He fished something out his jacket pocket. "Hold out your hand." When she did, Seth put a set of keys into it.

"You get the originals. I made a copy for myself."

Jenna stared at them in disbelief, immediately recognizing them. "Where—where did you get these?"

He rocked up into her then, pulling down hard on her hips and holding on, trying to distract her so she'd take the news well. "They're the keys to a house my future wife built for me—for us. You should see it. It's the most amazing house in the world. I can't wait to live in it with her. The fireplace is a freaking work of art."

Jenna's hand curled around the keys. He was the client. Seth was the client. The house she built was for Seth. The amazing house she had poured her creativity into by the buckets was now going to be hers. Her hands tightened painfully around the keys.

"I love you, Jenna," Seth said. "Every surprise won't be this big. You're just going to have to forgive me for keeping something like this from you. I had good reasons."

Jenna pounded on his shoulders with the keys in her hand. And then she cried, not little tears, but rolling sobs that began in her gut and forced their way up through her on their way out.

"Oh, don't do that—I can't stand to hear you cry. It makes me ill. It was supposed to make you happy, not sad. I wanted to help you make your dreams come true, but knew you needed to do it on your own. I thought maybe if you managed to have that much faith in your work, then you'd figure out how to have that much faith in us," Seth told her. "Now stop crying, and make love with me. Help me out here. You know it takes both of us to do this right."

Still crying, Jenna moved her hips on his and they rocked together until the world turned golden around them, and they found relief from their desire at last. But when it was done, neither of them wanted to break the connection.

"I'm sorry about a lot of things, but mostly that I haven't asked about your work. Who's Talia Martin?" Jenna asked quietly.

"She's a woman I hired who just made me three point five million dollars tonight. Oh, and I think Stedman is in love with her," Seth said. "Wait until you meet Talia's children. Her son is the smartest kid I've ever met."

"I saw the baby with Allen. There was a ton of material wrapped around him, and he was carrying her in it like a baby kangaroo," Jenna said, easing back to where she could look at Seth's face. "I probably look like hell. People are going to know I had a meltdown."

Seth inspected her face and turned her chin. "Yeah. Pretty much. Your makeup is ruined by crying, and I messed up your hair pretty bad when I was kissing you. Maybe we should just stay here in your room having make-up sex until everyone goes home."

Jenna laughed. "We can make up more later. Right now I want to go tell Mama and Casey that we're getting married. I love my wedding present." She opened her palm to look at the keys, which were still clutched in it.

"Oh yeah—married. Wait. I got caught up in the make-up sex and forgot," Seth said, patting his pockets. "Give me your hand."

"Why?" Jenna asked, pulling her left hand back in case Seth tried to take the keys from her.

"I'm not taking back the keys. Those are yours to keep forever. I told you I have another set. You are so stubborn. Give me your damn hand," Seth ordered, laughing and pulling her left hand into his.

He slid a diamond solitaire on it that gleamed in the light.

"Are you rich?" Jenna asked. "First the house and now a ring. I don't care about the money. It's just embarrassing to be the only one who doesn't know anything about your business. I'm sorry I haven't been more interested."

"Financially, I'm solvent. It's taken me several years, but I finally got there. But in every other way—yes, I'm the richest man I know," Seth said, cupping her hips in his hands. "I'm finally getting to marry the woman of my dreams."

"Well, I can think of at least one way I can add to your portfolio. We'll probably need to make a five year plan to get it done," Jenna said, sliding off his lap at last.

"What are you talking about?" Seth asked, laughing. "Since when are you in favor of a five year plan."

"Since I decided a few moments ago to marry a successful entrepreneur and have his children. I figured we'd space the kids apart a little bit," Jenna said.

"Perfect. Talia can give us lessons, and we'll get Allen to show us how to tie the baby wrap thing," Seth said, teasing. "If Steadman can pack a baby and still look masculine, I figure I can pull it off as well."

"Our children are probably not going to be very nice," Jenna said, closing her eyes. "Stubborn and persistent. Let's hope they get some recessive genes."

"I don't care how difficult they are. I still want them," Seth said, grinning at her worried expression. "I want my happily ever after."

"Fine. We'll start practicing tonight. First though, I'm going to try to repair my appearance, and then I want to meet the new woman in your life," Jenna said.

"She only makes money for me. Talia's in Allen's life more than mine. I hooked them up as kind of as a joke, but I actually think Steadman fell in love with her the first time they met," Seth said, standing and fixing his clothes. "How bad are my pants wrinkled?'

Jenna laughed and rolled her eyes. "They look fine. I thought your pants didn't matter to you when you were in bed with me?"

"Well, no—I mean, I wouldn't care if we were home. Stedman is already going to take one look at my face and know what just happened between us. I was hoping my wrinkled pants wouldn't announce it to everyone else," Seth said easily, watching as Jenna dabbed at her eyes and fixed her hair in the bathroom.

Jenna frowned at her reflection. She looked like she'd been crying for days, but at least her clothes and hair were mostly okay. It was going to be hell trying to keep her appearance up enough not to embarrass her husband-to-be.

"So do I look good enough to face your business crowd, Mr. Metro Man?" Jenna asked, when she saw Seth studying her closely.

Seth moved from where he was leaning on the bathroom door jam and crowded Jenna against the sink like he wanted to. He was never holding back with this woman again.

"You look like you're finally mine," Seth told her, bending to gently touch his lips to hers.

He ended up kissing her hard and staking his claim again instead.

Epilogue

At long last, it was finally going to happen.

Having helped plan most of it, Jenna had been looking forward to the perfect wedding for months. Now she couldn't believe she was spending the first third of the allotted time for the ceremony wrapped around the toilet throwing up.

"Seth, you don't have to wait for me," Jenna said through the stall door. "Go on, and I'll meet you in there. The sickness is passing now. I'll be fine in a couple more minutes."

"Jenna, I'm not leaving the mother of my child on her knees in a strange bathroom unless I'm with her," Seth teased, hoping to cheer her up so she could at least marginally enjoy this day. "When you're finished, I have some cold wet towels for you."

Jenna braced herself on the toilet seat and pushed herself into a standing position. Logically, she knew many women were sick all the time with their first child, but it was impossible not to feel sorry for herself when she was the one going through it. Lauren had rarely complained. Jenna was made differently.

She flushed one last time and pushed open the stall door.

"I hate being sick. The medicine helps, but doesn't get rid of all of it. Every time I get a little stressed, I spew. I don't want to do this anymore."

Seth was laughing when she exited, but his humor faded quickly when he saw how wiped Jenna looked.

"Honey, I'm truly sorry. I would do this part for you if I could," he said, seriously meaning it. Jenna was not a person who suffered anything in silence, but Seth felt she had a right to complain loudly about this.

"After making me this sick for three full months, this baby better be like Kendra and sleep all night," Jenna said fiercely, taking the towels from Seth and putting them on her face. She pulled them down and groaned when she heard the strains of the wedding march begin. "And now they're starting the wedding without us. That's just great."

Seth was openly laughing at the look of utter disgust on her face.

"Good thing I'm feeling like a caveman today," he said, bending and scooping Jenna up into his arms.

"Don't carry me," she complained. "I'm too heavy."

"No. I wish you were. You've lost weight and it's worrying me. When you can eat again, I'm going to feed you until you get big enough to fill up the great room in our house," Seth told her.

He elbowed the handicap accessibility panel, which opened the bathroom door automatically. Seth carried Jenna into the main vestibule of the church. Seeing the back pew was completely empty, he sat on the bench seat, and slipped off Jenna's shoes so her feet could rest on the seat beside them.

"Seth," Jenna whispered, wanting to protest the fact she was sitting in his lap in a church, but was silenced by his finger over her lips.

"Ssssh. . .they've already started," Seth whispered. "Lean your head back on my shoulder and watch. Doesn't Talia look great?"

Too weak to argue, Jenna did as she was told, promising herself that her bossy husband was not always going to have things his way. She might be suffering now, but her starring role in the whole baby production business would be ending in a few months. Jenna patted her small baby belly and smiled about how much fun she was going to have watching Seth learn to be the perfect stay-home dad.

"Do you, Allen Whitaker Stedman, take Talia Renee Walker Martin to be your wedded wife? To love, honor, and cherish her, so long as you both shall live?" the minister asked.

Before Allen could answer the question, a short blond spitfire wearing most of a baby harness streaked down the aisle heading straight for her brother as fast as her legs would carry her.

"Mason," Allen said in warning, looking down at the shortest and youngest best man in history. Kendra had managed to knock Mason down the first time she'd charged him, and now endlessly tried to do it over and over again.

"I see her," Mason said, resigned, stepping out to embrace being the target he knew he was for his crazy sister.

In the black suit Allen helped make and fit to him, Mason bent his knees a little and centered his stance like he was preparing for a fight. The heavy ankle weights sitting on his braces at least made him feel like he could handle what was about to happen. His sister squealed and flung herself at him, only to bounce backward off him in shock.

"Hey! It worked!" Mason announced loudly, looking up for confirmation and seeing Allen's smile and nod.

"You're getting stronger all the time," Allen told him, reaching down and picking up the stunned toddler by the back of her harness before she could do her kamikaze impression on her brother again.

Allen held Kendra dangling in the air in front of his face and stared at her until her loud squeal of protest faded to nothing. The rapt audience laughed at the family drama being played out while they waited to see what would happen next.

"Kendra, couldn't you have waited until I finished marrying your mother before wreaking havoc? We're only a few minutes away, monkey," Allen told her.

Kendra blew a raspberry with her tongue at him, grabbed Allen's face with both hands, and put her open mouth on his. Allen laughed, his mouth sputtering under the wet sloppy kiss while the church broke up in hysterical laughter.

Her grandfather finally got out of the middle of the pew with the other end of the baby harness hanging from his hand. Fighting to remove the grin on his face, Henry walked slowly to one of the best men he'd ever met. He certainly didn't want anything to stop Allen Stedman from marrying his daughter.

"Sorry, Allen, I think Kendra picked the bloody clasp," Henry said, letting what was left of his English accent become pronounced for the benefit of the crowd, making Allen laugh out loud as he handed Kendra over to him. He took the girl, who threw her arms around him and gave him a sloppy wet kiss as well.

"Is it time for the rings now?" Mason asked, sighing heavily as his grandfather carried Kendra away.

Allen sighed and smiled at the eager boy. "Not yet. Almost. You can get them out if you want. Never hurts to be ready."

He turned back to his bride, who was practically biting her bottom lip off struggling not to burst into unrestrained laughter over him and the kids. There was so much laughter in his life now, that Allen couldn't even imagine going one day without it. Less chaos would be nice, but he'd take that too if it meant he got to keep the rest of what he had found with them.

"Where were we?" Allen asked Talia. "I lost my place."

"Just say *I do*, son," the minister advised.

"Okay. I do. Of course, I do," Allen said, hearing giggling and snickering throughout the crowd.

The minister repeated the question, addressing it this time to Talia, who nodded, still fighting the laughter.

"A nod won't get the job done, I'm afraid. You need to say *I do*, miss," the minister said. "The assembly must hear your agreement."

Talia straightened and shook off the laughter. She took a deep breath. "I do. I absolutely do."

Talia smiled at her husband, and Allen smiled at his wife. Then he leaned forward and kissed her, wanting to see how it felt to have a legal right to do it. It was just as good as he imagined.

"Hey," Mason said, smacking Allen on the leg. "You said the kissing part came *after* the rings. Look, they are still in my hand."

Mason held the rings up to prove it.

The audience of onlookers dissolved into laughter again.

Allen pulled away from Talia and sighed. "Sorry, Mason. You're right. I—I got carried away."

"That's okay," Mason said wisely. "It happens to us men all the time."

More laughter from everyone had Mason sighing again.

Talia had her bouquet in front of her face now and one hand on her stomach. *Mine*, Allen thought, watching her fight for control. Playmate. Great mother. Friend.

He was the luckiest man in the world.

"Hurry," Allen ordered, turning to the minister. "Otherwise, we're going to be here all day trying to get this mission accomplished."

The minister laughed through the rest of the ceremony, but finally did manage to pronounce them husband and wife.

When Allen and Talia kissed at the end, the whole church broke out in applause.

# # #

Note from the Author

Thank you for reading my work. If you enjoyed this book, please consider leaving a positive review or rating on the site where you purchased it. Reader reviews help my books continue to be valued by distributors/resellers and help new readers make decisions about reading them. I value each and every reader who takes the time to do this and invite you all to join me on my Website, Blog, Facebook, Twitter, or Goodreads.com for more discussions and fun.

You are the reason I write these stories and I sincerely appreciate you!

Many thanks for your support,
~ Donna McDonald

Excerpt from *Dating A Silver Fox*

"Good evening, Mrs. McCarthy. I have a table for one available right now if you're ready," the hostess said.

Lydia nodded, deftly avoiding eye contact with the curious gazes of two couples waiting for a larger table. Widowed in her mid-forties, she had long ago grown accustomed to the pitying looks she received dining alone. At sixty-seven, the remaining discomfort was minimal.

She drew herself up to her full five-foot-six height and exhaled loudly at their rudeness, making sure they heard. Normally, she would have said something to dissuade them of openly expressing unwanted sympathy, but miscellaneous confrontations tended to ruin her dinner.

"Red wine, Mrs. McCarthy?" Andrea asked pleasantly, stepping around the hostess who had fled after pulling out the older woman's chair.

Andrea had been watching for her twice-weekly regular customer, not because she liked the woman and looked forward to serving her, but because kowtowing deference was simply expected. She had learned that the first time she'd served Mrs. McCarthy and received a hand written note with a list of improvements instead of a cash tip.

"Yes. Thank you, Andrea," Lydia replied formally, stiffening in her seat as the two couples from the lobby ended up at the table for four next to her. She shook her head over the bad judgment of the hostess, steeling her nerves to deal with the distraction they were sure to cause. Their current jabbering and laughter did not bode well.

"Chicken Alfredo, Mrs. McCarthy? It's excellent tonight," Andrea suggested, already writing it down, because this was Tuesday and she had long ago committed the meal rotation to memory. As the newest server on alternating evening shifts, she had inherited the unfortunate honor of always taking Mrs. McCarthy's table on her nights. Tips were better in the evening, but sometimes she was glad to serve at lunch instead. She made sure to have days when the bitter woman never came by.

Schooling her expression into a patient smile, Andrea kept her eyes trained on the menu as Mrs. McCarthy pretended to study it as if there might be something more appealing. It was a truth that the complaining woman had turned her into a better server, but her sorority hazing hadn't been as bad on her personal self-esteem. Now all Andrea could do was pray for a newer server to join the evening shift and relieve her torture.

"Fine. I'll have the Chicken Alfredo. Please make sure it doesn't sit too long before you bring it out this time. It was practically iced over when I got it last week. There's nothing worse than hardened Alfredo sauce on cold, slimy pasta," Lydia said, her attention drawn once more to the laughing group at the next table.

Oh there's worse, Andrea thought bitterly jotting down an obedient reminder on her pad, tightening her face at the rebuke until her fake smile actually hurt her cheeks.

"Yes, Ma'am. I will watch the timing tonight," she said, turning with a quiet sigh of relief to leave.

"Andrea?" Lydia called, rolling her eyes in exasperation.

"Yes?" Andrea asked, turning back and hoping like hell her irritation over the delayed escape wasn't showing because she needed her job.

Lydia handed her distracted server the folded menu that she'd forgotten to take away. "Are you feeling okay this evening? You seem a bit preoccupied."

"I'm fine. Thank you for asking," Andrea said politely, biting the inside of her jaw.

"Try to get some extra sleep, dear. Young people don't realize how much a lack of sleep affects their mental capacities," Lydia said, eyes darting again at the loud, bright laughter just beyond her as the sommelier arrived to pour the first glass of wine.

"Yes, Mrs. McCarthy. I'll keep that in mind," Andrea said, turning again and walking quickly away before the woman could stop her with another lecture.

Lydia frowned at the noise level caused by the incessant laughter that kept erupting from the group next to her. With their gray hair announcing their aging process, both couples looked to be close to sixty.

Not that being gray had obviously brought any true maturity to them, Lydia decided, watching the one couple being embarrassingly demonstrative with each other. They were holding hands like teenagers as they ate. The man had even leaned over and kissed the woman several times, once after he'd fed her a bite of something from his plate. The next time he leaned into her, he kissed her neck and the woman giggled.

Disgusting, Lydia thought. How could they act like that in public? People their age ought to have more of a sense of decorum.

She sipped her wine and tackled her dinner with gusto when it arrived hot and steaming perfect. But the laughter, the giggling, and the loud, bragging conversation were just too much to ignore long enough to enjoy her food. What was it going to take for her to finish her dinner in peace?

Finally, Lydia stood and laid her napkin beside her plate. Hoping a trip to the ladies' room would erase her unease and perhaps prevent her the unpleasant necessity of asking them to keep the noise level down at their table, she gestured to Andrea and held up two fingers. Her server nodded at the familiar signal indicating how long she'd be away and Lydia quickly walked to the bathroom with her purse tucked under her arm.

Lydia had just chosen the last and cleanest stall of three when the two noisy women from the table next to hers came into the room. They were sighing and laughing as they filled the other two stalls. Lydia sat in the stall, staring at the ceiling, and wondering why she was being punished this evening.

"Lana, you're not going to let that woman ruin your anniversary are you?" one asked. "She kept glaring at you and George all through dinner."

"Ruin it? Are you kidding?" the other answered. "I felt sorry for her. She was eating her dinner all alone, pretending like it didn't matter. Seeing her only makes me more grateful for my marriage. God, sixty-two is old, but most of the time I don't care about time passing. I've been with George half my lifetime and still think he's the greatest thing since sliced bread."

"I know. I admit I'm jealous. You two are so great. Have George talk to Len for me, will you? I think Len has forgotten what romance is," non-Lana said. "I can't remember the last time he kissed my neck and made me giggle. Maybe if I held the TV remote for ransom, he might get motivated."

There was more laughter, the sound of the stall doors opening and water running, and finally hands being washed. The rustle of paper towels filled a momentary silence without further chatter. Lydia sighed with frustration when they started talking again.

"I don't get it. I bet she's not even our age. Why would someone as good-looking as that woman not have a man in her life?" Lana pondered.

"Lord—that's an easy answer, which you would have figured out yourself if George hadn't scrambled your brain kissing you on the neck," non-Lana answered. "She's obviously a total bitch to live with. Did you hear the way she talked to her server? Who would want to put up with that bitchy criticism all the time? No one looks that good. Her last man is probably even now in bed with an ugly woman who talks all sweetie, baby to him."

"You don't even know her story. That's an awful thing to say," Lana said, laughing at her slightly drunk friend's joke.

"Yes—awful to say, but also probably true," non-Lana said with a snide self-confidence, bumping open the door. "Come on, I'm ready to go dancing. The guys are waiting. It feels like prom all over again."

Their laughter faded as they walked out the door and away.

Inside her hiding place, Lydia stared at the back of the stall door and breathed through the discomfort of what she had heard. The pain was familiar, but it had been a while since she'd overheard such a sharp critique of herself. Normally, criticism like that only came from her daughter.

But even Lauren cloaked her displeasure in innuendo instead of cold words.

As she tidied her clothes, Lydia ordered herself to shake it off. What did it matter if strangers thought she was a bitch? It wasn't the first time she'd accidentally heard bad news in a bathroom. Gossiping women was how she had discovered William had taken his first mistress. Hearing bad news had hurt then too, but the pain had dulled by the time the other two long-term mistresses had come along. William had told her about them himself.

It had been many years since she'd found herself thinking about William's indiscretions. After the first one, talk among their social group and friends had spread so badly that divorce had seemed the only dignified option at one point. Her mother's stinging reprimands about the social scandal had doused the flames of the personal anger that had flared inside her at living with a man who showed little remorse for replacing his wife with multiple bed partners. Lydia decided her sense of fairness had been beaten back only by her parents focusing on what everyone else thought about her circumstances. It was the only time in her life she could remember her mother had ever pleaded with her not to do something. It had been one more convincing reason to try to salvage her relationship, but it had cost her to win her mother's approval.

Choosing not to divorce a man she hadn't wanted in the first place had required she and William come to a civilized agreement about their relationship—or rather lack of one. He had told her that he intended to have his needs met and she could either deal with it or divorce him. If she had loved him, things might have turned out very differently, but she'd never really felt that about any male—or at least not that she could recall.

Now she was certain that she had done the right thing socially by staying, ironically becoming a more virtuous woman for her own lack of looking outside her marriage. But how could she with her husband's insistence that she was frigid and needed help echoing in her mind? His sexual criticism lingered still today, refusing to be banished even by his death and the passage of more years of widowhood than she could bear thinking about at times.

Maybe she should have sought another relationship, but she had never come across a man that had seemed worth the effort. Or the risk of failing again, and maybe with someone who would have told everyone she knew about it.

Not that she considered her efforts to be a good wife a failure.

Hadn't she always submitted to William's occasional attempts to be intimate, regardless of how they made her feel? Hadn't she done everything her husband had asked? It hadn't been enough, had never in all their years together been enough.

Nothing she had done had made him any happier with her. In the end, there had only been more and more women. By the time he had his first heart attack, all compassion for him had fled in the face of how miserable she was to be his wife. Though she'd kept him in the house for many months of his sickness, Lauren had visited him more than she had in the hospital during those last days. His death had been a sad liberation for her. She had not had in her to grieve him.

At William's request, they had kept the truth from the child they had created. Lydia had done all she could over the years to confront the wagging tongues and hurtful stares with the appearance of normality, but Lauren had found out about it in college anyway. The daughter of a woman William had dated ended up telling Lauren the truth about her father's philandering ways.

Lauren's confrontation with her about her part in maintaining the illusion was still one of Lydia's most painful memories.

And then history repeated itself. Everyone said so, and it certainly was the case with the women in her family, Lydia decided. When Lauren had married eventually, she had ended up with the same kind of bed-hopping husband. Like William, her son-in-law was not a bad man—just a weak one. Fortunately, Lauren had not had a child with Jared. If she had, she'd likely still be in that relationship and not have managed to find anything better.

Lydia frowned as she waited three more minutes, then walked out of the stall and to the sink, automatically running water and washing her hands—hands Lydia couldn't help noticing were trembling. Thinking about why, she decided it was the bitch remark that had stung the most.

No one had ever said it to her face, though she imagined several had thought it, especially when she spoke up to defend something. But then any woman who spoke her mind eventually got tagged with that moniker. Gone were the days of polite filtering.

Look at the two women Lauren kept company with most. Their language was punctuated with swearing. It wouldn't surprise her to learn Lauren adopted it herself when she was with them.

Really—when Lydia thought about it—what else but vitriolic words could be expected from the two laughing women at the next restaurant table? They had been drinking bottle after bottle of wine at dinner. They were probably just drunk and out of control.

Lydia studied her reflection, but saw only the same person she always did. Her carefully streaked hair was still in place and her lipstick fading appropriately with dinner. Her gray eyes held no more pain than she was accustomed to seeing in her gaze.

Ignoring the nagging voice inside her, shaking her head over the rationalization, Lydia was careful to avoid staring in the mirror as she finished up. As she left to return to the table though, she realized her appetite was completely gone. In its place was a knot in her stomach that felt like she'd swallowed a baseball.

"Everything alright?" Andrea asked, not meeting Mrs. McCarthy's gaze in case her own was not properly sympathetic.

"The food is fine. I just got really tired suddenly. I'll take the check and the rest to go," Lydia said.

Andrea boxed her food in record time. Lydia signed the check for dinner with a frown, then dug a twenty out of her purse and placed it on the table too.

The exorbitant tip was not out of guilt, she assured herself. The girl had been exemplary this evening and deserved to be rewarded. It was certainly not to prove the laughing women had been wrong about her, though Lydia did briefly wish they were still there to see her being gracious so they could find it out for themselves. That might teach them not to gossip so much.

She nodded briefly at Andrea's wide eyes landing on the cash and the softly spoken good-bye she received from the startled girl, not at all happy with the thoughts pushing forward in her mind.

More about Donna McDonald

WEBSITE

www.donnamcdonaldauthor.com

EMAIL

email@donnamcdonaldauthor.com

TWITTER

@donnamcdonald13 and @scifiwoman13

FACEBOOK

Donna McDonald Contemporary Romances
Donna McDonald SciFi Romances
Donna McDonald Recommends
Donna Jane McDonald

CONTEMPORARY BOOKS BLOG

www.donnamcdonald.blogspot.com

PARANORMAL/FANTASY/SCIFI BLOG

www.donnamcdonaldparanormal.blogspot.com

Contemporary Books

NEVER TOO LATE SERIES

Dating A Cougar (Book One)
Dating Dr. Notorious (Book Two)
Dating A Saint (Book Three)
Dating A Metro Man (Book Four)
Dating A Silver Fox (Book Five)
Dating A Cougar II (Coming 2013)

ART OF LOVE SERIES

Carved In Stone (Book One)
Created In Fire (Book Two)
Captured In Ink (Book Three)
Commissioned In White (Book Four)
Covered In Paint (Coming 2013)

NEXT TIME AROUND SERIES

Next Song I Sing (Book One)
Next Game I Play (Coming 2013)
Next Move I Make (Coming 2013)

SINGLE TITLE (NON-SERIES BOOKS)

The Right Thing
Quickies Volume 1

Paranormal/SciFi/Fantasy Books

FORCED TO SERVE SERIES

The Demon of Synar (Book One)
The Demon Master's Wife (Book Two)
The Siren's Call (Book Three)
The Healer's Kiss (Coming 2012)
The Demon's Change (Coming 2013)

SINGLE TITLE (NON-SERIES BOOKS)

The Shaman's Mate (Fantasy)

About the Author

Donna McDonald is a best selling author in Contemporary Romance and Humor, and lately has been climbing the Science Fiction list as well.

Science Fiction reviewers are calling McDonald "a literary alchemist effortlessly blending science fiction and romance". Contemporary and humor reviewers often write to tell her that the books keep them up reading and laughing all night. She likes both compliments and hopes they are true.

McDonald's idea of her highest success is to be sitting next to someone on a plane and find out they are laughing at something in one of her books. This would of course be while she was heading off to some new place on her next adventure to feed her creative soul.

17737623R00132

Made in the USA
Charleston, SC
26 February 2013